Opal Darkness

Francis reached underneath Clara's body and began moving his arm back and forth as he thrust more strongly between the fat, pink cheeks.

'Oh, my. Oh, lawks,' Clara squealed, her voice rising even higher as she pushed her hips backwards towards Francis's flat belly. 'Do me hard, sir. Oh, my. I'm spending!'

Francis threw back his head and went rigid. His buttocks were taut and his cock was buried to the hilt within Clara's body. Gritting his teeth he gave out a low satisfied moan.

At the exact moment that Clara and Francis reached a mutual climax, Rose cried out too. But her cry was one of shocked surprise.

'What the devil is going on here!' called out a strident male voice. 'Francis! Explain yourself at once.'

Sidonie almost fainted with horror. And Francis, already withdrawing from Clara and wiping himself on his shirt tails, turned around to meet the furious countenance of his father.

Author's other Black Lace titles:

The Captive Flesh
Juliet Rising

Opal Darkness
Cleo Cordell

BLACK LACE

Black Lace books contain sexual fantasies.
In real life, always practise safe sex.

First published in 1995 by
Black Lace
Thames Wharf Studios
Rainville Road
London W6 9HA

This edition published 2002

Copyright © Cleo Cordell 1995

The right of Cleo Cordell to be identified as the Author of
the Work has been asserted in accordance with the Copyright,
Designs and Patents Act 1988.

Printed and bound by Mackays of Chatham PLC

ISBN 0 352 33033 3

Chapter One

Sidonie Ryder watched the rain make snake-like runnels down the window-pane of the draughty sitting room.

She shivered and pulled the threadbare silk shawl more closely around her shoulders. On her lap, the open book lay forgotten. Leaning forward in the window seat she rubbed at the condensation with her palm, making a clear area through which she could peer at the garden.

Her spirits lifted as she saw that there was a patch of blue between the rain clouds. By the time she was ready for her art lesson all signs of the heavy shower would have gone. And thank heaven for it. The only bright spots in her week were the hours she and her twin brother spent in the company of Chatham Burney, ostensibly learning to draw and paint, but in reality completing her education in a way that would give her father apoplexy, should he ever get to hear about it.

Already a weak sun was sending dusty golden light through the tangle of trees and unkempt shrubs. As if to mirror Sidonie's thoughts a beam of light struck sparks from the rain drops, turning each one into a rainbow crystal.

She turned back to face the room, her heavy skirts and

1

petticoats making a rustling noise as she swung her legs forward and placed her feet on the shabby carpet. Catching Francis's eye she grimaced and was pleased to see his lips twitch as he tried to suppress an answering grin.

Poor Francis; he had the glazed look which she recognised as a mixture of boredom and introspection. And no wonder. The voice of the Reverend John Beecham was a dull brown monotone but only growing louder as he read from the book of Greek verse. The Reverend was so absorbed in his reading that he did not catch the look which passed between brother and sister.

Their tutor missed a great deal of what went on in the minds of his spirited young pupils. Something for which Sidonie was more than grateful.

She waved at Francis now, motioning towards the grandfather clock, whose loud ticks punctuated the flat tones of the Reverend's voice. Francis lifted one dark-brown, humorous eyebrow and pushed a lock of hair back from his forehead. He stretched and yawned loudly and the Reverend looked up in surprise.

'Goodness me. Is that the time?' he said. 'The bell for luncheon will be sounding in a moment. Off you go then, young master. I will see you tomorrow at eight sharp for Bible reading. Be sure to memorise the passage I set you, Sidonie. Good day to you both.'

'Good day, Reverend Beecham,' the twins mumbled in unison, Sidonie dropping a shallow curtsy and Francis clicking his heels smartly in what he imagined was a military-style bow.

As they hurried down the corridor towards the dining room, Sidonie reached for her brother's hand.

'Oh, Francis, you shouldn't tease the poor old thing like that.'

Francis shrugged, his fingers warm and firm against those of his sister.

'He didn't even notice anything different. I don't know why I bother to provoke the old fool. I'm sure I could have curtsied or even flashed him a glimpse of my bare

2

arse and he would just have treated me to that inane grin of his.'

Sidonie chuckled with delight at Francis's unexpected crudity as they entered the dining room and took their places at the table. She adored her wild and passionate twin and looked to him to take the lead in most things. Francis was the elder of the two by just fifteen minutes. And was fond of reminding her of that fact.

'I was so afraid that my art lesson would have to be taken indoors,' she said, quite unable to hide the eagerness in her voice.

Francis smiled knowingly. His eyes, so like hers in shape, but light blue while hers were a dark, satiny brown, crinkled attractively.

'Now that would have been a pity. The garden is so wild and romantic-looking just now. Just the thing to stir up artistic passions. And I'm sure that Chatham will be relieved to know that he won't have Smithers peering over his shoulder as he "tutors" you in the conservatory.' He paused and his lips curved in a wicked smile. 'Then again, perhaps Smithers would learn a thing or two from watching you together.'

Sidonie dimpled and a flush rose into her cheeks at the thought of the housekeeper, or anyone else, watching what she and Chatham did together. The only one who knew all her secrets was Francis. They had shared every thought, every experience, since the day they were born.

'She might learn even more from watching you and Chatham,' she said in a low voice, placing the table napkin on her lap as the housekeeper brought in the soup. 'I'm not the only one who's susceptible to his company and the pleasures he offers.'

'True enough,' Francis said without a trace of embarrassment. 'And I know how much you enjoy it when I tell you what we do together. Shall I tell you how it feels when he . . . Ah, you'll have to wait, after all. Luncheon is served. And what treats do you have in store for us today, Smithers dearest?' Francis gave his sister a theatrical wink.

3

'Brown Windsor soup, boiled ham and parsley sauce,' the housekeeper said, in her usual no-nonsense voice. 'And don't you be giving me any of your cheek, young master. I'll thank you to keep a civil tongue.'

Sidonie tried, without success, to muffle her laughter. Francis was incorrigible. Smithers gave her a haughty look before ladling out the soup. Leaving the tureen on the table, she disappeared into the kitchen. The twins began eating and for a while neither of them spoke. Sidonie let her mind rove free.

Chatham would soon be at the house. He was probably striding along the narrow country lanes at this very moment, a folder under one arm and a stout stick in his hand.

His handsome face, so sensitive with its broad pale brow, and slim, high-bridged nose were etched on her thoughts. His thick fair hair, worn fashionably long under his broad-brimmed hat and his velvet jacket marked him out as an artist and poet. A rare animal indeed in this region.

She was certain that her absent father would heartily disapprove of Chatham. And that, of course, added immensely to his charm.

Sidonie thought of the surprise she had planned for the afternoon's lesson and fairly trembled with anticipation. Up until now, she had simply been a willing pupil, happy to relinquish the burden of her virginity. But this afternoon was to be a watershed.

How perfect things were. It was difficult to believe that just a few short weeks ago she and her brother had been bored almost to distraction. The country house in Wiltshire was isolated and received few visitors. And the occasional tea party or game of canasta at the rectory was no diversion at all for two restless eighteen-year-olds.

She had written to her father to ask whether she and Francis might not be allowed to enjoy the London season, for surely it was high time they entered into society. How else were they supposed to meet the right sort of people? The reply had been short and to the point. No, they might not leave Wiltshire. But perhaps to soften the blow, their father had made arrangements for them to receive art lessons.

Now Chatham Burney's weekly visits were like an oasis in the desert of the twins' routine. He brought with him exciting news of the outside world. Sidonie could not wait to experience the wonders of the railway. Chatham had told her that there were passenger trains running between London and Brighton and Liverpool to Manchester. Everywhere there were new constructions of iron and steel.

It seemed that the 1860s were to be a time of change and expansion. She felt stifled by the dullness and the routine of the old house. The growth of industry was no more to her than gossip and here in Wiltshire they still travelled everywhere by coach and horses.

But Chatham himself was here, exciting and sophisticated. Sidonie sighed inwardly and shifted on her chair, aware of the pleasant tingling between her thighs and the tension in her stomach which had nothing to do with hunger.

As if he read her thoughts, Francis flashed her one of his special looks. The look which said, I'll make sure that I come into your room tonight and you can tell me all about it. She would of course. That was all part of the enjoyment. Huddled close under the counterpane, entwined in each other's arms and cushioned against the chill of the dark old house, the twins would talk long into the night.

Sometimes it seemed as if they were one person, not two. If I was a young man I would be Francis and if he was a woman, he'd be me, Sidonie thought.

The housekeeper left with the soup dishes and returned carrying a number of covered dishes, Sidonie tried to concentrate on eating, but the food tasted like sawdust. As she pushed the piece of boiled ham around on her plate, the excitement grew into a knot in her belly.

Soon now. Half an hour to go. It was all she could do

to stop from pushing away her lunch and running from the room. But she controlled her emotions, forcing herself to stay calm and to nod politely at Smithers as the used plates and cutlery were cleared away.

But although she clasped her hands tightly, meshing and unmeshing her fingers, she could not stop the disturbingly erotic images which flooded her mind; sunlight on naked muscled flesh; the wide sweep of strong, male shoulders; a slim hand caressing her breast and teasing the rosy nipple into a hard peak; that same hand sliding down her belly to toy with the dark reddish curls that grew on her mound of Venus.

Oh, God. Chatham. I cannot wait for you to touch me. What did Francis and I do before you came into our lives?

As he made his way along the path which led around the back of the house to the gardens, Chatham Burney whistled merrily.

He was looking forward to meeting Sidonie and he had brought something special for her today. In the folder beneath his arm, along with his artists' materials, he had a number of drawings. He was certain that Sidonie had never seen anything like them and he anticipated her response to his gift with marked excitement.

An image of her flashed into his mind. She was so beautiful with her pale skin, unusual dark eyes, and that marvellous froth of hair. It seemed to have a life of its own, so full and vibrant it was, gleaming with tones of copper, gold and palest peach.

He chuckled. It was a good thing that she was hidden away in deepest Wiltshire in that ramshackle old barn of a house. In London she would cause a sensation. Sidonie Ryder might not be aware of the fact, but she was the epitome of the perfect Pre-Raphaelite beauty. And his friends Rossetti, Millais and the others of the Brotherhood were ever seeking a new muse.

Chatham reached the wooden gate which led into the

old orchard. He pushed it and it swung open on rusty hinges. The lush green grass beneath the trees was still damp from the earlier shower and he had a sudden vision of Sidonie lying naked beneath him, her pale skin damp and fragrant.

He would love to sketch her like that, with the rain polishing her limbs and the violet shadows lying deep in the hollows of her body. Sometimes he felt guilty for awakening her to bodily pleasures, but he comforted himself with the thought that someone like Sidonie – so vibrant and eager for everything that life offered – was bound to give herself to a man at the first available opportunity.

That was true enough, but it did not explain his attachment to Francis. Chatham was not a man given to questioning his morals in any great depth. He allowed himself to be persuaded that it was Francis's uncanny resemblance to Sidonie that had captivated him. Was it *his* fault if brother and sister were so charming, so knowing, while retaining a refreshing innocence, so beautiful and so utterly captivating?

He was an artist, by God. A man who was acutely sensitive to beauty wherever he found it. How could he, a mere mortal, challenge the poetry of the flesh? Male or female, it was all one to him.

But today it was Sidonie he was meeting and all his thoughts were for her. Ah, she was waiting. He could see her there at the foot of the crumbling gazebo, her hair like a beacon shining through the trees.

She swept towards him, her shabby cloak brushing against the damp grass. Enamoured as he always was by her mere presence, he did not think to question the fact that it seemed too warm for her to be wearing the thick woollen cloak. She looked charming with her hair swept up with combs to reveal the slim column of her neck.

'Chatham! You're late,' she said reprovingly, her lower lip pushed out into a pout that made his pulses quicken.

7

God, just one look at her and he was so hard that it hurt.

'I apologise for my lateness. But I'm sure you'll forgive me when you know the reason why.'

'I don't know that I shall,' she said, sparkling at him. 'You had better have a good reason. I've a mind to punish you. Perhaps I'll just go indoors and forgo my art lesson today.'

'Then I must persuade you to stay,' Chatham said, reaching for her and drawing her into his embrace. 'If you must punish me, let it be with your kisses.'

She swayed against him, rotating her hips so that his erection rubbed against the base of her belly.

'Forward minx,' he murmured, then kissed her hard, pushing his tongue into her mouth, tasting and exploring her.

Sidonie made a sound deep in her throat as her tongue threshed with his. His cock pulsed in response and he put his hand down to adjust himself more comfortably.

'Let me do that,' Sidonie said, sliding her hand down between their bodies.

She rubbed her palm up and down his rigid stem, shocking him with her forwardness. Gently she squeezed him, her teeth caught in her bottom lip in a charming, childlike gesture of concentration.

When she drew away, she was breathing hard and her eyes were shining with excitement. Chatham had been going to show her the drawings as soon as they met, but now he was eager to lie with her. It was obvious that she needed no encouragement, nor did she need to look at pictures of nudes to get her into an amorous frame of mind. She had never been this demonstrative. Usually it was he who made the first approach.

Her wantonness thrilled and disconcerted him.

When he bent his head to kiss her again, Sidonie lifted her hand and placed her fingers against his mouth.

'Wait,' she breathed. 'I want to show you something.'

Taking a few steps backwards, she began to unfasten the clasp at her throat. The thick garment fell in folds to the ground. Chatham's eyes widened with surprise and pleasure.

Sidonie struck a pose. Her hand on one hip and her bent leg thrust forward.

'Would I do as a model for your London friends?' she said.

'Oh, yes,' Chatham said, trying to take in the vision before him.

She must have spent hours making the dress, although 'dress' did not describe the garment she wore. In shape it resembled a smock, such as farmers wore. The sleeves were wide and gathered into a low neckline and the fabric was so fine that he could see the contours of her body. As she straightened up and began to walk towards him the wide neckline slipped off one shoulder, laying bare a tantalising expanse of pale skin.

Chatham's breath caught in his throat as he realised that she wore no stays or drawers beneath the dress. Such a thing would have been daring even for an experienced artist's model in London. In someone of breeding and gentle birth, brought up with no idea of the existence of the bohemian society he knew well, it was doubly shocking.

Had he really thought her an innocent?

He watched entranced as each long, rounded thigh, the curve of her hips, and the slight pout of her belly were revealed as the fabric bunched into folds with her movements.

Sidonie stopped a few paces from him and gathered the fullness of the dress in both hands. Pulling the folds tight across the front of her body, she let him see the dark shadow at her groin. The neckline slipped further and the swell of one perfect rose-tipped breast came into view.

'Would you like to paint me like this?' Sidonie asked teasingly, her sensual mouth parted to reveal even, white teeth.

Chatham groaned and stepped towards her.

'Perhaps later. First . . .'

9

She was as eager as he was and fell back readily on to the rug which covered the dusty stone steps of the gazebo. Twining her arms around his neck, Sidonie arched against him, her thighs falling open.

'Do it to me at once, Chatham. I want you hot and hard within me.'

Speechless with desire and almost bursting with the need to possess her, he hardly registered her words. He pulled up the dress until it was bunched in folds around her slim waist.

'God. My God,' he murmured, looking down her body to her adorable quim.

He could never get enough of that place. The fine, silky hair which covered her mound was a darker red than the hair of her head. It did not entirely mask the entrance to her body, but revealed the softly pouting lips of her vulva. He had never seen a quim more generously offered. It was as plump as a ripe fig, and the scent of it was heavenly – musky and rich, like nothing else in the world.

He opened his fly and his cock sprang free. Sidonie's hands grasped his hips, pulling him towards her centre.

'Now. Do it now. I can't wait,' she urged him.

'Oh, Christ,' he breathed as he pushed the head of his penis into the closure of her flesh.

She was tight inside, yet yielding too. Her heat and softness surrounded him, drawing him in. As he began to move, he felt the subtle pulsing of her inner membranes and tried to distance his mind. He was going to spend, he knew it, and Sidonie would be left unsatisfied.

He felt ashamed of his eagerness. Usually he was not so lacking in finesse, but Sidonie normally acted like a shy country miss – not a tavern doxy. He could not stop himself thrusting into her. The contours of her vagina slid so sweetly against his invasive maleness.

The pressure boiled within him as he moved inexorably towards his climax. And Sidonie's gasps and moans urged him nearer and nearer still.

The first tearing spurts jetted into her and he dug his

fingers into the firm flesh of her buttocks, groaning deeply as he buried himself to the hilt in her moist darkness.

Serve her right. She had no business tempting him like that. A man could only stand so much.

Sidonie ground her hips against him, raising her legs and locking them behind his back. She began rubbing herself against the base of his belly, rocking back and forth, her head thrown back as her pleasure built. He felt her pubic bone digging into the base of his cock, her quim-hair mashing against him. Then she was gasping and crying out his name, her legs scissoring wildly and her vulva tipped upwards to extract the last drop of pleasure.

Chatham's rapidly shrinking cock slipped out of her, expelled by the force of her orgasm. For a second he felt affronted. By God – *she* had taken *him*. That had never happened before.

Rolling off Sidonie, Chatham took her into his arms. He did not know what to think. Should he be angry? Then he began to laugh. 'Well, it seems that the pupil has just bested the tutor,' he said. 'I must say it was a salutary experience.'

Sidonie kissed his chin.

'But you're really not sure whether you liked it or not? Let's rest for a while, shall we? Then I promise that you can roger me to your heart's delight. And, if you'd prefer it, I won't move a muscle! In fact, I promise that I won't enjoy it one little bit. It'll be all for you.'

Chatham kissed her soundly.

'Really? I've always loved women who don't keep their promises!' he said and, throwing back his head, laughed hugely.

Lying in bed later that evening, Sidonie went over the events of the afternoon.

A warm glow suffused her skin, a reminder of the potent pleasures of love-making. She turned on to her side and placed her linked hands between her thighs, hugging to herself the knowledge that she had passed her self-imposed personal test.

Up until the past few hours she had been Chatham's willing pupil, accepting each kiss and caress with a sense of wonder. The delight in watching herself unfold had been heightened by Chatham's reactions. His artistic sensibilities had moved him to poetic speech on more than one occasion.

That was all very nice, very romantic, and she would always look on Chatham with great affection, but she knew for certain that she was ready now for earthier pleasures. If only she and Francis were not compelled to live like church mice.

How could they hope to meet anyone of note? Every garment they owned was patched, worn or woefully out of date. Not that that seemed to bother Chatham. He seemed charmed by their air of shabby gentility. He probably thought that it was romantic.

She brightened. Surely even in the depths of the Wiltshire countryside there must be opportunities for sexual adventures. She would ask Francis about that. And she would write to Father again. The first letter had produced good results. It really was time that he was reminded of his duty to his children. How much longer could he leave them buried in this place? Didn't he care that they were so poor when he was so wealthy?

Just then the bedroom door opened and a gust of wind set the flame of her bedside candle fluttering.

Sidonie sat up and folded back the bedclothes.

'Get in quickly, Francis. Before you freeze.'

Francis shrugged off his quilted robe and stepped out of his threadbare slippers, then climbed in beside his sister and snuggled up close to her. He smelt of lavender soap and clean skin. Sidonie snuggled down next to him and he took her in his arms. His familiar, long body was hard against hers and the folds of his cotton nightshirt chilled her skin even through her voluminous nightgown.

12

'You're certain that Smithers has retired for the night?' she said.

He nodded. 'We won't be disturbed.'

Tipping up her head to him, she kissed him passionately on the mouth. His hand cupped the back of her neck as he returned her kiss, smiling against her lips and murmuring endearments.

It was comforting, as well as exciting, to kiss Francis. She was so used to his presence, his utter devotion to her. Thrown together in their loneliness and seclusion, the boundaries of their sibling love had broadened and deepened into an almost obsessive fascination with each other.

For just a moment Sidonie imagined life without her twin and was terrified.

'What is it, sweetheart? You're trembling,' Francis whispered against her hair.

'I was just thinking how awful it would be if we were ever to be parted. Oh, Francis. I think I'd die of a broken heart. Promise me that it will never happen. No matter who you meet and fall in love with, you'll always love me best, won't you?'

'Silly goose,' he said affectionately. 'Of course. Did you need to ask? I adore you. Now, tell me how much you love me.'

She smiled at him in the darkness. The faint light of the candle picked out the planes of his face. His blue eyes were shadowed and mysterious. He has my face, but the lines of it are harder, all the angles more pronounced and more chiselled, she thought. In him she saw herself reflected. His beauty humbled her.

'Tell me,' Francis insisted, when she remained silent.

He tightened his arms around her, until she whimpered with complaint. 'You're hurting me. Let me go,' she said.

His teeth flashed white when he grinned.

'I like to hurt you, but only a little,' he said huskily, bending his head to kiss her again, his firm lips moulding hers. In a moment he began kissing her cheeks, the tip of her chin and the hollow of her throat. 'There's something about you, an innocence that drives me to be cruel so that I can soothe away your hurt and kiss you better.'

Sidonie moaned as his hot mouth moved around to the back of her neck. When he bit her gently she arched her back and felt his heavy tumescence against her thigh. When Francis drew back finally she was breathless and shaking with desire for him.

'I love you, Francis. With all my heart and soul,' she said with a catch in her voice. 'No one will come between us, ever.'

Abruptly Francis rolled on to his back and lay looking up at the darkness which masked the ceiling.

'This is too dangerous, sweetheart,' he groaned. 'I think I had better go to my own room.'

Sidonie clutched at him.

'No! Don't go. I want you to stay. We can do . . . things to make ourselves feel better. Like we have in the past. Now that we are grown-up, it's so much sweeter to give pleasure to each other. It isn't a sin if no one knows what we do, is it?'

Francis chuckled and turned towards her, his chin propped on his hand.

'I doubt that the Reverend Beecham would agree with you, but I'm persuaded.' He put out a hand to stroke her face, his fingers cupping her chin. 'You've changed, Sidonie. You never used to be so bold. I suspect that Chatham had something to do with this new recklessness.'

Sliding her arms around his neck, Sidonie pulled his face down to hers.

'Why don't you tell me what you and Chatham did the last time you met,' she whispered. 'You know how I love to hear you say the words.'

'And you love me to do . . . this too, while I'm telling you every tiny detail, don't you?' Francis said, reaching down to slip his hand beneath the hem of her nightdress.

Sidonie drew in her breath as Francis's hand touched

her thigh. Pleasuring each other was somehow more arousing because it was forbidden. And yet, she told herself, the fact that they never lay together skin to skin, added a strange decorum. Both of them knew that if they ever stripped naked and came together simply as a man and woman, then there would be no hope of ever controlling their passions.

There was a single, dark area of their psyche where they feared to tread. Francis cared about Sidonie too much to ever put her in danger. And if she was to bear his child, he knew that something would die between them. It was a disaster they dared not contemplate.

As Francis's slender fingers tugged gently at the curling hair on her quim, Sidonie parted her legs and hid her face in the hollow of his shoulder. She could feel the moisture gathering at the entrance to her vagina, ready to make his probing fingers wet with her silky juices.

'Tell me about you and Chatham then ... oh,' she murmured, as he slipped a finger into the parting of her sex and began stroking her tender bud which responded by hardening until it resembled a tiny bead.

As Francis began speaking, she pushed herself towards his hand, the low, urgent tones of his voice adding an extra dimension to her pleasure.

'I met Chatham in the old conservatory,' Francis said, a quiver in his voice. 'It had been raining earlier and his clothes were soaked. As soon as our eyes met it was obvious what was going to happen. I had brought a towel with me, thinking that he would have need of it. It was just an excuse really, as if we needed one. Anyway, I told him to strip off his wet clothes and to spread them out to dry. I said that it would be a pity if he took a chill and I'd give him a rub-down to warm him up.' He paused and looked down at Sidonie's face.

Her eyelids were fluttering and her lips were parted as she emitted soft sighs of pleasure. His fingertips slid up and down her moist folds, now and then dipping into her body and exerting a subtle pressure on the firm pad

15

behind her pubis. He doubted whether she was actually aware of what he was saying. Just then she opened her eyes. They were drowsy, heavy with passion.

'Go on,' she whispered, sinking down on to his thrusting digit, her tongue snaking out to moisten her lips. 'Tell me what happened next.'

Smiling, he continued. 'When he had stripped off his jacket, shirt and trews and was dressed only in his under-drawers, I used the towel on his shoulders, belly and back. You know what fine, white skin he has? Well, it was buffed to a rosy hue by my ministrations and when I had finished, he was breathing hard as if he had been running. His cock was jutting straight out and he did not try to hide the fact. Instead, he took my hand and placed it on him so that I could feel the heat and the throbbing weight of it. My mouth dried as I looked at him. Before now I never desired another man. Perhaps it is because you and he are lovers – I don't know. But I felt an answering response within me. Chatham drew me to him, pressing his chest close to mine and we kissed.'

He paused, remembering. And Sidonie wriggled closer, her swollen nipples grazing his chest almost in imitation of the caress he was relating to her.

'When we broke apart,' Francis said, 'he put his hands on my shoulders and I dropped to my knees willingly. I knew what was going to happen and I was fearful and desirous at the same time. My fingers shook as I opened the buttons at his fly. His cock was thick and potent-looking, the skin covering the head of it was partly rolled back and the glans was moist and purplish.

'I could smell his arousal. It was like salt and clean sweat and there was an earthy undertone to his scent. I leaned forward eagerly, my hand coming up to rest on his slim hips and I opened my lips and drew his cock into my mouth. I can't tell you how it felt. The hardness of him, the male thrusting force deep in my throat. It was intoxicating. I clutched at his buttocks, kneading the taut flesh as I sucked and pulled at his phallus.

'God, Sidonie, that such an act between men is thought to be wrong! I did not feel any shame, only a glorious sense of freedom and pride and pleasure too. It was a privilege to be able to give such delight. And, somehow, I knew just what to do. It was a little like pleasuring myself.'

Sidonie clutched at her twin, her back arched and one leg twined around his waist, giving her freedom to thrust back and forth on his fingers which were buried deeply within her. Francis flicked the pad of his thumb back and forth across the straining bud, which had thrust itself free of its tiny hood and was so hot and erect. It ticked against him, like a tiny beating heart.

'And then ... Oh, yes. Don't stop that. And then ...' Sidonie gasped.

'Then I felt his hands moving in my hair and caressing my cheeks, moving bonelessly down to my mouth and tracing my lips which were stretched open to contain his delicious flesh. I did not know that I could take so much of him in.

'But I did it. His pubic hair grazed my lips and my chin and he was moaning, his buttocks clenching and unclenching. I cupped his balls then, feeling how tight they were, ready to give up his jism. Then he spent and his seed gushed into my throat. I swallowed all of it and relished the last drops.

'When I stood up, we kissed and embraced. Chatham rubbed his tongue around the inside of my mouth, no doubt tasting the faint traces of his essence. He smiled crookedly at me then and my heart gave a great lurch, because I realised that he wanted to fellate me in turn.'

Francis paused and held her close as she climaxed, uttering sharp little cries and throwing her head from side to side.

'Oh, Sidonie, my darling.'

He pressed kisses to her throat, holding her until she was quiet. How he loved her face when she came. It made him feel so tender and protective towards her.

They lay together, still embracing and cushioned on

17

the pillow of Sidonie's spread hair. In a moment she adjusted her position and smiled wickedly at her twin.

'That was divine. I thought I was going to melt with pleasure. And now to attend to you. What is it that Chatham calls it – fellating? I did not know that there was a name for what I do to you.'

Francis lay on his back, his hands linked behind the back of his neck. Sidonie pushed up his nightshirt until it was raised above his waist. She studied the column of flesh, which he had various pet names for, calling it his cudgel and his pego. His cock – so hard inside, but with its velvet-soft skin – fascinated her, just as the intricate shape of her quim fascinated him. Ever since their first exploratory, childhood games, they had been charmed by the differences in their bodies.

Sidonie stroked Francis's cock lightly, her fingers moving up and down the rigid shaft. She smiled with satisfaction when it twitched and leapt in her hand. As she bent forward and gave the swollen glans a long, loving lick, she murmured, 'Oh, Francis. Whatever happens, whoever I meet, I'll always love you the best. Only you.'

Francis let out a long sigh as her hot mouth closed over his straining cock-head. The sensation was exquisite and he closed his eyes, letting the feelings wash over him. It was an effort to speak, but he just managed to get the words out.

'Me too, my pet. Never forget that I'll always care for you. We belong to each other.'

Chapter Two

Sir James Ryder looked down at the letter in his hand and experienced an unusual flicker of conscience.

This was the second missive from Sidonie in a little over a month. Were the twins unhappy then? He had to admit that he had hardly given the matter a thought. His business commitments took up much of his time and that which was left over was filled most admirably by the company of Lady Jennifer Haversidge, wife to an aged member of Parliament and his mistress for the past two years.

Perhaps it was time he paid his children a visit. They must be thirteen, fourteen? No probably more. He realised with a sense of shock that he did not know exactly how old they were. How the years had fled since their mother died.

He had been too wrapped up in his own grief to give a thought to his children at first and then he had thrown himself into his work. London could be exhausting with its round of social engagements, but it was necessary for a man in his position to move in the right circles.

And now, of course, there was Jenny.

He liked to think that Jenny had softened him, rubbed away some of the hard edges of which he was once so proud. Sir James was a stubborn, self-made man. Everything he had achieved he had worked hard for. The twins did not know how lucky they were to be free of his worries. They were clothed decently, fed, and their time was their own.

The sound of a discreet yawn and a slight rustle of bedclothes alerted him to the fact that his mistress was awake. It was typical of Jenny that she did not fling back the counterpane, sit up and rub her knuckles in her eyes then scratch her armpits, like many a drab he had taken to his bed in the past.

His mistress was a lady of breeding and the delicacy of her manners was something he loved best about her.

'What's that you're reading, James?' she asked, the soft husky tones of her voice raising the hairs on the back of his neck.

'Just a letter from my daughter, dearest. Seems that she's set on reminding me of my fatherly duties. I have the uncomfortable feeling that I might have been remiss in leaving the twins to their own devices for so long.'

Jenny propped herself up on the pillows and patted her hair into shape. One blonde, corkscrew curl fell artlessly over one shoulder and tumbled over the exposed swell of her breasts.

'How old are the twins now?' Jenny asked.

Sir James looked shamefaced. 'Somewhere in their early teens I believe. Hardly more than children really.'

'Oh, James, you scoundrel. Don't you know how old your own children are?' Jenny chided. 'You have only one date to remember after all. I expect you've been forgetting the twins' birthday too. I see by your face that you have. This really won't do. You'll have to go and visit them. Fancy leaving them buried in the country all this time. They must be introduced to society, fitted for new clothes. Sidonie must have a coming-out ball. However else is she to meet people of breeding?'

Sir James looked worried. All this was quite beyond him. He had planned to just look in on the twins, perhaps increase their allowance a little. Jenny had made him see that there was a lot more involved.

Jenny smiled fondly at him. 'Would you like me to come to Wiltshire with you?'

He brightened. 'Oh, would you, darling? It would be a great help to me. I can handle Francis, but young women scare the daylights out of me. Perhaps if you would speak to her?'

'Of course. I'd be glad to. I'd really enjoy the change. The country air will put roses into my cheeks. And when Sidonie comes back to London with us, I'll take her to my personal dressmaker. She's just imported some dress patterns and some wonderful figured silks from Paris. Monsieur Worth, very *à la mode*, don't you know.'

Jenny struck a pose, one hand on her hip and the other in the air in imitation of a dress mannequin.

Sir James beamed at his mistress. There was nothing at all to worry about. Jenny would take Sidonie under her wing and he would see to Francis. All a young man needed to get into the right set was to join the required gentleman's club. He had plenty of influential friends and many of them would be sure to look kindly on Francis.

Yes, it was certainly high time that his son took his place in the family business. He even found himself looking forward to it.

'What would I do without you, my dear,' he said, his voice soft with affection. 'I owe you a great deal.'

Jenny's blue eyes sparkled as she untied the blue ribbon at the neck of her chemise. Slowly she slipped the lace-trimmed garment down her upper arms, uncovering first the deep well of her cleavage and then baring her breasts.

'You could show me how grateful you are if you wish,' she said, her full lips curving and the tips of her pearly teeth glinting in the early morning light.

Sir James took a step towards her, the blood pounding in his ears, his eyes on her magnificent bosom.

The full, creamy globes were pear-shaped and slightly up-tilted. Jenny's nipples were large and quite dark in colour, the areolae as clearly defined as two copper pennies. She held out her arms to him and he sat beside her for a moment, just looking at her, thinking how blessed he was to have the affection of such a handsome woman.

And how extraordinary it was that she should mean so much to him. He had always been a bluff, cold man with a no-nonsense attitude to life. Jenny had changed all that. He was like butter in her hands and could deny her nothing.

'Come here, dearest,' Jenny said, her husky voice soft and full of promise. 'Come to Mama.'

Sir James gave a strangled groan and put his head in her lap. His cock was hot and throbbing and he longed to lie between Jenny's soft white thighs, push himself into her quim and lose himself in the glory of her flesh. But first there was the usual ritual to go through.

It was partly because Jenny had discovered his weakness and given herself up to it so readily that her body had retained its hold over him.

Oh, God in Heaven, how he relished this act.

Jenny lifted one generous breast and held it towards him, a finger curved on either side of her nipple so that it was pushed between her digits. The semi-erect teat jutted out provocatively, offered up to his questing lips. With her other hand she steadied his head and drew him towards her.

Sir James lay quiescent as she rubbed the swelling nipple against his lips until it hardened fully. For a few moments he savoured the sensation of the warm morsel, which jabbed gently against his mouth as if it were actively seeking to gain entrance.

Opening his lips, he licked the nipple, flicking at it and collaring it with his tongue. It was a rigid cone, a wanton little nub, and it tasted faintly of Jenny's perfume. For a moment longer he teased himself by denying entry to that which he most desired. Then he could not bear to wait any longer; he opened his mouth in submission and Jenny placed the nipple in his mouth.

A dart of pure lust speared his belly as he began to

suckle like a baby. His soft sighs of enjoyment and the smacking of his lips were the only sounds in the room.

'There, there, dearest,' Jenny murmured, stroking his damp forehead as his cheeks worked in and out.

Her cheeks grew pink with pleasure as Sir James worked away at her nipple, little groans of enjoyment rising in his throat. She rested her head back on the pillows and allowed the sensation of the sweet, nearly-painful pulling to spread through her.

'That's it now,' she said, after a while. 'Is my naughty boy getting hard for his mama? I think I had better feel you and see.'

Sir James trembled and sucked ever more strongly as Jenny slipped her hand inside his dressing-gown and thrust it into his groin. Her cool fingers closed over his thickened shaft and gave it a friendly squeeze. James moaned, aching for her to feel him under his nightshirt, to stroke him more firmly or to cup his balls, but feeling a surge of joy when she removed her hand.

That meant that the game would last longer. The anticipation of pleasure made it all the more sweet. Jenny had taught him that too.

'My, what a big boy you are,' Jenny said. 'I think you're almost ready for me. I have a soft, warm place between my thighs where you can put that rod. A special place which is already growing wet and swollen. But first, you must have the other breast. Be a good boy. And do as Mama says now.'

Obediently Sir James shifted position and laid his head in the crook of Jenny's arm.

The nipple he had been suckling was warm and wet, pulled out into a little, brown-red tube by his ministrations. The delicate skin was shiny, polished by his saliva. He shuddered with eagerness as he looked at the other breast, the virgin peak which hovered a few inches from his mouth. The nipple was still not fully erect. He imagined that it was waiting for his tongue to tease it into a vibrant erection.

Oh, he just knew that it would feel cool and dry. He

ached to suck it, but Jenny began pinching and stroking it between her fingers.

Sir James was compelled to harness his impatience, whilst all the time watching her movements avidly. His eyes followed every slow stroke of her long, white fingers with their pale, almond-shaped nails. His cock twitched and he felt the weight of it against his thigh. Soon now, when he had suckled enough for her satisfaction, she would give him permission to roll down the bedclothes and raise her chemise.

He felt almost faint at the thought of gazing on her rounded belly. The urge to bury his face between her thighs and lap at the fragrant, rain-tasting flesh of her quim was so strong that he clenched his teeth until the feeling faded.

'There now,' she purred, when the nipple stood out proud and firm. 'You *have* been patient. You may take the other teat into your mouth now.'

Sir James closed his eyes and bit her, ever so gently. Jenny laughed huskily and called him 'my greedy boy'. As he suckled, he felt the reflection of the strong pulling sensation in the throbbing at his groin.

The full weight of her breast was warm against his cheek and nose and he sighed in ecstasy at the glorious firmness of the nipple on his tongue. If only he had met her when they were both young enough to have another child. What joy he would have experienced in suckling milk from her, in having her squirt the sweet, bluish liquid on to his tongue.

The thought of it caused him to spasm with an erotic pulse which was so strong that he almost ejaculated. When, after a few more minutes, Jenny slid her little finger into the corner of his mouth and eased the breast free he almost groaned aloud at the feeling of loss.

'That's enough. Mama is ready for her naughty boy to pleasure her now,' Jenny said softly. 'You know what to do. Be good and I'll reward you.'

Raising himself up, Sir James folded back the bedclothes, easing them down Jenny's body inch by inch. As he had been longing to do, he lifted the exquisite, lace-trimmed chemise and rolled it up to lie in folds on her stomach.

'Oh, Jenny dearest. I adore you,' he breathed as he stroked the firm white skin of her belly and thighs. 'Open your legs, so that your devoted boy can suckle that salt teat between the lips of your quim.'

Jenny did so and he breathed in her musky scent, his mouth actually watering at the thought of tasting her. The hair on her mons was dark-blonde in colour and the lips of her vulva were plump and well developed.

He exerted a gentle pressure and Jenny bent her knees and drew her legs open more widely. Sir James gazed on the glistening red folds and the shadowed opening of the vagina. The inner lips were finer and darker in colour and there was the little bud, covered by its tiny hood.

The object he called her 'salt teat' was firm and well developed. It drove Jenny wild when he sucked it gently.

Dipping his head he closed his mouth over the spread-open quim and moved his lips in an erotic kiss. The taste on his tongue was wonderful: rich and salt-sweet. Jenny always perfumed her pubic hair and he detected the faintest tang of sweat under the perfume. Divine.

Jenny clutched at his hair, little sighs emitting from her. As he pushed his tongue inside her, feeling how the flesh walls trembled, he rubbed the tip of his nose against the hard button of her pleasure bud and thought how much he relished this act.

The full white thighs brushed against the sides of his head as Jenny drew them together, her hips bucking as she reached the crest of her passion. With her trembling wet quim pressed to his mouth, he felt every pulse and jerk of her climax.

Not until Jenny had sunk back, sighing with repletion, did he lift himself into position and thrust his bursting cock into her vagina. His plump buttocks pounded back and forth and the sweat stood out on his forehead. After just a few strokes he emptied himself, burying his face in Jenny's neck and gasping out his thanks.

As he lay beside her, Jenny stretched out her hand and ruffled his hair.

'You were a good boy,' she said softly. 'Mama is very pleased with you.'

Sir James smiled proudly. With Jenny he had discovered that it was even more satisfying to give pleasure than to receive it.

Francis awoke first and looked across at the sleeping face of his twin.

Sidonie looked so childlike in sleep. Her mouth was soft and a trifle sulky in repose. There were faint violet shadows under her eyes and in the hollows of her cheekbones. The adorable dimple in her chin was not so pronounced.

He felt such a surge of affection for her that his eyes stung with emotion. His beautiful sister. His companion of eighteen years. Nothing would ever hurt her while he lived.

Suddenly he was afraid; she seemed so still. He sat up and shook her gently. She awoke with a jerk and he smiled down into her unusual brown eyes, thinking that they were the exact colour of strong coffee, rare on someone with her hair and skin.

'What? What is it?' Sidonie said. 'Why did you wake me? Did you hear the breakfast bell?'

'Oh, it's nothing. I just felt lonely,' Francis said.

She laughed softly and put her arms up to draw his head down to hers. They kissed deeply.

'How can you be lonely? We share my bed every night now. Did you remember to ruffle the bedclothes in your room? We don't want Smithers getting suspicious.'

'I remembered, but it hardly matters. No one cares what we do.'

Sidonie laughed delightedly. 'How reckless you are, Francis. I do believe that you're getting worse. Is it true what you told me last night – about the chambermaid, I mean?'

Francis looked annoyed. 'You know I never tell you

lies. Other people perhaps, but I always tell you everything.'

Sidonie clasped her hands behind her head and beamed up at him.

'In that case, you won't mind proving that to me.'

'What do you mean, proving it? How can I? You can't mean . . . You do! You want to watch, don't you?'

Sidonie nodded and clapped her hand to her mouth, her brown eyes dancing with amusemant. When she lowered her hand her cheeks were flushed.

'Oh, Francis, you sound so shocked. What's the matter? Aren't I allowed to be a little reckless too?'

'Well, yes. But it's different for you.'

'Because I'm a girl? That's utter rot and you know it. Don't I enjoy doing all the things we do to each other as much as you do? I'm just like you, my darling brother. And don't you forget it. I shall find it very tedious if you start keeping things from me – for my own good.' She punctuated each of the last four words with a pointing finger. 'Don't you dare start treating me like you're my guardian!'

Francis's blue eyes widened with respect.

'I wouldn't dream of doing any such thing. Very well. How can I refuse? I'm meeting Clara and Rose in the old wine cellar at eight this evening.'

'Both of them!' Sidonie had the grace to look scandalised.

Francis grinned, his mouth curving with unashamed pride. 'Oh, yes. They like it better that way. One likes to watch while I do her friend. Sometimes I watch them stroke each other.'

'Two women, together? I had not thought it could happen. But I didn't know that men pleasured each other until you told me about Chatham. How fascinating. There's so much to find out, isn't there? I shall go to the cellar early and hide. I cannot wait! Be sure to take enough candles with you. I want to see absolutely everything.'

Francis swung his legs over the side of the bed, then jerked the bedclothes off Sidonie.

'You're a monster, do you know that? Now out you come. That *was* the breakfast bell. I had better go to my room before Rose brings my hot shaving water and Clara comes in here to help you dress.' He saw the gleam in his sister's eye and grasped the tops of her arms. 'Don't you dare say a word to Clara or the whole thing's off! Understand?'

'Very well,' Sidonie said sulkily, rubbing her arms.

Really, Francis did not know his own strength sometimes. At her next words her voice took on an edge of sarcasm.

'I can't think why you're worried that I'll tell. After all, I have the whole day studying the Greek classics with that old fool Reverend Beecham to look forward to. I'm sure that I can hardly concentrate on anything else at all!'

As Francis walked quickly across the room, his muffled laughter floated back to her.

'Don't ever change, Sidonie,' he said, having to almost choke out the words. 'You're priceless.'

While Sidonie read through the passages set by the Reverend, she thought of her last meeting with Chatham. Strangely it was not the erotic act they had shared that stayed in her mind, although that had been satisfying to them both, it was the things he told her about his circle of friends.

How she longed to go to London and meet the poets, writers and artists he knew. Women were welcomed amongst them apparently. Chatham often praised her unusual looks, comparing her with someone called Elizabeth Siddal who was a favourite model of the artist he admired most, Dante Gabriel Rosetti.

Sidonie felt that it was probably vain of her, but she loved to hear Chatham's compliments. There was no one, other than Francis, to notice how she looked. And he looked too much like her himself to be overly impressed. It was not that he did not think her beautiful, it was just that he saw her every day. He was accustomed to her in a way that Chatham was not.

She hoped it was not disloyal of her to long for male company. It was different for Francis; he had his own private appreciation society in the form of Clara and Rose. Then there was Smithers, who sometimes had a twinkle in her eye when Francis was around, despite her sharp tongue.

Well, there were compensations for having such a wicked self-indulgent brother; she smiled as she thought of what she was to witness in the old wine cellar. If she had not been so certain of her place in Francis's affections she might have given way to pangs of jealousy. But that would be absurd. Both she and her twin had an unspoken rule about each of them taking other lovers.

Their love for each other was unshakeable. Sexual dalliances were just pleasant diversions to be shared, examined and used as a spur for their personal satisfaction.

She gave a little shiver as she remembered the caresses she and Francis had exchanged last night. He was becoming quite expert in arousing her. Sometimes it seemed as if he knew her body as well she did. And now she knew why. Whilst he had been pleasuring Clara *and* Rose, he had no doubt been learning new techniques as well as furthering his studies of intimate female architecture.

Goodness, Francis was turning into quite a rake. No matter, as long as *she* reaped the benefits. Given the opportunity she might have followed suit. But the only other males she came into contact with, besides Francis and Chatham, were Hodgkins the gardener and Tillworth the coachman, both of whom were grizzled, stoop-shouldered and positively ancient.

One day, she promised herself, she would have more lovers than she could cope with. And she would treat them with haughty disdain, accepting their slavish attentions as no more than her due.

Was there a female equivalent for 'rake'? She did not think so, at least nothing that sounded pleasant. Perhaps she would make up a name for herself.

A woman of pleasure, she thought, that's what I'll become. A worthy she-rake – even better. Liking the sound of the phrase she consigned it to her memory, then opening the book on her lap, turned her attention to her Greek studies.

The day passed slowly. After a break for a luncheon of cold roast beef, followed by apple pie and cheese, which she took with Francis in the dining room, she was obliged to go over the following week's menus with Smithers.

The ritual was a formality only as it was obvious to everyone who was the real mistress of the house. Smithers ran things in her own way and the household tasks were accomplished with the regularity and smoothness of a well-oiled machine. All Sidonie had to do was to approve the dishes, then listen and nod sagely, while Smithers discussed the range of produce which was in season and could therefore be purchased most cheaply from the suppliers.

Smithers seemed in a hurry to get the meeting over with, which suited Sidonie. She wondered idly why Smithers was in such a flap. Already the woman was stuffing her notebook into the capacious pocket of her apron and hurrying from the parlour as if she had a hundred and one tasks to perform before dinner.

She shrugged, forgetting about Smithers' agitation almost at once. The housekeeper's problems did not concern her.

It was a relief to go up to her room to wash and change before dinner. Clara brought clean towels and a jug of hot water, which she tipped into the china washing bowl on the dresser.

Sidonie looked at Clara from the tail of her eye, seeing anew her buxom, freckled good looks. The dark, high-collared dress and snowy white apron did nothing to disguise Clara's rich curves. At the thought of watching

Francis thrusting into the housemaid's willing body, while Clara sighed and surged against him, Sidonie felt quite weak at the knees.

'Thank you, Clara. Be so good as to come back in ten minutes to help me dress,' she said, surprised to find that her voice was steady.

'Yes, ma'am,' Clara said, her eyelids lowered respectfully as she dropped a curtsy before leaving the room.

Sidonie was bursting to ask her questions: How many times have you lain with my brother? How does it feel when you stroke Rose? And, most importantly, tell me what it feels like when you spend?

As she stripped and washed herself all over with a piece of flannel and some rose-scented soap, she thought how she had never discussed such things with another woman.

Francis was her confidant, her only other source of information. Did other women get a warm, tingly sensation in the base of their bellies when they experienced their peak of pleasure, as she did? She had never thought to ask him about such things.

Tonight she would watch closely while Francis had Clara and Rose and observe all of the subtle signs of the women's enjoyment.

The inside of the coach smelt strongly of leather and more subtly of Lady Jenny Haversidge's perfume – Lotion de Guerlain, which was redolent with the scents of *chypre* and patchouli.

Jenny adjusted her position. Her back was aching and the whalebone ribs of her corset were pinching unpleasantly. She would be glad when they reached the house. The journey had been long and tedious. And they had been held up on two occasions: once by a fallen tree and once when one of the horses had become lame.

The light was failing now and the coach lamps cast a faint golden glow outside the window, obscuring the view of the Wiltshire downs. The sound of hooves on the road and the squeaking of the coach-springs was

grating on her nerves. All she could think of was a soft
bed and a hot drink. It was typical of her that she did
not give vent to her irritation, but said only, 'It's getting
rather late to arrive without notice, Jimmy. Nothing will
have been prepared. Shouldn't you have warned Smithers that we were coming?'

Sir James smiled and patted the back of her elegant,
gloved hand.

'Don't worry, m'dear. Smithers is expecting us. I
instructed her to get the west wing ready, but to be
discreet about it and tell no one that we are coming – not
even the maids. I want to surprise Sidonie and Francis.'

'Won't they hear the carriage arrive?'

'Not if we alight at the gatekeeper's lodge and walk
up to the house. Do you mind, dearest? It's a fine night.'

'Of course not,' Jenny said, thinking that it would be a
mercy to stretch her legs and rather romantic to walk
along the tree-lined drive with the moonlight shining
down through the branches.

She squeezed Sir James's hand, knowing how nervous
he was about facing his children. Well, she was here to
help him.

'I'm so looking forward to meeting the twins. I'm sure
that Sidonie and I shall be the greatest of friends.'

Sir James smiled worriedly and peered out of the
carriage window.

'Ah, here's the gatehouse now,' he said.

Jenny drew her full, silk skirts together and reached
for her reticule as the coach drew up in a flurry of
chinking harnesses and stamping horses. Quickly she
checked her appearance, wanting the twins' first sight of
her to be favourable. After all, they were not aware of
her existence. It would no doubt be something of a shock
for them to discover that their father had a gentlewoman
companion.

By the time they reached the main house, both Lady
Jenny and Sir James were a little out of breath. Smithers
had been keeping a look-out and opened the front door

before they had a chance to lift the lion-headed, brass knocker.

'Good evening, Sir James. Your ladyship,' she said. 'I have your rooms ready. Please come this way.'

Jenny stripped off her gloves and hat as she entered the suite in the west wing. She saw that there was a fire burning in the grate and the fresh smell of lavender polish filled the air.

'Her ladyship is rather tired from the journey. Bring her some tea, will you, Smithers?' said Sir James.

'Yes, sir. And something for you? A hot toddy?'

'Nothing at the moment. I want to speak to the twins if they have not retired yet. You didn't tell them that I was coming?'

Smithers rose up to her full height and said, a trifle indignantly, 'I did as I was told.'

'Very good. Now, you attend to her ladyship. I'll go and find the twins.' He waited until Smithers had left the room before turning to Jenny. 'I want to speak to Sidonie and Francis before I introduce them to you, m'dear. You don't mind my leaving you alone for a while, do you? You'll be in safe hands.'

Jenny sat back in the comfortable armchair and stretched her feet towards the fire.

'Don't worry about me. I'll be perfectly comfortable. Oh, you might bring back a bottle of that Spanish malmsey you've told me about. That is, if you have any left in the cellar here. We could share a glass or two before retiring.'

Sir James felt a ripple of desire at the thought of bed. The malmsey was a good idea. He imagined trickling the strong, sweet wine over Jenny's breasts, then licking the sticky liquid from her nipples.

'Right you are. I won't be long. Enjoy your tea.'

From her vantage point in the cellar behind the racks of wine, Sidonie watched the tableau unfold, her knuckles pressed to her mouth to hold in her murmurs of surprise.

In the wildest flights of her imagination she had not

33

pictured such a scene of wantonness. Francis was plainly the worse for drink and surely Clara and Rose had been allowed to drink from the same bottle.

Both women were partly clothed, their hair awry and their cheeks flushed with colour. Two bottles of wine, in fact, lay on their sides on the floor, the last of the red liquid seeping out on to the flagstones. Sidonie gave a muffled, scandalised giggle. It was a good thing that the cellar walls were thick; there was no likelihood of anyone upstairs hearing the sounds of enjoyment.

'Come on then, Clara. It's your turn to go first,' Rose slurred, pulling at the remaining hooks on the back of Clara's gaping dress.

Clara, who had been dancing in circles, her breasts bobbing and her skirts raised up to expose her sturdy knees and calves, spun around and knocked Rose's hands away.

'Leave off, you,' she said, squirming out of Rose's grasp. 'It's Francis who says what's to do. In't that right, sir?'

Francis grinned and caught her around the waist.

'That's the way of it, Clara. But I've a strong mind to have you first. Have you any objections?'

Clara clamped both hands to his cheeks and kissed him soundly.

'I'll take that as a no? Shall I?' Francis said, grinning when she drew back.

Clara pushed the flat of her hand against his chest. 'Ooooh, you're sharp, you are. Mind you don't cut yerself.'

She began pulling down the bodice of her dress and freeing her arms. Rose helped her disrobe and soon Clara was dressed only in a knee-length chemise and a stout cotton corset. Her big round breasts jiggled under the chemise as she moved, the prominent nipples making little peaks in the fabric. She faced Francis with her hands on her hips, her bottom lip stuck out in a pout.

'Well? How d'you want me?'

'You're frisky tonight, Clara,' Francis said with mock disapproval. 'What shall we do with her, Rose?'

Rose's thin face lit up with a crafty smile. Flicking back a lock of dark hair, she said, 'I think she ought to be punished for her cheek, sir.'

'I quite agree, Rose. Capital idea. Come here, Clara, and lean over this bench.'

Clara sidled over to him, pushing back a strand of straw-coloured hair which had flopped into her eyes. Holding eye contact with him, she bent forward and pressed her belly to the rough wood. The curves of her broad behind became visible as the chemise was pulled tight.

While Francis looked on, Rose began rolling up the chemise until it lay in a sausage shape in the small of Clara's back. The full globes of her buttocks and her shapely thighs were laid bare. Clara giggled and waggled her bottom, parting her legs a little to expose the pouting, split-fruit shape of her quim.

Sidonie watched in fascination. She had never seen a woman undressed like that. Clara had a lot of hair between her legs. The cleft between her buttocks looked deep and the skin there was a darker, pinkish colour.

'How many slaps do you think, Rose?' Francis said. 'Tell you what, I'll leave that to you.'

Rose flashed him a lecherous grin, her eyes fastening on his fingers which were unbuttoning the fly of his trousers. Stepping out of them, Francis cast them aside and put his hand down to pull up the tail of his shirt. His cock stood out like a poker, red and potent-looking.

'Ooooh, sir,' Rose whispered. 'You is ready now. Are you goin' to do her while I spanks her?'

Francis squeezed himself, running his cupped hand along the shaft of his member. As he smoothed back the skin from the purplish tip, a tiny drop of clear fluid appeared from the slitted mouth.

'I might just do that, Rose. Get started, will you? I'm a bit quick on the trigger tonight. Must be the blasted wine.'

Rose set to with a will, slapping Clara's broad white backside while Clara squealed theatrically and called out protests. 'Ow! That one 'urt! You don't have to be so rough, you girt lummox!'

Sidonie was spellbound. Clara was obviously enjoying the spanking, even if it was somewhat painful. Her back was arched, so that her bottom was pushed out towards Rose's hand. In a moment she began weaving her hips back and forth, bending her knees and thrusting forward to rub her pubis on the overhang of the wooden bench.

'Oh, look, sir. She's being ever so lewd,' Rose said, giggling.

Francis swore softly. He was breathing hard when he took up position between Clara's spread thighs. He placed both hands on her reddened cheeks and circled the firm, dimpled flesh. Then he slid his hands in towards the moist cleft and eased the heavy globes apart exposing the generous quim and the tight, wrinkled opening of her anus.

'Fore or aft,' he said jauntily. 'What's it to be, Clara?'

'Oh, Gawd. Do me up the back-end, sir. But rub me with your fingers too. Oh, I can hardly stand it, I'm so near to spending.'

Francis dipped his fingers into her wet folds and smeared the pearly juices around the head of his cock. Easing the swollen glans towards her anus, he pressed forward gently until the tight ring of muscle gave. Clara gasped and jerked as he slid more deeply into her and began to move slowly.

Watching, Sidonie bit her lip. She was so aroused that she had to squeeze her thighs together to try to still the pulse which was beating in her quim. But that only made the feeling worse. Her dew was seeping out of her, soaking the folds of her chemise. Lord, she had not known that there could be such pleasure in watching others doing it.

Francis reached underneath Clara's body and began moving his arm back and forth as he thrust more strongly between the fat, pink cheeks.

'Oh, my. Oh, lawks,' Clara squealed, her voice rising ever higher as she pushed her hips backwards towards Francis's flat belly. 'Do me hard, sir. Oh, my. I'm spending!'

Francis threw back his head and went rigid. His buttocks were taut and his cock buried to the hilt within Clara's body. Gritting his teeth he gave out a low satisfied moan.

At the exact moment that Clara and Francis reached a mutual climax, Rose cried out too. But her cry was one of shocked surprise.

'What the devil is going on here!' called out a strident male voice. 'Francis! Explain yourself at once.'

Sidonie almost fainted with horror. And Francis, already withdrawing from Clara and wiping himself on his shirt tail, turned around to meet the furious countenance of his father.

Chapter Three

Sidonie cowered behind the wine racks too terrified to move, while her father grabbed Francis by the scruff of the neck and hauled him towards the cellar stairs.

Clara and Rose broke out into noisy sobs, cowering away from Sir James whose face was almost purple with rage. Clara was trying to struggle into her dress, while Rose had thrown her pinafore over her face.

As soon at the two maids had hurried up the steps and disappeared, Sidonie came out of hiding. She felt sick at the thought that her father had discovered Francis in such a compromising position and heartily relieved that he had not known that she was watching, but she could not leave Francis to face this alone.

Stealthily she made her way towards the parlour, from which came shouting and the sound of a scuffle. There was the sound of a hand striking, a low moan of pain, and then Sir James's enraged voice crying, 'You're a dashed bounder, sir! I ought to take a horse whip t'you! You utter swine. You depraved little beggar!'

'Father! Stop, please. Listen to me!' Francis had a frantic note in his voice. 'Ow! Please stop. That bloody well hurt! Stop hitting me this instant or I swear I'll hit you back!'

'You dare face me down. You bloody foul-mouthed young whelp! I'll thrash you within an inch of your life!'

Trembling, Sidonie approached the door and pushed it open. Francis stood with his head bent. One arm was held up defensively and the other curled into a fist. His shirt was hanging out of his trousers and there was a livid mark across one cheek. Blood from a split lip trickled down his chin.

He looked crushed, but defiant and very young. It hurt Sidonie to see her arrogant, dashing brother looking like that. She rushed into the room and stood beside Francis crying out, 'Stop, Father. Please. Don't hurt him any more.'

Sir James, his hand raised to deliver another blow, arrested the motion in mid-air.

'Sidonie! Leave the room at once. This is none of your affair. I'll deal with Francis.'

'Best do as he says, Sidonie,' Francis said, his voice quivering. 'I can fight my own battles.'

Throwing her arms around Francis, Sidonie turned to face her father.

'I won't go. You can't make me, either of you. Whatever concerns Francis, concerns me.'

'Sidonie! Obey me at once!' Sir James bellowed. 'I will not countenance such defiance.'

'I'm sorry, Father,' she said evenly, 'but I must do as I think fit. I'm staying here. Perhaps you'd like to thrash me too!'

Sir James looked perplexed. He dropped his hands to his sides and frowned at his children. Francis, white-faced and trembling with emotion, was struggling manfully not to cry, while Sidonie was blazing at him with such spirit that, for a moment, he felt a surge of parental pride.

They were a handsome pair and no mistake. And, apart from the difference in colouring, as alike as two peas. Both of them wore the same look of stubbornness.

Lord, what was he to do with the two of them? Francis's behaviour could not go unpunished, but he could hardly berate the boy and beat him in front of Sidonie. And it was out of the question to beat his daughter, despite her unfeminine behaviour. He became aware that Lady Jenny had stepped into the room and he felt a great surge of relief as her husky voice brought some sanity into the fraught atmosphere.

'I hope I'm not intruding, but I couldn't help but hear all the fuss. Can I be of any assistance?'

Sidonie looked at the stranger who stood in the doorway. She saw a tall, well-built woman, who was dressed in an exquisite peignoir of eau-de-Nil lace. Although past her youth, the woman had a soft-edged, comforting beauty. Her curly blonde hair was pinned up to leave her neck bare and dressed with ribbons of the same greenish-cream.

'Come in, m'dear,' Sir James said. 'I'm glad you're here, Jenny. I'm in sore need of your level head and good sense.'

Sensing that she had found an ally, Sidonie rushed over to the woman and was immediately swept into her soft, perfumed embrace. Despite the dreadful situation, Sidonie was drawn to the stranger, who she felt instinctively to be kind and generous of spirit.

She began at once to cry, her shoulders shaking with emotion. Although she was hoping to stir the woman to pity, her tears were not entirely fabricated.

'There, there, my dear,' the vision in lace murmured. 'Don't upset yourself. I'm sure we can sort out this mess.'

'May I introduce Lady Jennifer Haversidge,' Sir James said stiffly. 'A dear friend of mine and someone whose opinion I value highly. I wanted you all to get to know each other. But this is a long way from the pleasant reception I'd envisaged.' He sighed deeply. 'I'm very disappointed in you both. Whatever will Jenny think of you? I can promise you that strict measures will be needed to put things right here.'

'We are all tired and a little strained, James,' Jenny said gently, glancing at Francis who still standing rigid with fury. 'Would it not be better for everyone if we discussed this in the morning? A night's sleep has a way of making things seem clearer.'

Sir James nodded. 'Very well. Francis go upstairs at once. You are confined to your room until further notice. Smithers can see to your needs for the time being. I don't want you within a mile of the maids. They will have to be dismissed of course.'

Francis flashed Sidonie an agonised glance. She attempted a reassuring smile, but her lips were trembling badly. Reaching for his hand as he walked past, she gave it a squeeze and mouthed silently, 'Don't worry.'

'I'll take Sidonie up to her room,' Jenny said. 'It'll give us a chance to become acquainted.'

Sidonie managed a grateful smile and allowed herself to be led from the room. She did not dare glance back at her father who stood watching her, his hands linked in the small of his back.

Once inside her bedroom Sidonie threw herself on her bed and began to cry bitterly. Jenny sat beside her on the counterpane and waited until her sobs subsided. She handed Sidonie a lace-trimmed handkerchief. Sidonie sat up and mopped her eyes, trying not to stain the fine lawn cloth.

'What'll happen to Francis?' she said. 'Father was beside himself with fury. If I hadn't gone into the parlour, he'd have beaten Francis most severely.'

Jenny smiled. 'Your father's an impulsive man. By tomorrow morning he'll have calmed down. But, tell me. What did Francis do to so enrage his father?'

Sidonie blushed hotly and looked down at her lap.

'Oh, I see. A woman? And your father caught him *in flagrante delicto*? Is that it?'

Sidonie looked puzzled.

'In the act of committing the crime?' Jenny explained. Then, when Sidonie nodded, she went on, 'Well, perhaps that's not too bad. It is, after all, expected that a young man will sow a few wild oats. No doubt your father was

41

shocked to find Francis so ... forward in the manner of his ... personal education. James – Sir James – was under the assumption that you and your brother were still little more than children. It must have come as a dreadful shock to find that he was greatly mistaken.'

She reached out and picked up Sidonie's hand. Entwining her own soft white fingers with Sidonie's, she said, 'You look so worried. Is there something you're not telling me, my dear? Come now. If we're to become firm friends and I just know that we are, you must learn to trust me. You can tell me anything. Anything at all. And rest assured that you can rely on my complete discretion.'

Sidonie was silent for a moment longer. She had never met anyone so sophisticated or so understanding. It was also plain that Lady Jenny was a woman of the world. Sidonie sensed that nothing she had to say would shock her.

'It's worse, far worse than you think,' she began hesitantly. 'Francis was in the cellar with both maids, Clara and Rose. Rose had spanked Clara and Francis was ... you know ... with Clara, while Rose watched. He ... he was not having Clara in the usual way. But in the way that is supposed to be a sin.'

'I see,' Jenny said in a matter-of-fact voice. 'No wonder Jimmy was so incensed. He must be worried that Francis is a sodomite. And how do you know the details?'

She took in Sidonie's puce face, her trembling lips and nodded sagely. 'You were there too, weren't you?'

'I was just watching. It's hardly any different from seeing the farm animals coupling. How else am I to know what happens between men and women? I hid behind the wine racks. Francis did not know that I was watching. He would never have allowed that.'

Sidonie's eyes slid sideways and Jenny knew that Sidonie was giving her a censored version of the truth. If she was any judge, and she flattered herself that she was, the little minx and her twin were far more experienced than Sidonie was making out.

And no wonder. The two of them were breath-taking and ripe for the plucking. Something like this had been bound to happen. She blamed her lover for neglecting his children for so long.

It was probably best not to pry too much. She had a feeling that Sir James could not cope with knowing the whole truth.

Drawing Sidonie close, she kissed her forehead. What a lovely creature she was. Quite startling with that great mass of red-gold hair, narrow white face, and enormous dark eyes. Jenny felt a pang of unaccustomed envy.

'It's time you got some sleep now. Let me handle your father. Everything will be all right, I promise. You can rely on me. Remember that.'

Sidonie gave Jenny a hug.

'Thank you, Lady Haversidge. I'm so glad you're here.'

'Call me, Jenny, my dear. Sleep well. I'll see you at breakfast.'

Jenny closed the bedroom door behind her and made her way towards the west wing. The situation was going to need careful handling, but she already had a plan in mind. It was obvious that Francis and Sidonie were not ready to be let loose on society. They had been allowed to run wild and must now be educated in the virtues and manners expected of them.

There was a time-honoured way to instil culture, poise and sophistication into the minds of young adults of good breeding and Jenny could think of no better way to handle the situation.

Francis and Sidonie would be sent on the Grand Tour.

Sir James listened to what Jenny had to say. As usual, she made perfect sense. He had balked at first at the mention of the Grand Tour. What Jenny proposed was going to cost a deal of money, but he could afford it. Besides, he owed the twins that much after all the years of neglect.

As he became accustomed to the idea, he realised that

there would be many extra costs. They would need a complete new wardrobe. Underwear, outer-garments, shoes, everything. It had been a shock to see how worn and patched were their clothes. The dress Sidonie was wearing had frayed cuffs and had obviously been let down at the hem. Even then it was too short and revealed neat ankles in darned stockings and a pair of down-at-heel shoes.

Francis was attired in no better fashion. His trews were far too tight for modesty and his shirt had been washed so many times the fabric was almost transparent. He felt a pang of guilt. It was not a pleasant sensation.

There were other things to see to. He would have to engage a bearleader – a travelling tutor and chaperon. A quite obscene amount of money was involved.

Unexpectedly he found the thought of showering the twins with luxuries quite gratifying. He smiled inwardly.

'So. It's decided then?' Jenny said. 'I'm sure you're doing the right thing, dearest. Sidonie and Francis will benefit greatly from the experience. No one can visit Paris, Florence, Venice, see all those works of art and go to the opera and remain unmoved by the experience.'

'I'm sure you're right,' Sir James said, relieved to have the decision made for him. In truth he had no idea how to deal with the twins. He was fully aware that this situation would not have come about if he had taken more of an interest in their welfare. Well, perhaps it was not too late. Francis was merely high-spirited and lusty – a little like himself in his younger days.

One sexual encounter with a chit of a girl did not provide proof of irredeemable moral weakness. Francis needed to get out into the world and put some of his excess energy to use. Sidonie too would benefit from mixing in the right circles. She was a little too spirited and bold for his liking. Men did not like women to be cleverer than they were themselves.

No doubt Sidonie would meet someone who she could respect and who would teach her modesty and forbearance in return. There would be many other English people on the Continent, many eligible young men, all of them frequenting the right sort of hotels and gatherings. He must make certain that the travel arrangements were meticulous.

As if she had read his mind, Jenny said, 'Would you like me to make all the arrangements, dearest? I have a frightfully good agent in London. He has served the family well for many years and arranged my own tour in my youth. Leave it to me. You need not worry about a thing.'

Sir James nodded and stretched out his feet towards the hearth where the leaping firelight was reflected in the black lead of the grate. He felt relaxed and at ease. Jenny was a gem, an absolute diamond.

He reached for the silver tray which stood on a small table next to his easy chair. 'Will you take a glass of malmsey with me, my love?' he said.

Jenny laughed. 'You remembered to bring a bottle up from the cellar? Why, James, how naughty of you.'

Sir James poured two glasses of the red-brown wine and handed one to his mistress. Her eyes gleamed as she took a sip and then opened the front of her peignoir. The deep cleavage of her breasts was visible above the low neck of her Paris nightgown.

Deliberately she tipped the glass slightly and let a trickle of wine flow on to the white skin of her chest.

Instantly Sir James's cock stirred into life. The heaviness at his groin was hot and throbbing. He could imagine the taste of her wine-sweet nipples, the thrilling sensation of her soft breast nudging against his mouth as he suckled. 'Come to Mama,' Jenny said huskily.

With a muffled groan, he crossed the room and took Jenny into his arms.

Chapter Four

Sidonie tried to stand still while the dressmaker pinned a seam on the evening gown of embroidered blue silk.

Although she appreciated that she must be fitted for a multitude of garments, she was thoroughly bored with standing on the chair and gazing absently out of the window. The only sound in the room was the ticking of the carriage clock on the over-mantel.

She glanced down at the assistant who was on her knees, moving around with the marked stick used to adjust hemlines. If only the women could work faster.

Sidonie sighed. Surely she had enough clothes now. Her room was already filled to bursting with suits and gowns and her chest of drawers bulged with underwear from Paris: chemises, corset covers, frilled petticoats and fine silk stockings.

In a few short weeks the lives of Francis and herself had been turned upside-down. There was hardly a spare moment for reflection. The change was due in the main to Lady Jenny. Sidonie was well aware how close they had come to disaster. Even Francis, chastened by his narrow escape, was extremely circumspect in his actions these days.

She was excited by the thought of the coming journey.

If all was ready, they were to depart for Paris at the end of the following week. Her one regret was that she would not have time to take a proper farewell of Chatham Burney. With things as they were, it was much too risky to arrange a private meeting with him.

She and Francis must bide their time. And harness their passions – a much more difficult endeavour. Soon enough there would be ample chance for adventure. And, she determined, as soon as they were free of their father's jurisdiction, she and Francis would resume sleeping together.

She missed her twin's long, muscular body. It was comforting as well as arousing to have him curled around her in bed, the two of them fitting together as neatly as two spoons. Her body stirred with latent hunger, but she pushed away the images that rose to mind.

It was no use either to think of Chatham's pale, aesthetic body and the pleasures they had shared. There must not be the slightest hint of a scandal.

Lady Jenny was almost too astute. Sidonie knew that the older woman was not fooled by half-truths and veiled lies. In Lady Jenny, Sidonie saw a kindred spirit. Jenny had been wild and adventurous when she was young, she just knew it, and no doubt she had been pursued by any number of handsome men.

That her father adored his mistress was obvious. Sidonie wondered what hold Jenny had over him. Her father was not the stuff that erotic dreams were made of, although she supposed he had a stolid, country-squire sort of attractiveness. The thought of Jenny and her father doing *it* made her laugh aloud. She imagined Sir James's florid face twisted with passion, his plump buttocks pumping away between Lady Jenny's spread thighs.

'Ouch!' she said, as a dressmaker's pin pierced her skin.

'If madam would just keep still,' the dressmaker said coolly, raising her eyebrows.

'I'm trying to,' Sidonie said, smiling inwardly.

If only the vinegar-faced old harpy knew what she was thinking about.

Perhaps some time in the future, when she had settled down to married life, she and Jenny might have the kind of frank woman-to-woman talk she longed for. But until then, Sidonie must curb her own wildness and impatience.

Think of Paris, she told herself. How wonderful it will be. Paris.

The only blot on the blank page of the forthcoming adventure was that they had yet to meet the man whom Father had engaged as bearleader. The name Thomas Hibbert had been mentioned. Sidonie hoped that he was young and handsome, then she could twist him around her little finger. And, if he was not young, then let him be of the mould of Reverend Beecham – vague, affable, someone she and Francis could lead a merry dance.

Thomas Hibbert slung an arm around the meaty shoulders of Martha, the serving girl at the Wig and Pen tavern in the Seven Dials district.

'Lean on me, Master Hibbert,' Martha said affably. 'I'll see you safe upstairs to your cot.'

'Thank you, lass,' Thomas mumbled, his tongue feeling too big for his mouth. 'You're too kind.'

The room swam as he began to move and his stomach gave an ominous lurch.

It was the second time that week that he had been too drunk to attempt the short walk back to his lodgings. He had not meant to drink so much, but the company had been good, the porter excellent, and the hours had flown by.

Martha took a breath and heaved Thomas over the last step. Edging the door open with her foot, she managed to get Thomas into the narrow room where the innkeeper let the straw mattresses out for a few pence a night to good customers like Thomas.

The room was low-ceilinged and dark. A tiny leaded

window gave out on to the narrow alley beyond. Rows of cots covered with grimy mattresses were ranged down each side of the room. Many of them were occupied and snores and rustles came from those nearest the door.

A carpet of soiled rushes covered the floor. There was a smell of sweat and the acrid stench of vomit and urine. Martha did not flinch. She was used to such smells.

Manoeuvring Thomas on to the nearest empty mattress, she reached for the nearby stub of a candle, set in a cracked saucer and giving out a faint yellow light. After setting it down beside the cot, she studied Thomas's face.

He was well gone, was Master Hibbert, but there was life in him yet and she knew right enough how to rouse a man. Thomas was generous when he was pleasured. She might have to wait for payment and make her mark on the slate with the rest of his tally, but he always settled his debts in due course.

Fumbling with the buttons she opened the waistband of his trousers and pulled them and his under-drawers down to his knees. Taking the flaccid cock between her palms she began to roll it gently back and forth.

Almost at once she felt a response and she smiled with satisfaction. Thomas was one of those rare men who could get it up even when he had drunk himself into a near stupor. She had such an itch on her that she could think of nothing else all evening. Thomas was the lucky man she had chosen to scratch it.

'That's it, my bully boy,' Martha murmured. 'Get good and hard for me now. That's as fine a gully-raker as ever I've seen on a cove.'

Thomas groaned loudly and opened his eyes. He managed to lift his head a fraction and look down his body. A bleary smile flickered over his face as he saw Martha rubbing his cock energetically.

'Bless you for your generosity. But I beg you to spare me, lass,' he slurred. 'I haven't the juice to whet your whistle. The demon drink's done for me.'

Martha giggled. Oh, Thomas did have a way with

words. He was a real scholar. He rarely used bad language. And he was clean. His under-linen was white and fresh-smelling. Not like some of the malodorous riff-raff she was forced to lie with.

Thomas's cock was standing up thick and strong now. It twitched against her hand and the bulbous tip was moist and throbbing. On impulse she bent over and took him into her mouth, her thick lips moving down to encompass the whole of the cock-stem.

Oooh, Master Hibbert had a cudgel on him and no mistake. She curled her tongue around and flicked the under-side of the plum-like glans. Slipping a hand between his thighs she stroked the heavy scrotum, then reached further back to the tight little aperture between his buttocks.

'Christ!' Thomas grunted, his hips lifting off the bed as Martha sucked him and the tip of her finger wormed its way into his anus.

Martha's finger sank fully into him and pressed on some nameless spot inside him. A jolt of intense pleasure shot all the way down his cock and centred in the pulsing red end. It was all he could do to contain himself.

'Christ! Oh, Christ,' he said again.

There was a cackle from one of the other cots.

'He won't 'elp yer none! If you need any 'elp, Abe Cotter's willing. Here, Martha girl. Leave that toff and come over 'ere to me.'

'Shut yer 'ead, you,' Martha said affably, sitting up and removing her hand long enough to raise her skirts up to her waist.

Straddling the low cot, she positioned herself over Thomas and bent her legs. She sank down until her pubic curls brushed against Thomas's member. Then, with one hand still holding up her skirts, curled her fingers around the cock and brought it to rest between the spread lips of her quim.

Oh, she was ready for it right enough. But she liked to savour her pleasures. The men liked that too. They paid more and asked for Martha instead of one of the other girls if they thought they were something special. Instead of bearing down until her quim met Thomas's belly, she fed the cock into her bit by bit until he was fully lodged inside her.

'There my fine lusty gent. How's that feel?' she said, her breath leaving her in a long sigh of pleasure.

Thomas gave out a loud theatrical groan which was met by an oath from one of the other occupants.

'Can't a body get no peace?'

Ignoring the interruption, Martha began moving up and down. Leaning forward, she placed her palms on Thomas's chest to brace herself. His hands came up to close over her heavy breasts, kneading and squeezing the opulent flesh as Martha rode him.

She was breathing hard, little groans of pleasure escaping her open mouth. The big glans was nudging against her innards and the rough, almost-hurting feeling added to her enjoyment. Grinding her quim against the base of the cock on each downward stroke she urged herself onwards to her own release.

Thomas threw his head back, gave a great shout and shot his seed into Martha's capacious vagina. Shuddering and grunting she reached her own climax. Even before she had climbed off him and was wiping herself clean on the skirt of her chemise, he was half asleep.

Somewhere in the fuddled recesses of his mind was the knowledge that he must remain sober on the morrow. He had an appointment with Sir James Ryder at his country house in Wiltshire. First thing tomorrow he must catch the train.

The offer of work was a potent lure for a man in his state of financial embarrassment. It was important that he make a good impression. With a great effort of will he managed to rouse himself and mumble under his breath, 'An extra threepence for you, Martha, if you are sure to wake me early.'

'You can rely on ole Martha,' she said, bending over and patting Thomas's quiescent organ affectionately. 'And now I bid you good night.'

Fluffing her skirts and swaggering a little, she walked around the cot. At the door she blew him a kiss, then went out into the corridor.

'Thank Gawd for that,' came a voice from across the room. 'The drab's had her oats and the toff's lost his wits. Now we might get some blessed shut-eye!'

It was late afternoon before Thomas reached the house in Wiltshire.

Every bone in his body seemed to have been shaken loose by the coach journey from the railway station and his stomach felt as if it had been massaged by a large hob-nailed boot. Reaching for the hip flask in his inside pocket, Thomas took a deep pull of the geneva.

Screwing up his face, he said aloud, 'Mother's ruin. You'll be the death of me yet.'

The gin settled his stomach and he felt almost human as he walked towards the servants' entrance of the house.

Sir James Ryder stood with his back to the fire, his coat tails lifted to expose his backside to the warmth of the flames. He came forward to shake Thomas's hand and wave him to a seat.

'A glass of something to warm you after your journey?' he said.

With a supreme effort, Thomas refused. His hands were shaking slightly and he linked them in the small of his back so that Sir James would not notice.

'Never touch a drop until the evening,' he said stoutly. 'Perhaps some tea?'

Sir James reached for the bell-pull which would summon a maid. He seemed gratified.

'Very commendable, Hibbert. I should not wish to employ a man who is not master of himself. The position I am thinking of offering you is one of great responsibility. As well as acting as tutor to my son and daughter, I expect you to introduce them to the right people and guard against them mixing with the wrong sort, if you get my meaning.'

'I do indeed, sir,' Thomas said. 'You may rest assured

that I will give my whole attention to the task – should I prove suitable. I have a great deal of experience in these matters. Perhaps you would like to see my letters of reference?'

Sir James took the bundle of documents and sat down to study them. The tea arrived and Thomas sipped a cup, watching for any sign of an adverse reaction in his prospective employer. There ought to be no problem. The letters were very good forgeries and had cost a deal of money.

He hid a secret smile. For all the signs of his outward poise, Sir James Ryder was a desperate man. Anyone other than Thomas might not have noticed the subtle, tell-tale signs, but Thomas was so accustomed to recognising desperation in himself that it was hard to miss it in others.

He imagined the scenario which had preceded his visit. Some sort of family scandal, possibly the son had put a swelling under the apron of a local girl or maybe the daughter had formed an unwise alliance with some-one of the tradesman class.

It happened all the time, even in the best of families. And now Sir James was eager to pack his offspring off on an improving tour of European cities. In his opinion, a dull or slow-witted person gained little from travel. And Sir James's children, having never been seen in the social circles of London, surely fell into that category.

But he did not intend to give voice to such sentiments. Who was he to argue with a wealthy man like Sir James?

A bubble of elation rose inside him which he quelled at once. Best not to seem too eager, even though he was certain that the position was his. Unless Sir James decided to check his references, and Thomas did not think that likely, he had nothing to worry about.

'Everything seems to be in order,' Sir James said, looking up. 'If you are agreeable to my terms the position is yours.'

Thomas permitted himself a triumphant smile.

'I shall be honoured to accept.' He and Sir James shook hands.

'Well, my good man. Have some more tea. I'll ring for Francis and Sidonie to come and join us. Might as well take this opportunity for you all to become acquainted.'

The sound of the bell ringing somewhere in the depths of the house was muffled. In a few minutes the door opened and two of the most exquisite creatures Thomas had ever seen stepped into the room.

Mercy, they were twins. Why had Sir James not warned him?

Sidonie wore a gown of emerald silk overlaid with white lace, which even he could tell was of the latest fashion. Her great mass of reddish hair was pinned up and held by enamelled combs. Francis, in corduroy suit and snowy shirt, was dark-haired and light-eyed, a taller, heavier-built version of his sister.

'Pleased to make your acquaintance,' Sidonie said, her dark eyes dancing with merriment.

'Likewise, sir,' Francis said, taking Thomas's hand and giving it a firm shake.

For a moment Thomas was speechless.

Even as he thought of changing his mind and telling Sir James that he had suddenly remembered a prior commitment, a wooden smile was spreading over his face. To refuse the position of bearleader was impossible. His creditors were almost breathing down his neck.

There was nothing for it but to brazen it out. God help him. For the two strapping, rather dull, country-bred children he had expected to meet had turned out to be slender, groomed creatures of a disturbing ethereal beauty.

Sidonie seemed to glow with an inner vivacity and Francis was possessed of a tightly leashed energy.

By the time they all returned from Europe he would have earned every penny he was being paid. For, with every bone in his body, Thomas Hibbert knew that Sidonie and Francis were going to be trouble.

Chapter Five

Sidonie stood at the window of her hotel room and
looked out over the slate-blue roof tops of Paris. The
many attic windows and little red chimneys were lent a
softness of tone by the early morning mist which was
already changing from blue to champagne.

She still could not believe that she was there. Would
she ever lose the joy and simple delight in every moment
of freedom? She thought not. It was the years of being
shut away in the house in Wiltshire that gave a sort of
crystal edge to every experience, every facet of their
journey.

The days had passed by in a welter of excitement. She
had been sick during the Channel crossing and Francis
had sat and patted her hand, mopping her face with a
lavender-scented cloth, and holding up a chamber-pot
for her to vomit in. Thankfully he had proved himself to
be a hardy traveller and had suffered no ill effects.

Before reaching the hotel they had experienced the
horrors of some French inns in the remoter countryside,
but now they were safely resident in the impressive
stone building on the Faubourg St Germain.

Walking across her room, Sidonie shrugged off her
peignoir and stepped into a skirt of grey serge, decorated
with violet braid. A matching jacket of violet, trimmed

with grey fur, went over the skirt. She patted her newly coiffured hair and used a rabbit's foot to smooth a tiny amount of rouge on to her cheeks. On impulse she rubbed a dab of colour on her lips. In England such a thing would be considered 'fast' but in Paris everyone wore face paint.

Feeling extremely daring, she went down the hall and knocked on the door of Francis's room. There was no reply to her knock, so she inserted a key in the lock and pushed open the door.

She saw at once that Francis was still in bed and, by the look of the humped shape buried beneath the sheets, he was still asleep. Moving quietly across the room she approached the bed. The hump did not move. Stretching out a gloved hand, she took hold of a corner of the sheet and whipped it back.

Francis turned over on to his back and gave her a sleepy grin. He was naked and an impressive erection jutted upwards from his groin. His cock was dark and flushed-looking, the thick shaft lying almost flat against his belly.

'You were awake all the time, you horror!' Sidonie said, laughing. 'And having wicked thoughts by the look of . . . that.'

Francis sat up and ran his hand through his tumbling brown locks. His hair had grown in the last few weeks and the strands brushed against his shoulders.

'Sister mine! I've been waiting for you to come and get into bed with me.'

He stretched out his arms to Sidonie, his eyes shining with invitation, but she avoided him neatly. Francis's expression changed.

'What's the matter? Are you angry with me?'

'Firstly, nothing is wrong. And secondly, no I'm not. Madame Dupont, the hair-dresser, called this morning. You know how long *she* takes. Then I had to get dressed. There was no time left to come and dally with you. Besides, I wasn't sure whether you were back. I heard you and Thomas go out very late last night.'

56

'Aha! So you *are* cross with me. Do I detect a note of disapproval in your voice?'

'Of course not,' Sidonie said tightly, turning her back. 'You can do as you wish. It's just that . . . Well, I thought we're supposed to share everything.'

'Come here, you silly goose,' Francis said affectionately. 'Sit beside me for a moment. I want to tell you something.'

Sidonie sat on the bed, her gloved hands clasped in her lap.

Francis laughed and chucked her under the chin. 'I adore you, when you're sulking. Give me a kiss.'

She did so and his firm lips opened under hers, his tongue pushing strongly into her mouth. The taste of him always excited her. When she drew back she was breathless and the blood was pounding in her ears.

'Oh, Francis,' she murmured, relaxing into his embrace. 'I thought you'd found someone else to share all your secrets with.'

'Who? Oh, you mean Thomas? I've just been getting the measure of our bearleader. It seems that as long as he's settled with a pint of wine before him and a pretty woman on his knee he's no hindrance to us. We just have to pretend to do as he says, but in reality can do as we like. My poor darling. Did you really think that I'd changed towards you in so short a time?'

Sidonie dimpled. 'Not really. I suppose I was annoyed at being left out. There are so many distractions for a young man in Paris.'

Francis smiled tenderly. 'But we are one, my love. Whatever I do, you shall share. And I absolutely insist that you include me in everything you do.'

'Very well,' Sidonie said, rubbing her cheek against his bare chest and smiling with relief. 'What was it you were going to tell me?'

Careless of the fact that she was creasing her new suit, she climbed on to the bed and lay cradled in Francis's arms. She stroked his chest, playing with the silky hairs that sprinkled his pectorals and snaked down in a fine line towards his groin, as he told her about the fashionable restaurant he had discovered.

'It's called the Frères Provençaux and they offer a most unusual menu. It's frequented by all manner of interesting people and I've made reservations for us for tomorrow night.'

'Another restaurant?' Sidonie pulled a face.

'I can promise you that this one is very unusual. The most beautiful courtesans of the *demi-monde* and various pillars of Paris society go there. So you see that I have been thinking of your enjoyment. Satisfied now?'

He was suddenly serious. 'You remember that we swore to be true to each other above all else? Well, never forget that. Other women mean nothing to me. They are just playthings, pretty toys to throw away when broken. If either of us ever begin to feel differently, we must tell each other at once. Promise me now.'

'I promise,' Sidonie said. 'But I can't imagine a time when I don't love you the best. Oh, Francis. I'm sorry I doubted you. It's just that there is so much to take in. So many new sights and experiences. I'm just so happy that we're together to share all this.'

Francis glanced down at his erection, which after Sidonie's gentle touch on his chest was even bigger.

'And I'd be completely happy too – if only you would take pity on me. And do something about my aching pego.'

Sidonie took off her kid-leather glove and curled her fingers around her brother's cock. Francis sank back on to the pillows with a sigh as she began to stroke him in the way he liked best.

Smoothing back the skin from the glans, she saw that there was a drop of clear fluid at the little mouth. Even as she watched, the seepage brimmed over and trickled down the groove towards the under-side of the shaft. She captured the silvery thread on the ball of her thumb and used it to lubricate the tender purplish end.

For a while she worked the skin of the stem back and forth over the rigid centre, then when she judged that

Francis's level of arousal demanded it, began to stroke him more firmly.

Francis dug the back of his head into the pillow and tensed the muscles of his thighs until they stood out like cords under the skin. His belly too was taut with the rising tide of his excitement.

Continuing to move her hand back and forth, Sidonie bent over and put out her tongue to flick at Francis's chest where his tight male nipples stood out like brown pips.

Arching his back Francis moaned, 'Suck them. Bite them.'

Sidonie obliged, using the edges of her teeth to nip at the firm little buds. Tremors passed over the flat belly and the cock leapt in her hand.

'Ah, I'm spending!' Francis called out, contorting his body into a bow-shape as a gush of creamy liquid shot into Sidonie's hand.

Closing her mouth over his, Sidonie absorbed his cries of pleasure, loving the way the sound vibrated all the way down her throat. It seemed as if she absorbed part of the very essence of her twin.

While Francis lay spreadeagled, recovering, Sidonie crossed the room to the dresser and poured water on to a towel. A moment later she returned to the bed and dumped the wet towel on Francis's groin.

He emitted a yell and sat straight up.

'Hell's teeth! You little cat! That's freezing!'

Sidonie smiled serenely.

'You deserve it. That will teach you to give me cause to worry. Now, brother dear, I shall help you to dress. Thomas has planned for us all to take a boat-ride down the Seine to visit the cathedral of Notre-Dame.'

'Hmmph,' Francis snorted, as he climbed out of bed and began splashing himself with cold water. 'He really is determined to try and drum some culture into us, although I would have thought by now that he'd have given up. I suppose we had better humour him. After all, that's supposedly the reason why we're here.'

'I'm glad you think that,' Sidonie said. 'Because tomorrow we're to visit the Louvre and the Tuileries to study the fine art collections.'

Francis flashed her a grin. 'After tonight at the Frères Provençaux, I doubt that you'll be able to concentrate on the canvasses in the Grand Gallery! And somehow I don't think that Thomas will be on time for his appointment with us this afternoon.'

'Francis, I know that look!' Sidonie said. 'Where is Thomas? You did bring him back with you to the hotel last night?'

'Well, no actually,' Francis said, laughing dismissively at Sidonie's look of outrage. 'I left him on the steps of a brothel after paying a coachman to wait until he emerged. Don't worry so much. We'll just go on to Notre-Dame and trust that Thomas will join us there later.'

Thomas groaned and opened one eye experimentally.

No flare of daylight seared his retina and he judged it safe to open both eyes. A thick gloom surrounded him, punctured at intervals by odd glimmers of candle-light.

Where in Hades was he?

His head throbbed dully and his mouth tasted as if a rat had died in it. A body next to him stirred and then he felt himself being shaken.

'Come, monsieur. Monsieur, if you please.' It was a softly accented female voice, belonging to someone he vaguely recalled.

The smell of sweat, sex and cheap perfume coloured the air. He remembered now. The whore. Ah, yes, the drunken fumbling. A tight aperture, pert breasts and a willing mouth. The girl had been named Minouche or something similar.

'We must go into the salon,' Minouche said, her voice rising with agitation. 'Madama Vigonette has clients waiting to use this cubicle. Hurry, please. Or I shall be in trouble.'

'Wh. . .? Go where?' Thomas muttered, then as he gathered his wits, full understanding came back to him.

He was still in the brothel. What time was it? Through the fug of a hangover he remembered Francis being with him. He must go and look for him. God forbid that any harm should come to the boy.

Pushing himself to his feet, helped by Minouche, he tottered forward and pulled back the curtain. The light was brighter in the corridor and he squinted as he edged along the wall. The stairwell, when he reached it, presented an almost insurmountable obstacle, but he managed to descend the stairs step by step by hanging grimly on to the banisters.

Downstairs in the salon there were a number of people in various stages of undress sitting around on couches. Scantily clad girls moved to and fro serving shallow dishes of coffee and plates of food.

'Can I get you a *café*, monsieur? Or a cup of *bavaroise*?' Minouche asked.

Thomas blinked and turned his head slowly. Hell's teeth, how old was she? She looked no more than sixteen. Remembering her valiant attempts to give him pleasure the previous night, despite the amount he had drunk rendering him almost senseless, he felt a surge of warmth for the girl.

'*Café au lait*, if you please, Minouche. *Merci*.'

Minouche flashed him a smile before disappearing behind the screen which hid the kitchen.

Thomas looked around the salon, but there was no sign of Francis. Perhaps he was still in one of the upstairs cubicles. The whores must have fought over who was to have the honour of pleasuring him.

Stretching himself out on a *chaise-longue*, Thomas fumbled in his waistcoat for his pocket watch. Damn thing did not seem to be working. He tapped the face with his forefinger, then held it to his ear. It was ticking regularly. But surely that was not the time?

Addressing one of the other gentlemen, a Dutch soldier with an amply proportioned woman sitting astride him and feeding him slivers of chocolate croissant, Thomas motioned to him.

'Time? *Quelle heure est il?*'

The Dutchman passed Thomas his watch. Thomas's eyes bulged as he looked at it. Good Lord. His watch wasn't wrong. It actually was four – but four in the afternoon. He had almost lost a whole day.

Sidonie would be waiting for them. She must be frantic with worry by now. He returned the watch and stood up unsteadily.

The shock had sobered him somewhat and he hurried back up the stairs, pulling aside curtains and peering into cubicles as he swept along the corridor.

'Francis?' he hissed. 'Where are you? Francis.'

Curses and cries of outrage met him as he continued to peer into the various cubicles. In one was a grossly fat man lying on his back while the whore who was straddling him bounced up and down. In another two women were lying on a narrow cot, too engrossed in each other to notice the interruption.

Thomas's cheeks burned as he threw back the curtain of a cubicle to reveal a well-built, muscular man who was kneeling on the floor while a young boy pissed into his mouth.

'*Merde!*' the man uttered and shook his fist in Thomas's face. 'You want to watch, you pay!'

'Sorry. So sorry,' Thomas muttered, letting the curtain fall back.

Where the hell was Francis? He distinctly remembered him accompanying him to the brothel. In fact, it had been Francis's idea that they go there. They had walked up the steps together, and then ... He groped for the memory. Ah, he had it now. What an idiot he was.

Francis had left him there, after assuring him that he had paid a coachman to wait as long as necessary. That angelic face hid a devious mind, Thomas knew that already. He ought to have been forewarned about something like this happening. Even slight acquaintance with the twins had borne out his initial doubts about them.

They were steadfastly loyal to each other, but anyone else was fair game. He did not think that they were intentionally cruel. It was just that they did not care if they hurt people. They used them, then threw them away.

He hurried back down the stairs and almost crashed into Minouche.

'Your *café au lait*, monsieur,' she said.

'No time for that now. You have it. Here, take this.'

He pressed a number of coins into her hand, hardly bothering to check the amount. Minouche looked down at her palm.

'Thank you, monsieur. Be sure to come again,' she said, smiling delightedly. 'And ask for Minouche. I will give you a good time. *Oui?*'

'Er yes. *Oui*. Right. Must dash.'

Outside the coachman was still waiting. As Thomas climbed aboard he thought that Francis must have paid the man handsomely, obviously having anticipated the long wait. What an utter fool he was to reinforce the twins' view of himself.

They treated him with a sort of contemptuous affection which was worse than dislike. At least if you disliked someone, you could still respect them.

You're a weak-minded, drunken wastrel, Thomas Hibbert, he told himself. If only he'd had the strength of character to follow Francis straight back to the hotel. He would have loved to see the look on his face.

The sad thing was that Thomas knew that in similar circumstances he would behave in exactly the same manner. He felt a surge of self-hatred. How pathetic he was.

As the carriage sped towards the Faubourg St Germain, he put his head in his hands.

Chapter Six

Sidonie dressed carefully for the evening, choosing an evening dress made of tiers of pure-white, barèges fabric, especially imported from France on Lady Jenny's orders. The neckline was low, showing an almost unseemly amount of bosom, and was decorated with garlands of silk gardenias. More of the flowers trimmed the bustle and train.

With her new hair-style and wearing some of the jewellery lent to her by Lady Jenny, she was confident that she looked just as chic as any of the Parisian women.

Francis and Thomas were waiting for her in the foyer. Both looked dashing in dark frock-coats and white waistcoats, top hats completing their ensemble.

Thomas, looking chastened, gave her a sheepish smile. She felt rather sorry for him. The disaster of the previous day had not been entirely his fault. Francis's sense of humour could be waspish at times.

Giving Thomas a beaming smile, she linked arms with him and Francis.

'How lucky I am to have two such handsome escorts,' she said, gratified to see that Thomas brightened considerably.

Although his thin cheeks looked sallow and the bags

under his eyes were more than usually prominent, he held his head high and managed to look quite debonair.

'May I also compliment you on your appearance this evening, Sidonie,' he said. 'You look quite splendid.'

'Why, thank you, Thomas,' Sidonie said, sparkling at him. 'Aren't we all grand! This is going to be a wonderful evening.'

'It will be a surprising one. I'm certain of that,' Francis said, causing Thomas to flash him a sharp look.

Francis laughed, his sculpted lips parting to reveal even, white teeth.

'Don't look so suspicious, old fellow. I have it on good account that this is *the* place to go in Paris. An officer of the Garde Impériale, whom I met in a café, tipped me the wink. Apparently there's to be a special floor-show tonight. He promised to reserve us a very good table.'

'I'm sure he did,' Thomas said dryly. 'It's amazing how you find these things out, Francis, when I doubt that you could tell me the name of a single French artist, despite the number of art galleries I've taken you to.'

Francis ignored the slur on his cultural shortcomings, only saying with barbed lightness, 'I must say, you're still looking a bit liverish. Perhaps you should stay in the hotel and have an early night. You could have a bottle sent up. Hair of the dog, eh?'

Sidonie pinched her brother's arm. 'Do stop teasing Thomas, Francis. It's really too bad of you.'

'I feel perfectly well since you ask,' said Thomas with dignity. 'Besides I wouldn't dream of leaving you and Sidonie alone. Part of my duties is to chaperon you. I fear I have been lax on that score this past week. But be assured that I intend to take the responsibility of guarding your morals seriously from now on.'

'The devil you do!' Francis said, with a harsh laugh. 'I'll do as I dashed well like! Don't get above yourself, Thomas. I should hate to have to mention ... certain weaknesses of yours in my letters home to Father.'

Sidonie stamped her foot. 'Will you two stop bickering! The carriage is waiting outside. Are we ready to go, or shall I go on alone and leave you here to face each other down?'

'Sorry,' Francis said, sounding just the opposite and grinning from ear to ear. 'Pax, Thomas? I didn't mean that, you know – about ratting on you to Father.'

'Consider the comment forgotten,' said Thomas. 'I apologise also, Sidonie. It's most unseemly to bandy words in public. Don't know what I was thinking of. Come, let's see if we can get through this evening in a civil manner.'

The doors of the Frères Provençaux stood open to the street, a blaze of light cascading out into the night.

A number of carriages were drawn up outside and richly dressed men and women were alighting and being shown into the restaurant. Sidonie had not expected anything half so grand. It seemed as if all Paris society was converging on the restaurant for the evening.

Sidonie watched in amazement. Many of the carriages sported coats of arms and there were some very handsome horses. In particular a maroon carriage, drawn by a pair of matched greys, caught her eye. The door opened as she watched.

A tall, blond-haired man with rakish good looks and wearing a flowing, black evening cloak alighted from the carriage. He looked up and caught her staring.

Sidonie blushed as the man tipped his hat and smiled appreciatively. It really was disconcerting to be assessed so openly. It was something she had noticed about Parisians in general. No one cared if you caught them staring. They were quite blatant in the way they looked you up and down.

Aware that her English upbringing was showing, Sidonie found herself looking away quickly. But it was as if an image of the striking man was retained on her retina. He had been tall and well-built and had the unmistakable air of old money about him. Although she tried not to show it, she was very impressed.

When she dared to glance back at the man, he was

striding towards the restaurant, the cloak thrown back over one shoulder to reveal its scarlet lining. He was holding a black, silver-tipped cane. The doorman greeted the guest by name, but Sidonie did not hear what he said.

She pulled at Francis's sleeve. 'Who is that man?' she asked in a low voice, not wanting to attract Thomas's attention.

Francis glanced in the direction she indicated. He grinned. 'Handsome brute, isn't he? And look at his cane. Must be a sword stick, quite the last word in elegance. Taken a fancy to him, have you? Don't be too eager to lose your heart, my pet. There will be plenty more like him inside.'

You're wrong this time, she thought. There'll be no one *quite* like that man.

'And plenty of pretty women to take your eye?' she whispered aloud.

'Indeed,' Francis said. 'But none of them will be as beautiful as you are.'

They were shown to their table which was placed next to a small, silk-draped stage set in darkness. Two candelabra held unlit candles. The main body of the restaurant was ablaze with gas-light, which was reflected back from floor-length mirrors, all of them framed with cut crystal. Almost every surface seemed to be decorated and gilded. The effect was of an almost decadent opulence. White, floor-length cloths covered the tables and lengths of ruched, deep-cream velvet hung around the walls. In the centre of the restaurant there was a marble fountain surrounded by trees. Nightingales in cages hung from the branches.

An army of waiters, dressed in white shirts, black trousers and enormous white aprons, moved between the tables carrying silver trays bearing drinks. Sidonie had hardly taken in the details of the surroundings before a waiter appeared bearing a bottle of champagne in a silver cooler and three glasses.

He placed the bottle on the table and began to pour.

'But we have not ordered anything,' Sidonie said.

The waiter smiled. 'Compliments of the gentleman, mademoiselle.'

Sidonie turned around. The blond man she had seen getting out of the carriage raised his glass to her and inclined his head. He looked even more handsome without his top hat. His shirt, bow-tie and evening jacket were all white. The blond hair, swept back from a broad forehead, accentuated the angular jaw and strong features.

Sidonie smiled her thanks and sipped her champagne.

'A conquest already,' Francis said delightedly. 'You're going to have your work cut out keeping an eye on Sidonie and myself tonight, Thomas.'

Thomas smiled over the rim of his champagne glass.

'Perhaps it was a foolish notion to even consider doing so,' he said ruefully.

'Oh, don't sound so down-hearted,' Francis said. 'Just think about enjoying yourself and leave Sidonie and me to ourselves. We're used to looking out for each other.'

Thomas nodded glumly and refilled his champagne glass.

The food was excellent and Sidonie ate with relish, enjoying the rich yet delicate flavours. After a lifetime of sensible English cooking, the subtlety of French cuisine was a delight to her palate.

Now and then she glanced towards the table of her fair-haired admirer, conscious that he was watching her despite the presence of his elegant dinner companion. Once, Sidonie caught the eye of the woman – a creamy-shouldered vision in an extravagant gown of satin and feathers – and sparks flew between them. She looked away hurriedly, unused to such an open display of hostility.

Francis had not noticed the exchange. He was flirting with two young women at the next table and Thomas was working his way gradually through his second bottle of champagne. At that moment the house lights dimmed and someone touched a taper to the candelabra on the little stage.

The sound of laughing, glasses chinking and low banter did not abate. It seemed to Sidonie as if the entertainment was something which was to be simply taken for granted.

Two women, both dressed only in diaphanous veils came on to the stage. Each of them carried a basket which was piled high with orchids. They began strewing them on to the floor. More young women followed them and soon the stage was covered with a layer of the fragrant blooms.

There was an appreciable difference in the atmosphere now. Sidonie detected a tension as the sounds of revelry began to die away. Only when there was silence did a woman step on to the stage.

She was tall and slender and her unbound hair streamed over her shoulders to her waist. A wreath of lilies adorned her head, but apart from that, she was naked.

Sidonie was profoundly shocked. Even on the stages of the most notorious London music halls, the women did not appear naked. They were clothed in flesh-coloured stockingette and draped with flowing scarves.

No one appeared to be scandalised by the dancer's nudity and soon Sidonie forgot her own discomfort. As the woman began to dance, dipping gracefully and then rising again, Sidonie followed her movements. Now and then the dancer struck an attitude as if allowing the audience to fully appreciate her beauty.

Whistles, claps and the banging of glasses on tables signalled the audience's approval. Such reactions seemed, to Sidonie, to be rather coarse and out of place, yet somehow *anything* would have been excusable within the confines of the fashionable restaurant.

Sidonie found herself envying the woman's statuesque figure, her finely moulded limbs, the rich curves at breast and buttock, and the pearly tinge to her skin. How would it feel to be naked in front of so many people? And to have men looking at her with lust-filled eyes?

The thought sent a shiver of excitement down her back.

The dance became more abandoned as the woman lifted up her arms and performed a pirouette. The heavy tresses of hair spun outwards, giving the audience the first clear view of her body. Although the gesture seemed artless it was designed to show her figure to advantage. Her large white breasts jutted outwards, the rouged tips looking as bright as cherries. Her waist was indented deeply, accentuating the generous swell of her hips and the prominent, rounded buttocks.

Finally the woman swept downwards and collapsed gracefully to the floor, bringing the dance to a dramatic climax.

The applause was deafening.

'Bravo! Bravo!' Francis shouted along with the others. 'More! More!'

Sidonie clapped enthusiastically as the dancer came to the edge of the stage and took a bow. She realized only then that the woman was covered from head to foot in a sort of sparkling powder. Seen close to, her nipples were a brilliant red. As she straightened up, Sidonie saw a flash of the same colour between the woman's legs and thought, she has rouged the lips of her quim; how enticing that looks.

When the applause subsided, an enormous silver tub was carried on to the stage. The dancer, her shoulders still heaving with exertion, turned her back on the audience as two young women came on stage to attend her. In a few moments her luxurious hair had been pinned up and a number of orchids pinned amongst the tresses.

Glancing coquettishly over her shoulder, the dancer climbed into the silver tub. As if on a given signal, there was a mad rush towards the stage. Some of the guests emptied their glasses into the tub, others brought full bottles, popping the corks so that jets of frothy champagne fizzed over the woman's shoulders and breasts.

Laughing and kicking up her legs she bathed in the sweet liquid. Francis and Thomas, realising that the race was on to fill the tub with champagne, hurried to add their contribution to the silver bath.

Overcome with curiosity, Sidonie leaned across to the next table.

'Excuse me. Who is that woman?' she asked.

'That's Thérèse Grammont – otherwise known as Nymphia. She's the most celebrated courtesan in Paris.'

A whore? Sidonie was shocked. In London such a creature would be shunned by polite society, not fêted. She had thought that she was becoming accustomed to new ways, but she realised that there was still so much to learn. How sophisticated everyone seemed. In Paris it was not thought of as a crime to enjoy the delights of the flesh.

In the tub, Nymphia had risen up and arched her back, pushing her hips forward and parting her thighs. To cheers and cries of increased delight the streams of champagne were poured directly on to her exposed sex.

Like a number of other men, Francis was leaning forward, shaking up the bottle in his hand and letting the jet of white foam wash up and down the parted quim-lips. The rouge, diluted by the liquid, ran in pinkish rivulets down the firm, white flesh of Nymphia's inner thighs. Similar pink trails snaked down her ribcage and pooled in the slight pout of her belly.

Nymphia smiled and splashed, now and then smacking a hand which attempted too intimate a caress.

Yet again, Sidonie felt the eyes of the blond stranger on her. Was he the only man in the building whose attention was *not* on the stage? She was flattered and intrigued.

A moment later, a tall figure appeared at her side. As he bent down to place a card on the table in front of her she caught the scent of him: expensive cologne and a subtle, woody odour of hair oil.

'Permit me to introduce myself, mademoiselle,' the blond man said in a heavily accented voice. 'Will you accept my card?'

Not sure how to react Sidonie picked up the mono-grammed card and read the name. 'Gunter Eckart' was followed by an address on one of the new boulevards in the most expensive and fashionable part of Paris.

'Thank – thank you,' Sidonie stammered, wishing she knew what was the proper response.

If Thomas had still been sitting next to her, he would have advised her. She could see him from the corner of her eyes directing a stream of champagne on to Nymphia's cleavage. By his crooked smile and unfocused eyes, she could tell that he was very drunk. There was no hope of help there.

She slipped the card into her evening bag and smiled up at Gunter. Gunter's well-shaped lips curved as he said, 'I look forward to seeing you at my residence, mademoiselle. Or receiving your invitation. Let it be soon.'

Then he bowed, clicking his heels together smartly and went back to his table.

Sidonie felt a mixture of alarm and anticipation. It seemed that she had just given Gunter the impression that she approved of his interest in her. Oh, well. It would be fun to have an admirer. She had wanted to become as sophisticated as Nymphia – who must have countless lovers – and it seemed that she was soon to have the chance.

She looked towards the table where Gunter had been sitting, planning to give him her most seductive smile, and was disappointed to see that he was no longer there. Then she caught sight of him. He was in the process of ascending the white wrought-iron staircase, leading to the balcony which ran around three sides of the restaurant.

He was alone, his dinner guest, the woman in silks and feathers, was nowhere to be seen.

As Sidonie watched, a door opened in a room upstairs and Gunter, after a brief look back into the restaurant, went inside. Intrigued by Gunter's last backward glance which seemed to be somewhat furtive Sidonie kept her attention focused on the upstairs balcony.

Waiters carrying trays of food and drink moved in and

out of the rooms. She deduced that these must be private function rooms. If only she had the nerve to go and look into one of them. She had a suspicion that she would see something even more shocking than Nymphia's champagne bath.

Francis and Thomas were still on stage and she felt a flicker of annoyance at their joint desertion. Hadn't they had enough of the over-fleshed whore yet? The noise and bawdy laughter, Nymphia's shrieks as a champagne cork found an intimate receptacle were beginning to pall.

Having no impetus to join in the fun, Sidonie was becoming profoundly bored by the spectacle on the stage. Goodness, how soon the unfamiliar became commonplace; the risqué toilette had degenerated into a lot of wet drunken fumbling.

Men could be so crass sometimes, she thought loftily.

On impulse she stood up and pushed back her chair. Thomas and Francis could hardly take her to task for deserting them if she decided to go upstairs and investigate. It was their own fault for leaving her alone at the table.

It took only a minute or two to climb the stairs. Lifting her full skirts up in both hands she marched purposefully along the balcony. The train of her gown rustled on the polished wood floor. There were one or two raised eyebrows as she passed, but no one passed comment.

Ah, that was the room. Gunter was behind that door.

'I regret that entrance is by invitation only, mademoiselle,' the doorman said, his hand on the door, as Sidonie attempted to push past him.

Sidonie was annoyed. It had taken an effort of will just to walk up the stairs. Her nerve was wavering, but she had come too far to be turned away now. Besides, she wanted to be able to taunt Francis with her daring when she went to his hotel room to report later that night.

He would be annoyed to have missed out on anything. Well, it would punish him for his obsession with Nymphia.

'I have an invitation,' she said boldly.

'Then an apology may be in order,' the doorman said with studied politeness. 'You will not mind if I check, mademoiselle? That way there will be no mistake. Your name, *s'il vous plaît*? And you are the guest of . . . whom?'

'Sidonie Ryder and I am the guest of Gunter Eckart. You may go in and ask him if you wish,' Sidonie said, her voice level and her eyes unwavering.

'*Pardon*, mademoiselle. That will not be necessary. I'm sure you understand the need for discretion? Please to go in.'

The door opened on to a room which seemed lined in red velvet. It was dimly lit by a single gas lamp. In the gloom it was possible to see that a number of men and women sat around on couches, sipping glasses of a greenish liquid. There was a sweetish smell in the air, like incense or some kind of burning herb. A pall of bluish-grey smoke hung over everything.

Sidonie closed the door and walked across the room. She passed people sitting or lying in various attitudes that suggested they were sleeping. How curious that seemed. Other couples were engaged in sexual acts, openly caressing and kissing each other.

Not daring to look too closely at what was taking place between those who were seated, Sidonie walked boldly up to an empty couch and sat down.

A waiter appeared at once and asked if she would like him to bring her something.

'Oh, er yes,' she said. 'Bring me whatever they are drinking.'

'Absinthe? Very good, mademoiselle.'

While she was waiting for her drink, Sidonie chanced a look around. Directly in front of her sat a man and woman who were too absorbed in each other to notice anyone watching them. The woman, who was dark-haired and buxom, rested against the back of the couch, her head tipped back and soft sighs of pleasure escaping from her lips.

Her partner had one hand buried beneath the voluminous skirts of her dress, while the other was plunged

74

into the unlaced bodice. Sidonie blushed as the woman changed position, sinking even further back on the sofa, drawing her skirts up above her knees to reveal shapely calves clothed in silken stockings, then pulling them even higher and opening her thighs.

The man's hand worked back and forth and Sidonie imagined that his fingers were pushed deeply inside the woman's vagina, moving slickly in and out while he rubbed at her bud of pleasure with the pad of his thumb. As the woman began to thrash and moan the man drew a breast free from its confinement and rolled the nipple between finger and thumb.

Pushed out by the stays beneath it, the breast jutted out provocatively. Sidonie experienced a sharp spasm of excitement. Never had she seen such a nipple. It was bark-brown and covered at least a third of the woman's breast, seeming somehow to encompass the very essence of femininity.

Sidonie wished that she had nipples like that. They must be very sensitive, because the woman began moaning more loudly as her partner leaned over to lick and nuzzle them.

Sidonie watched in horrified fascination. How could the woman bear for the other people in the room to witness her arousal? She seemed oblivious to anything but her pleasure. Now the other breast was freed, standing proud of the rim of stiffened cloth as was its twin, making the woman look more enticing than if she had been completely naked.

Sidonie felt a surge of heat between her thighs as she imagined taking the woman's place.

How awful, how shameful it must be to be so excited and eager for a climax that you did not care who watched you.

The woman was opening her knees even wider and thrusting her pelvis into the air. The pale skin of her rounded thighs was revealed, hardly obscured now by the froth of petticoats. The woman murmured words of pleasure and rose up, surging against the back of the couch. Her knees sagged apart and Sidonie glimpsed a dark patch of pubic hair, which glinted with silvery moisture and saw thick male fingers dipping into the shadowed sex.

Soon now, the woman would surely spend. Sidonie found herself longing for the moment of release. She was so involved in the scene that she did not notice that the waiter had returned.

'Your drink, mademoiselle,' he said, coughing politely to gain her attention.

Sidonie jumped and took her drink. '*Merci*,' she managed to say and took a gulp from the glass.

At once she began choking. The liqueur was strong-tasting and with a bitter-sweet after-taste. People turned to look in her direction as she fumbled for a handkerchief and wiped her streaming eyes.

'Can I be of assistance? Mademoiselle is indisposed?' the waiter asked.

'No. I am well. Thank you,' Sidonie said, managing to get her coughing under control.

Her cheeks flamed. What a fool she must look. And how humiliating that the waiter had seen her staring at the couple making love. Then she realised that he had moved away, his face expressionless.

Of course he must be used to such sights. She felt suddenly gauche and entirely out of her depth. Sipping the absinthe more slowly, she savoured the unusual taste. She was not sure that she cared for it, but its effect on her was almost immediate. The room began to swim and there was a pleasant buzzing in her ears. People were no longer looking at her and she began to feel more at ease.

Glancing towards the couple opposite she was disappointed to see that the woman had pulled down her skirts and covered her breasts. The man was kissing her cheek as she laced her bodice. Sidonie was annoyed. The interruption and her fit of coughing meant that she had missed seeing the woman spend. She had been so looking forward to the moment of climax, her own erotic tension keeping pace with the woman's sighs and the frankly lewd thrusting movements of her hips.

Now that the spectacle was over, Sidonie was left in a state of heightened arousal. She adjusted her position on the sofa in an effort to ease the throbbing pressure between her legs, but the movement only made her even more aware of the slippery wetness of her quim.

A shadow fell across her and she looked up to see a large woman wearing a red taffeta gown trimmed with rubies. The woman was handsome, rather than pretty, with broad features and well-groomed hair of a most surprising shade of yellow. Without asking whether Sidonie wished to have company, the woman sat on the sofa beside her.

'Did you enjoy that spectacle, *ma petite*?' she said without preamble. 'It can be enticing to watch another woman receive pleasure, no? I have been watching you. I have not seen you here before. Might I know your name?'

The woman's smile and easy, friendly manner put Sidonie at ease, although she was mortified to think that someone had seen her reactions.

'I am Sidonie Ryder – ' she began.

The woman put a plump, be-ringed hand on her bare arm.

'First names only here, *chérie*. It is a house custom. I am Marceline. I arrange these intimate tête-à-têtes for special customers and I know that you were not on my guest list. I would not have overlooked such a lovely young Englishwoman.' She leaned close and said in a soft voice, 'Forgive me, but you seem such an *ingénue*. *Pardon* – an innocent. How did you get into this room?'

Sidonie turned crimson. Lord, it seemed that she had hardly *stopped* blushing since she set foot into this place.

'I . . . I told a lie,' she said, for somehow the woman invited confidences. 'I said that I knew a man who I saw enter the room earlier.'

Marceline smiled, her full, rouged lips curving with

77

satisfaction. 'I thought so. And may I ask who that man was?'

'Gunter. Gunter Eckart – Oh, forgive me. First names only?'

Marceline flapped her beautifully manicured hands in a dismissive gesture.

'No matter. I know Gunter well. He is one of my regular patrons. But, tell me, how do *you* know him?'

'He gave me his card downstairs in the restaurant and invited me to call on him.'

'Ah,' Marceline said, in a way that spoke volumes. 'Then you do not know Gunter well?'

'No, but he seemed perfectly charming and he's so handsome and cultured.'

Marceline gave a short laugh. 'Oh, he's all those things – rich too – and a lot more besides. Every young woman's dream, eh?'

She leaned over and patted Sidonie's cheek. 'Such skin. There are no complexions like the English. Just like the softest silk,' she said. 'Such beauty should be appreciated.' Rising to her feet in a rustle of skirts she reached for Sidonie's hand.

Sidonie allowed herself to be drawn to her feet. 'I have friends waiting for me downstairs. Where are we going?' she asked.

'Into the holy of holies,' Marceline said with a husky laugh. 'This will not take long. Oh, la – you really are such an innocent. You remind me of myself, so long ago. Come with me, *chérie*. You think you have seen something shocking tonight? You have not. But you are about to. If you are considering responding to Gunter's invitation, then I think it wise that you know *exactly* what you are letting yourself in for.'

Her heart thumping painfully, Sidonie followed Marceline to the area of deepest shadow at the back of the room.

Chapter Seven

*E*ven before Marceline pulled back the heavy velvet drapes, Sidonie heard the sound of muffled cries and something else – something she did not immediately recognise.

The alcove was more brightly lit than the main room. Iron sconces around the walls held a number of candles. A soft yellow glow illuminated the three people who made up a startling tableau.

Two women were kneeling before a wooden bench. Both were naked except for their knee-length stockings and their shoes. Their hands were secured at the small of their backs. Each woman was bent over at the waist, stretching forward so that her hips were tipped up. The bench was narrow and looked as if it bit cruelly into the women's soft bellies. Without any support the two sets of breasts hung down, rocking gently as blow after blow was directed on to their unprotected buttocks.

The sound of leather hitting flesh was loud in the confined space. This had been the sound she did not recognise.

Perhaps because she had been forewarned by Marceline, Sidonie was not too surprised to see that the man wielding the lash was Gunter. He had stripped off his evening clothes and wore only a pair of fine woollen drawers tucked into riding boots. His muscular physique was marred only by a softness at his waist and a slight thickening of his torso.

He did not once glance towards the heavy curtain which partly hid the figures of Sidonie and Marceline. His whole attention was centred on the two kneeling women. Sweat poured down his handsome face and his eyes looked glazed and unfocused.

It was obvious that Gunter was very drunk. He did not look as handsome or as imposing as he had on first sight.

Sidonie felt the effects of the absinthe in herself. Whilst she felt light-headed, the surroundings seemed to have an unnatural clarity. Somehow her reactions had slowed down. She felt a curious lethargy, a reluctance to leave the alcove although she found the sight before her disturbing.

The positions of the women, so submissive and helpless, seemed to her to be appalling. And yet she could appreciate the perfect symmetry of their pale skin against the unyielding surface of the wooden bench. The way their buttocks were forced outwards and upwards, their plump thighs parted to reveal the shadowed valley of the inner cheeks and every detail of their quims, the pear shapes of their hanging breasts, and even their stocking-clad calves all seemed to have a kind of dreadful harmony.

Two things affected her deeply. The deep red stripes that covered the women's bottoms and the fact that both women were shaved between the legs.

The red marks against soft white skin were startling. She imagined that they would wear the evidence of their beating for days to come. And those shaved quims – she had never seen a sex looking so stark, so offered up to view. The puffy outer lips, the darker flesh within, and even their most intimate body openings were revealed. And how different were the two women. She studied them in fascination, never having realised that there could be so much variation in the female pudenda.

One of the women had a neat oval-shaped quim with small, pinkish inner lips which did not protrude overmuch. The other had a larger, more generous-shaped vulva, with deep-red inner lips which hung down a little, looking enticing and very sexual against her pale skin.

At that moment, Gunter gave an order and each of the women opened their thighs wider, striving to arch their backs and offer up their buttocks even more readily for punishment. Gunter laid down the lash he had been using and went to a slim wooden wall cabinet, unnoticed by Sidonie until now. He opened the door to reveal a number of beautifully crafted whips and canes.

Selecting an object which had a stout handle of bound leather and which flared out lower down into a number of leather 'tails', he returned to his former position. Sidonie had seen a drawing of a similar instrument. The object resembled the 'cat' used on board ship to administer a rough and ready justice to recalcitrant seamen.

She watched with awed fascination as Gunter trailed the thongs almost gently over the women's buttocks while they squirmed and wove their hips from side to side. In a moment he began to whip them lightly but directly on the spread-open flesh of their quims.

Sidonie shuddered, imagining the smarting heat, the exciting feeling of the leather strands as they brushed smartly against the pushed-out little buds of pleasure.

How had Gunter persuaded those women to let him abuse them for his sole amusement, she thought. Probably he had paid for their services. Then she realised that things were by no means as simple as they looked. Each naked quim, although rosy now from the mild abuse, was shiny with the slippery outpourings which she recognised as a sign of arousal.

And the gasps and little cries which both women emitted as the lash flicked up and down their most sensitive membranes were not altogether of pain or distress.

Dear God. How must that feel? Sidonie squeezed her

own thighs together, trying to allay the heavy pulsing there. Her breasts burned and the nipples tingled with only the slightest scraping against the lace of her chemise. She was alarmed by the ferocity of her responses.

It was a surprise when Marceline spoke. Sidonie has quite forgotten the woman who stood beside her.

'So now you see, little one,' Marceline said, slipping her arm around Sidonie's slender waist and drawing her close. Even through the layers of garments the other woman's body felt hot and solid.

'Gunter is a man of jaded and singular passions,' Marceline went on. 'Think twice before you accept any invitation from him. It is his delight to seek out young, untried women and bend them to his will. At least now you know who you are dealing with. Have you seen enough?'

Sidonie did not trust herself to speak.

Marceline looked closely at her, taking in her high colour and shining eyes.

With a low laugh, she said, 'Ah, I see that you have not. Not as innocent as all that, eh? You wish to stay until the finale. *Très bien*. Stay here as long as you wish. Where else should you get such an education, except in Paris? Come with me, *chérie*. Marceline will take care of you.'

Sidonie slipped inside the room and followed Marceline behind a lacquered screen. There was just room for a two-seater couch. Perching herself on the edge, she leaned forward and looked through the strategically placed cut-outs in the screen.

'Oh, my Lord,' Sidonie murmured under her breath.

She realised that she had almost uttered the words aloud and pressed her fingers to her mouth, for Gunter was pushing the handle of the 'cat' into the vagina of one of the women. The woman moaned and threshed as he worked the thick handle deeply inside her and left just the last few inches sticking out. The leather tails dangled obscenely between the plump thighs.

Gunter made a sound of satisfaction and began to

spank the spread buttocks while rotating the buried object with his free hand. The impaled woman emitted a series of sharp little cries and flexed her thigh muscles. The rim of her vagina was stretched around the thick handle and her juices ran in silvery trails over the circular binding.

Marceline pressed close to Sidonie, her heavy taffeta-clad thigh brushing against Sidonie's leg. The gesture was at first furtive, then more insistent. When it became heavy with promise Sidonie could no longer ignore it. A little alarmed she sat quite still as Marceline slipped a plump arm around her waist, her spread fingers just touching the under-swell of her breasts.

She could feel the warmth of Marceline's body and smell her exotic perfume. The heady sweetness of it was cloying and made her head swim. Sidonie tensed her shoulders, wishing that the older woman would move away but unwilling to say anything to offend her.

'You are hot for love, are you not, *ma chérie*?' Marceline purred. 'Watching Gunter has thawed the famous English reserve, no? You imagine how it would feel to have a man push the handle of a whip inside you and how it feels to reach a climax while being spanked. Oh, la. Do not look so stricken. Nothing shocks me. I have seen everything in my time. That is how I know that you burn and long for your own release.'

Her voice grew soft and cajoling. 'Marceline knows how to pleasure beautiful young women. Why not lie back a little and make yourself more comfortable? You can still watch Gunter and the women through the screen. See there? There are more spy-holes lower down. I will attend to your needs and you shall do nothing but relax and enjoy it.'

Not at all sure that she wanted Marceline's attentions, Sidonie edged away until the arm of the sofa stopped her progress.

'You are too kind,' she whispered. 'But really, this is not necessary.'

'Oh, but it is,' Marceline said and for the first time

there was a petulant note to her voice. 'It is the price I exact for my generosity. For I have been generous, have I not? You lied to get into this place, but I did not mind. I brought you here, so that you would be armed against Gunter should he ever call on you. And now I ask only that you let *me* give *you* pleasure. Is that unreasonable?'

Put like that, Sidonie could think of nothing to say. Perhaps it would not be so bad. She need only close her eyes and imagine that it was Francis who was making free with her person.

Marceline took her silence as agreement.

'*Ah bon*,' she said. 'You will not regret this, I promise you.'

She positioned Sidonie so that she was half-lying on the couch. Suppressing a shudder, Sidonie allowed Marceline to roll up her skirts. Despite Francis's earlier mention of the two maids, Clara and Rose, stroking each other and her initial interest in the process, she felt no inclination at all to sample the caresses of a woman.

But it seemed that she had no choice.

She focused all of her attention on the view through the spy-holes, trying to ignore the feel of Marceline's plump hands as they raised her petticoats and began to ease her thighs apart.

Gunter had withdrawn the handle from the woman's vagina and was holding the 'cat' to the second woman's mouth. He nudged open the closed lips, urging her to lick off the female juices. The woman complied, her eyes seeking his face as if searching for his approval.

Withdrawing the handle, Gunter turned his back. It was evident from the tented appearance of his drawers that he was strongly erect. Cupping the bulge in one hand he stroked himself, then took a step back and began to loosen the buttons at his waistband.

Sidonie felt Marceline's hot breath on the inner surfaces of her thighs and despite her reluctance began to anticipate a more intimate caress. She could only see part of the woman's broad back and a wide expanse of taffeta ruffles. Marceline's top half was hidden by her

84

own voluminous skirts. It was easy to pretend that the hands on her flesh were those of some anonymous male.

Dragging her attention back to the screen, she saw that Gunter's cock was not over-long, but it was thick and veiny. It reared up from a thick tangle of dark-blond pubic hair. Around the base of it, close to his body, he had wound a leather thong. The effect of it was to make his cock bulge with the pressure contained within it. It looked shiny, almost angry and extremely potent.

Bending down briefly, he freed the first woman and handed her the 'cat'. Then he walked around the bench and knelt at the head of the second woman. Grasping her full breasts, he drew them together so that a deep cleft was formed between them. Leaning forward he pushed his cock into the cleft and began working it back and forth.

As if on a signal the released woman began to lash her companion between her widely spread legs.

Sidonie barely suppressed a gasp as she felt Marceline's lips brush against her thighs. The tiny soft kisses moved over the sensitive inner surfaces. The sensation was very arousing, but something was odd. It took another moment for Sidonie to realise what that was.

The plump facial cheeks which, now and then, came into contact with her flesh were slightly rough with the stubble of a newly emerging beard.

Good God. Marceline was a *man*?

Of course. That would explain her size and her large features.

How stupid of her not to have realised. But she had never met any man who dressed as a woman before now. She wanted to laugh, but was too engrossed in what was happening to Gunter.

His cock-head, moist and shiny with the fluid of pre-emission, was emerging from the valley of the woman's breasts. Faster and faster he rubbed, squeezing the breasts together tightly around his straining shaft.

Gunter's mouth was open and his normally hollowed cheeks were puffed out with pleasure. The woman he knelt before was crying out more loudly. It seemed that her companion was beating her more thoroughly on the quim than Gunter had.

Little ripples of sensation passed over Sidonie's skin and her sex fluttered with eagerness as Marceline worked her way inwards and mouthed the damp pubic curls. And then came the first touch of a hot tongue on her labia. Sidonie drew her breath in sharply as one long, tantalisingly slow lick was followed by another.

Marceline was an expert. She used a gentle pressure to ease Sidonie's pleasure bud up towards her stomach, all the while holding open the puffy, outer lips and smoothing her thumbs up either side of the jutting nub. Now and then she used her lips to nuzzle the pleasure bud or sucked it, varying the sensations by also flicking it back and forth and grazing it with the very tips of her teeth.

The absurdity of the situation no longer mattered. She did not care whether Marceline was a man or a woman.

Her quim felt so swollen and receptive. The fragrant juices must be dripping out of her. The movements of Marceline's mouth and tongue were driving her wild. Her legs scissored madly as she mashed her pubis against the firm lips that possessed her.

Never had she been so desperate to come.

At that moment Gunter gave a hoarse cry and his creamy seed shot into the air, spattering the woman's breasts and chin. The woman was crying now; great tearing shudders passed over her entire body. Sidonie could see that the spread quim was very red and swollen. Silvery drops of wetness trickled from the thick lips.

'Please. I beg of you. Do it . . .' she murmured between sobs.

Her female tormentor put aside the 'cat' and leaned forward, mouthing the abused buttocks. Her tongue poked into the flesh-valley and sought out the tight hole there. The movements of her head were slow and tender as she licked the anus and then moved downwards to kiss the heated, swollen labia.

'Now. I beg you,' the woman pleaded.

Clasping the scalding globes of her buttocks, her tormentor pulled them open to fully expose the sore and reddened quim. For a moment she regarded the vagina, which was forced to gape a little, then plunged both thumbs into the wet, inner darkness.

The woman screamed and jibbered with pleasure, her bottom bucking and mashing against her tormentor's face while her feet drummed on the floor. Droplets of Gunter's jism slid down her pendulous breasts, which swung freely back and forth as she writhed and spasmed.

Sidonie could hold out no longer as Marceline's tongue exerted a rhythmic pressure on the little stem of her pushed-out bud; she drew up her knees and gave herself up to the deep contractions of a satisfying orgasm.

'Where on earth have you been?' Francis demanded to know as Sidonie took her place at the restaurant table.

She smiled serenely and reached out to pat his cheek. The effects of the absinthe had not quite worn off and she felt very relaxed. Her vision was still lightly fogged.

'Wouldn't you like to know?' she said, smiling crookedly. 'I've such things to tell you, darling. But not now. Wait until later. When we're alone – together.'

Francis grasped her hand, squeezing until her fingers began to ache. His eyes glittered coldly.

'This isn't amusing,' he said. 'I've been looking for you everywhere. You were gone for over an hour. Why did you not take me with you? We do everything together, remember?'

'Really?' She glared at him. 'I seem to remember that I have cause for complaint. The last time *you* went off without *me*.'

'Well, I won't do so again. I told you that in the hotel room. Have you been with a man? No. Don't bother answering that. I can see by your face that you have.

Damn it, Sidonie! I *have* to know about everyone you find attractive. It's my right. We agreed on that, remember? And I've promised not to take a lover unless you approve of her.'

Sidonie pressed her lips together with characteristic stubbornness. Really, Francis sometimes took the 'older brother' stance too seriously.

She suppressed a wince as he squeezed her hand again, rolling the bones together until they grated. He would always do that as a child when she failed to agree with him. She found the gesture strangely endearing. It was a measure of how upset he was. He was hurting and so he wanted to hurt her back.

To spite him she made no sound although her eyes watered and her lips whitened at the edges. Her lack of reaction was calculated to punish him.

'And what if I choose to do exactly as I wish?' she said teasingly. 'Just how are you going to stop me?'

'You can treat Thomas like a lackey if you wish, but don't try that with me,' Francis said in a voice that dripped ice.

'Where is Thomas?' she said. 'And you can stop squeezing my hand now. You've made your point.'

Francis loosened his grip and began to massage her sore knuckles. Bringing her hand to his lips he kissed the tip of each finger.

'Our valiant bearleader has gone to ask someone to search the cloakroom,' he said.

'Oh, really!' Sidonie snatched away her hand. 'What did you think had happened to me? That I had been carried off by white slavers! There's no cause to make such a melodrama out of this. I'm surprised that you even noticed my absence. You were so captivated by that flesh-pot on the stage!'

Francis grinned then and the fierceness slipped from his face. 'So that's it. You were jealous of Nymphia, so you thought you'd go in search of an adventure. And did you find one?'

Sidonie's mouth curved in a voluptuous smile.

'I certainly did. Just wait until you hear about it. You're not going to believe what happened to me – '

'Whatever it was,' Thomas, returning at that moment, cut in, 'I don't think I want to hear about it. But I do know this. That is the last time you disappear like that. Do you hear me? I want your word on it. Otherwise I'll write home to your father this minute and tell him that I resign my position forthwith. Without a chaperon you'd have to return home at once.'

Sidonie and Francis stared at Thomas in open-mouthed amazement. There was an uncomfortable silence. Thomas looked furious. Lord what a fuss, Sidonie thought, but did not judge it prudent to remind him that she had slipped away for merely an hour or so.

'Why, Thomas, old man. Stap me, but I've never seen you in such a froth,' Francis drawled affectedly.

'Be quiet,' said Thomas in a dangerously controlled voice. 'I know what you both think of me. And it's true that I drink too much and I'm susceptible to a pretty face and a well-turned ankle. And perhaps I'm not able to exert a strong influence on you. But I tell you this. I simply will not put up with your spoiled ways, your unwitting contempt and your utter lack of concern for anyone's feelings except your own.'

'I'm truly sorry,' Sidonie said, startled into an uncomfortably honest reaction. 'I did not mean to worry you. Surely you can see that no harm's done? Here I am safe and sound. Can we not forget this and try to salvage what's left of the evening? Please, Thomas? I promise that I'll behave impeccably from now on. We have only a few days left in Paris. Let's not spoil them '

Thomas looked unconvinced. His hair was flopping forward on to his forehead and his face was shiny with sweat. Although his bow-tie was crooked and there were wine stains on his waistcoat, he seemed to have sobered up entirely.

For the first time she felt a pang of guilt. Thomas really *had* been worried. How sweet of him. Perhaps there was more to him than she and Francis gave him credit for.

She laid her hand on his arm.

'Please?' she repeated, giving him her most winning smile. 'Am I forgiven?'

'Oh, tell her that she is, why don't you,' Francis muttered, bored with the conversation. 'This is a gale in a commode after all.'

He picked up Sidonie's evening bag and took out the white card which was protruding from the opening.

'What's this?' he said. 'Gunter Eckart. Aha. If I'm not mistaken that's the name of the blond Adonis we saw alighting from his carriage. Mystery solved, Thomas. Sidonie has simply been courting an admirer! All the time we were wondering where she had got to, imagining that she had stepped outside to be accosted by some disreputable old roué, she was with Gunter promenading around the balcony and roof garden.'

'Is this true?' Thomas said, looking somewhat mollified.

'In a manner of speaking,' Sidonie said, snatching the card from her brother's hand. 'Gunter came over to our table and gave me his card. After ... spending a little time in his company, I have decided that I do not care a whit for him. And I shall not be accepting his invitation to visit. So there!'

Tearing the card into fragments she tossed them on to the white cloth.

Thomas looked relieved, while Francis seemed impressed.

'That's done with then,' Thomas said. 'Let's hear no more about it. I hate there being bad feeling between us. Is anyone thirsty? I'll order more champagne.'

'Quite the socialite, aren't you, my pet?' Francis said.

On the pretext of kissing her cheek, he bent close to whisper into her ear. 'You might have fooled Thomas, but I don't believe a word of it. I recognise that softness in your face and a certain gleam in your eyes. You've been pleasured by someone – and recently. I'll come to

90

your room tonight and you can tell me what you have *really* been doing!'

She laughed and turned her face towards him so that for a moment their lips met. At the slight contact Francis's eyes darkened and she felt an answering pressure between her legs.

'Why, Sidonie. If I'm not mistaken that's absinthe on your breath. Take care, my pet. Did you not know that over-indulgence in that green-souled liqueur leads to madness?'

Sidonie had hardly undressed, washed and donned her nightgown before the bedroom door opened and Francis slipped inside.

Grasping her around the waist he strode across the room and bore her with him. Clasped tight to the cool, padded silk of his dressing-gown, she felt the hardness of his slim body beneath the fabric. He was newly bathed and his face was smooth from a recent shave. His dark hair, smelling of lavender and lemon, curled damply on to his shoulders.

They landed in a heap on the bed, rucking up the silken counterpane, Sidonie shrieking with muffled laughter as he tickled her unmercifully, rolling her about until the bedclothes were tangled around them.

'Stop! Stop! For pity's sake . . .' she gasped between giggles as his fingers reached into ever more intimate recesses.

When he stopped at last, he was straddling her, his hands on her shoulders holding down. Breathlessly she lay under him, excited by the wildness and beauty of his face. She seemed still to feel the places where he had touched her skin. Her breasts burned and throbbed and she was wet with desire for him.

Swooping down he claimed her mouth and she accepted his tongue, sucking it deeply into the hot depths of her mouth. Their tongues meshed and entwined, tasting, exploring. As the kiss went on, she began to move under him, lifting her hips provocatively.

In a moment Francis drew back, his lips drawn wide in a grin.

'No you don't. You temptress! You'll not get around me like that. Now, you wretch, tell me everything. Why, for instance, did Marceline take such a fond farewell of you as we were about to leave the restaurant?'

Sidonie squirmed and arched her back. 'Later, Francis. I'm dying for you. I'll tell you, but after we – '

'Oh no. I'm afraid, my pet, that there's to be no pleasuring for you until I know every – little – sordid – detail.' Each of the last words was punctuated by a kiss on her nose, chin and eyelids.

'Ooooh, Francis . . .' she said, drawing his name out into a caress.

He wavered and she grinned, nipping her bottom lip with her teeth. Then she saw that he meant to hear her out before he laid another finger on her.

'Oh, very well,' she said sulkily. 'What a bore! Get off me then. I'll tell you it all now – if I must.'

Obligingly he rolled clear, then pulled her into his embrace. They lay closely entwined and she told him everything; about the small upper room with its haze of perfumed smoke and waiter who served glasses of absinthe; about the couples caressing openly; and about Gunter's secret vice.

'And the women really seemed to enjoy this kind of spiked sexual pleasure?' he asked incredulously. 'It sounds too harsh for my tastes. But the latter part was . . . interesting. Tell me again what Gunter did with the whip-handle.'

So she told him, feeling the hardness of his erection pressing against her thigh through the thin fabric of her nightgown. Relating the events made her feel all hot and tingly and by the way Francis was rubbing himself gently against her she knew that he was having difficulty controlling the urge to caress her.

Finally she told him about her discovery about Marceline.

Francis laughed as he imagined her surprise.

'It would have been more of a shock if Marceline had suddenly produced a stout cock from under her silken skirts! Oh, I wish I could have seen your face. You really did not know? Marceline is a well-known figure in certain circles. He always dresses as a woman and prefers to be addressed as mademoiselle. The French have a name for it – *travesti*.'

'He – she, was very kind and charming,' Sidonie said. 'But for her intervention I might have accepted Gunter's invitation.'

'I am grateful to Marceline,' Francis said softly and earnestly. 'Surely now you are persuaded that you need me to look out for you? It is out of love that I speak, not because I think that I own you. Although we are bound to each other by our shared blood, you can do as you please, my darling. Take all the lovers you like. Only let me get to know them. No one will ever hurt or betray you while I have breath in my body.'

Sidonie sighed and snuggled into Francis's embrace.

'Very well. I was a little foolish to go off like that. I promise that the next time I have an erotic dalliance or take a lover, you'll be the first to know. In fact you can vet him for me!'

As Francis began to kiss her, she responded with passion. She felt once again warm and cherished.

Whenever she and her twin had a disagreement, however mild, she felt ill at ease until they had returned to their usual equilibrium. Francis was more than brother, lover, father-confessor – he was an actual part of her. Arguing with him made her feel as if she was at war with herself.

Francis's breathing quickened and she slipped her hand between their bodies to stroke the thick stem of his cock. He groaned with need and she waited for him to say the words, loving it when he asked her to pleasure him.

It surprised her when he pushed her hand away gently and got off the bed.

'What's the matter? Is something wrong?'

Francis shook his head, flashed her a grin and reached for his padded dressing-gown which lay crumpled on the floor. After feeling in the pocket, he climbed back on to the bed, an object wrapped in scarlet silk in his hand.

'I bought something for us earlier today,' he said. 'It was to be a surprise, but I am so hot for you after all you've told me that I have to use it on you now.'

Unfolding the layers of silk, he held up the object which was revealed to be shaped like a column with a flaring tip. Sidonie had never seen anything like it.

'It's a false cock! Wherever did you get it?' she asked, amazed and intrigued. She examined it as he gave it to her to hold. It felt just like the real thing and was obviously made by a craftsman. It was made of wood and covered with the softest, red kid-leather. The stitches down its length were so fine as to be almost invisible.

Lying in the discarded folds of scarlet silk there was a sort of harnesss which had straps attached to it. Sidonie regarded them with wonder, holding them up and examining the way the phallus fitted into the harnesss.

Francis smiled at her obvious delight.

'I see that you appreciate my efforts. My friend in the Garde Impériale obtained it for me. Seems that his mistress, a pretty little *midinette* – she's a milliner I believe – loves to use one of these on *her* female lover, while the officer watches them and rouses himself to a stiff erection!'

'Lord. It could only be a subject for discussion in the cafés of Paris,' Sidonie said giggling. 'Oh, this thing's so wicked-looking, Francis. One can play with it as it is or strap it on and use it to penetrate a lover. Lord, I can become a man with this! What is it called?'

'There are many words, but I'm told that "dildo" is one most frequently used.'

'You are so clever,' Sidonie said, her eyes dancing with delight. 'Are you going to make love to me with this . . . dildo?'

'That's why I bought it. There will be no danger of any unwanted complications for you,' he said.

Sidonie was touched. The one act she longed for was forbidden to them as brother and sister. This way they could indulge their passions along new byways. She could even use it on Francis. Her blood quickened at all the possibilities. She imagined him writhing under her, his tight buttocks pressed up hard against her belly, his face bound by an expression of pained bliss.

'Use it on me now,' she said eagerly. 'Oh, Francis. I can imagine that it is *you* inside me, how wonderful.'

Pulling up her nightdress, she lay on her back and parted her legs. Francis positioned himself so that he was lying on top of her. It felt so good to lie with him belly to belly, something they hardly ever did for fear that their passions would flare out of control.

He positioned himself so that he straddled her hips high up, his shoulders looming over her head and his hard cock trapped between their bodies. She was aware of every ridged muscle of his torso pressing against the soft flesh of her breasts.

'I'm ready now,' she said. 'I'm so wet and swollen. Put it into me, dearest.'

She arched her back and drew up her knees. Francis reached around and felt between her thighs.

'I can't reach in this position,' he said. 'We'll have to lie on our sides.'

They changed position, Sidonie eager to assuage the longing which made her whole lower body feel like a throbbing pit of warmth. Her quim was liquid and swollen, eager for the thrust of the leather-covered glans. The dildo was a most delightful toy.

'Why don't I use the phallus on myself while you rub your cock against my belly?' she said. 'That way we can both spend at the same time.'

'Put it in first. I want to see you do it,' Francis said huskily, lifting one of her legs to expose her quim. 'Oh, darling. You're as soft and swollen as a ripe plum. I love to see you like this.'

He stroked the scant, red-blonde fleece on her pubis before using two fingers to ease her labia apart. The

95

slight pressure he used to press back the fleshy lips caused her nub to stand proud of the surrounding folds. Sidonie's breath came fast as the firm cone jutted free of its tiny hood and began throbbing almost painfully.

Moving his fingers down Francis pressed on either side of her vagina, so that the shadowed orifice opened to his gaze.

Sidonie shuddered as she felt her dew seep out on to her twin's fingers. She always felt a mixture of shame and delight when Francis looked at her *there* and saw the physical evidence of her desire for him. The signs of a woman's sexual arousal were more secret, more subtle than a man's, and therefore all the more fascinating to uncover.

She knew that she would never lose the feeling that this was a doubly forbidden act – sister-love, brother-love was perhaps the last taboo – and the pleasure to be found in Francis's touch was all the more enticing because of it.

Bringing the head of the dildo to her vagina she began slowly to insert it. Francis watched as the leather glans breached the closure of her flesh, was collared by it and then accepted into the deep, wet interior.

The shaft went into her and Sidonie whimpered as the thickness of it pushed aside her inner membranes. It filled her completely. Slowly she began to move it back and forth, loving the internal pressure and the way her pleasure bud bulged outwards because of it.

'Oh, it feels heavenly,' she sighed. 'It's almost too big, but I'm getting used to it now. Hold me close and rub your cock against my belly.'

Francis took her in his arms and began to move, but stopped after a few moments.

'What's wrong? Doesn't it feel good?' Sidonie asked, reluctant to change position again.

The warm feelings were pooling inside her lower belly and she knew that she would spend soon, but she wanted Francis to share the experience. She could see that he was a little perturbed by her delight in the phallus. His face was turned away from her and his erection was subsiding.

Perhaps he was jealous of the toy. After all, this act of penetration was the single thing they could not share. She could not bear to see the look of defeat on his face.

'You enjoy yourself. Don't mind about me,' he said, trying to sound as if he did not mind and beginning to pull away.

'Stay with me,' she whispered against his mouth. 'Nothing feels right unless you're here beside me. Shall I put this dildo away? We don't have to use it. I really don't care.'

'No. I want to see you use it. It's just that I can't seem to . . . Oh, I don't know. This has never happened before.'

She had a thought. 'I know what we need. Go over to the dresser, darling. There's a pot of cold cream there.'

Francis returned with the cream, scooped out a large blob and rubbed it into Sidonie's belly. Smearing some of the cream on to her hands, he placed them around his cock, Sidonie rubbed him gently, smoothing the cream into his shrinking stem and squeezing the life back into the fat, oily glans.

She kissed him deeply, reassuringly, murmuring endearments, calling him 'my potent lover' and 'darling, beautiful brother'.

Soon he was rigid and throbbing against her palm. When they were once again positioned face to face with his straining organ trapped between their bodies, he began to thrust back and forth. The oily cream provided a slick warmth and a measure of friction. Francis arched his back and began pumping his hips in short muscular bursts.

'It really feels as if I'm inside you now. Oh, Sidonie. If only that were possible. I long for it so.'

Sidonie's eyes pricked with tears. 'I too. But it isn't possible, beloved. And it never will be. It does not matter, I can imagine that this leather cock is your sweet flesh. And you must imagine that you are pushing into me at this moment. Can you feel how my juices run down your shaft? How my silken muscles are squeezing you tightly – so tightly.'

Excited by her own words, she thrust the dildo back and forth, imagining in turn that it was her twin's own pulsing cock that nudged against her womb and drew down the pleasure from her body.

'Sidonie. Oh, God . . .'

With a groan Francis came, spattering her belly with his creamy emission. At the same time Sidonie spasmed and surged against Francis, her inner contractions gripping the phallus.

As soon as they were both quiet, Sidonie drew out the phallus and put it aside. It might become a welcome toy, but she knew that she would have to be very careful how she used it. How odd that she had discovered her twin's fragility during a moment of light-hearted sex-play.

She had always thought of them as one entity, but the differences in their gender were becoming more apparent. As he took the role of protector more seriously, she was becoming his nurturer.

Enfolded in each other's arms, they kissed and caressed until they grew calm again. Just before they slept, Sidonie thought how strange it was that with so much they could do together, the one forbidden act was the thing they both craved the most.

Perhaps it's in our very nature to be perverse, she thought. She smoothed back the tumbled dark hair from Francis's forehead and kissed his closed eyes. His sculpted lips were lifted slightly at the corners as if he smiled in his sleep.

At that moment, her heart hurt with love for him.

Chapter Eight

*F*or a few days, after the incident in the Frères Provençaux, the twins behaved with unusual decorum.

Thomas knew that the state of affairs could not last, but it was pleasant to imagine that he was, for the moment, performing the task to which he had been appointed. He arranged visits to the theatre and the opera, short tours of the city to visit more art galleries and, just to please Sidonie, he went out of his way to discover the whereabouts of the establishments of Monsieur Houbigant and Monsieur Guerlain.

His efforts seemed to be appreciated and Sidonie and Francis showed every evidence of having enjoyed the entertainment. He even flattered himself that they might have learned something – proving his own adage that culture must be absorbed naturally and not forced down a person's throat.

Sidonie spent an enjoyable afternoon at the famous perfumers, emerging with a selection of cut-glass bottles of exquisite fragrances. She had bought presents of lavender toilet-water and lemon soap for Francis and Thomas and a stock of Lady Jenny's favourite perfume to send home to London.

'Oh, it was so wonderful,' Sidonie said, kissing Thomas lightly on the cheek. 'Like an Aladdin's cave of scented treasures. I could have spent a week in those shops. What a dear you are for thinking of it.'

Thomas was most gratified by the vehemence of her thanks. It was a new experience for him to feel appreciated.

It cannot last, he told himself, waiting for some out-burst of rebellion. But Francis seemed content to seek his company and made no further efforts to abandon him on their evening forays and Sidonie made no attempt to go anywhere by herself. Indeed, she made a point of asking his opinion on anything she was considering doing.

Charmed and completely won over, Thomas grew confident of the fact that he was beginning to establish a relationship of sorts with the twins. As they packed their bags and prepared to leave Paris, he felt light of heart.

He was eagerly anticipating the weeks of travel down to Italy, culminating in a stay in Florence. At this time of the year there would be many English residents – artists, poets, writers, as well as those there simply to enjoy the sights. There would be receptions and soirées aplenty and invitations to dine at many of the villas that thronged the hills surrounding the city.

Such a place was Florence with its many ancient palaces and churches. Everywhere there were archaic stoneworks: statues, cupolas, urns, grottos and cunningly devised structures for waterworks. Thomas looked forward to showing the twins the River Arno with its sumptuous bridges, in particular the Ponte Vecchio, which was lined with goldsmiths' shops and the factories which produced silk damasks, velvets and exquisite embroidered brocades.

His only regret was leaving behind Honorine, the serving maid whose bed he had warmed for the past three nights – each time making sure that he returned to his own room well before morning. With his new-found air of responsible, if slightly shabby, gentility he wanted nothing to mar the twins' good impression of him.

Honorine, a rosy-skinned country lass, had a generous heart contained in a pleasingly rounded package of flesh.

He had slept off the effects of many a glass of apple brandy pillowed on the crest of her breasts and known great delight in lying between her sturdy thighs and thrusting into her fat, pink quim. She was the juiciest woman he had ever had.

Ah well, there were many women waiting for him to discover them in Italy.

Sidonie fell in love with Florence at first glance.

The city shimmered softly in the afternoon heat haze. The many colours and hues of stone – cream, honey, yellow-ochre, sand – were a perfect foil for the deep purple of the Apennines in the background.

Thomas pointed out the magnificent cupola of the Duomo, which crowned the clustered palaces.

'There, see? That's the tower of the Palazzo Vecchio,' he said eagerly. 'And behind the Palazzo Pitti you can see the dark foliage of the Boboli gardens. We must go there. They are some of the most fabulous in Europe.'

His enthusiasm was infectious and Sidonie looked forward to their stay. Instead of the usual hotel, Thomas had arranged for them to stay at a villa situated on the nearby heights of Fiesole.

The 'villa' was soon revealed to be a good-sized house, with spacious, high-ceilinged rooms; floors and pillars of marble; exquisite furnishings and a wonderful view over Florence. A number of servants were waiting to welcome them and before long Sidonie and Francis were relaxing on the terrace with cool drinks, the dust of the journey having been sluiced away with hot perfumed water.

'Two whole months in this glorious place,' Sidonie mused happily. 'I wonder what Thomas has planned for us.'

Francis grinned ruefully. 'More of those improving visits to art galleries and gracious buildings I expect. I'm heartily sick of flexing my brain. Other parts of me are being woefully neglected! Don't you think we've done enough to convince him that we're paragons of good behaviour? He's been walking round with that same self-satisfied smirk on his face for weeks.'

'I think he trusts us now,' Sidonie said. 'It ought to be easy to find some pleasant diversion that will keep him out of the way for a time so that we can go our own way. He responded well to Honorine and I'm certain that he had no idea at all that we knew all about that particular dalliance.'

Francis laughed and took a deep swallow of the chianti. 'What a capital idea of yours that was, my darling. Keep Thomas supplied with a variety of flesh-pots and his favourite tipple and he's as happy as the proverbial pig.'

'I do confess that I'm quite looking forward to this evening's entertainment,' Sidonie said. 'Thomas has sent out cards to suitable families inviting them to supper. Apparently we are to be graced with a visit from a number of English families who are staying in Florence for the season. I expect that this is the accepted way of notifying the "set" of one's arrival.'

Francis affected a look of disdain.

'I suppose we're expected to be gracious to any number of dull, plain, eligible daughters and sons of the aristocracy!'

Sidonie squeezed his arm, her eyes glinting with devilment.

'They can't *all* be plain and boring. And it's high time that we had a little fun at Thomas's expense, don't you think? I for one am heartily bored with behaving well.'

The capacious rooms of the villa were ablaze with candle-light and every door and window stood open to the sweet summer air. Marble-topped tables groaned under the weight of a cold buffet and a quartet of musicians played tasteful music in the background.

Sidonie wore her lightest gown of printed muslin in the palest shade of violet-grey and took the daring step of wearing only a single, hoopless petticoat underneath it. Instead of flaring out into the more usual bell-shape the gown fell in graceful folds around her hips and legs and trailed some way behind her. Her heavy red-gold curls were pinned up high on her head and threaded with ribbons which matched her dress.

Thomas looked worried when he first saw her walk into the room.

'Ah hem, Sidonie,' he began. 'I do not wish to appear to criticise you, but is that gown *quite* suitable for this occasion? I would have thought that something ... perhaps a little more formal?'

'But it's so hot, Thomas. Surely the rules of formal dress are a little more relaxed here than in England. If you think I look a fright I'll go and change of course. But I thought I looked quite attractive.'

'You do. Absolutely ravishing, as always, but that's not the issue – '

'Thank you for the compliment,' she cut in, hiding a smile and tapping his arm with her folded fan. 'That's settled then. I value your opinion in all things, as you know. But you really must allow a woman to be the judge of her own wardrobe.'

The first guests were to arrive at any moment and if she were to be ready to receive them as good manners demanded, then she had no time to go and change – something she had made certain of in advance.

Francis appeared at her side, resplendent in a light-weight dinner suit of charcoal-grey. His silk shirt and bow-tie were in the exact same shade of pale grey violet and his tie-pin was set with amethysts. His dark hair was swept straight back from his forehead and fell in curls over his collar.

Sidonie slipped her arm around her twin's waist. As so often happened they had unwittingly chosen to wear the same colours. Francis looked stunning. It was always a shock to see how handsome he was and to realise what an impression the two of them must make on any initial meeting.

'Here come the first guests,' Francis said softly, then

gave a groan of dismay. 'Oh, Lord. Just as I thought. Master and Mistress Portly and pig-faced daughter! And behind them is Lady Dim-wit and pudden-headed son!'

At her brother's acid wit, Sidonie suppressed a giggle only with the greatest difficulty. A bubble of laughter seemed to have lodged in her chest.

'Oh, don't,' she hissed. 'Or I shall never last through the next hour. Put on your most gracious smile and think dutiful thoughts.'

An hour or so later the villa was buzzing with activity. The low hum of conversation and the clink of plates and glasses was masked by the playing of the string quartet. Elegant figures in evening dress moved through the rooms. The silken gowns of the women were like inverted tulips, the colours of them in every shade of the rainbow.

Thomas moved amongst the guests, smiling and nodding and accepting the eagerly offered calling cards.

'Just look at him playing host,' Francis whispered to Sidonie, drawing her away from a group of admiring young men. 'He's in his element. Every moment of our stay in Florence will be accounted for in no time and he'll stick to us like glue.'

'Oh, I think not,' she said in a low voice. 'Look there.'

Thomas seemed to have been cornered by a large woman with frizzed, light-brown hair. Her gown of ruby silk was cut low across the bosom to reveal a large expanse of creamy shoulders and the top of extremely generous breasts.

Thomas's normally pallid face sported a flush across the cheekbones and his rather dull features were enlivened by a broad smile.

'Looks as though we need not look for an Honorine,' Francis said, winking conspiratorially. 'He seems to have made the perfect match.'

He moved off to approach a group of young women who were simpering at him with open admiration.

Sidonie and Francis were the centre of attention for the whole evening. The prettiest women and the most handsome men gravitated towards them, pouring out compliments and offering invitations to dine, go horse-riding, or to see the sights of Florence.

By the time the last guest left, Sidonie felt exhausted. She could remember hardly any of the names of those who had been dancing attendance on her. Thomas had disappeared and so had the woman in the red dress.

Excusing herself, she went to her room. The maid helped her undress and brushed out her hair, then set out her night things before bobbing a curtsy and leaving the room. Shrugging on a nightgown of figured silk, Sidonie padded barefoot down the corridor to Francis's room. The marble tiles were deliciously cool against the soles of her feet.

Francis's window stood wide open to the terrace and the floor-length drapes of muslin blew inwards carrying with them the scent of the garden. Francis was sitting by the open windows drinking a final glass of wine before going to bed.

She went over to him and was enfolded into his embrace. They kissed, the taste of wine mingling in their mouths.

'So, who is to be your first conquest?' Sidonie said, when she was settled on his lap, her head resting against one muscled shoulder. 'Have you decided? No, don't answer. Let me guess. The pretty, slender young woman with hair like spun sugar and a petulant mouth. What was her name? The Honourable Elizabeth Bexham – but she likes to be called Liza. Am I right?'

Francis grinned and nuzzled her neck, his teeth just grazing the tender skin beneath her ear.

'Have I no secrets from you? Yes, it's to be Liza. She's delicious, isn't she? Frightfully spoiled and used to getting her own way. I can't wait to share her with you. We're to go riding tomorrow. And you? Let me see. A tall young man, wide shoulders and strong features. Not the best-looking man in the room, but a trifle serious and sensitive-looking. Lord Robert – something or other ... Was it not? Ah, I see that I'm correct.'

'What a coincidence. We're going riding too,' Sidonie said with a shiver. Francis's kisses were becoming more passionate, sapping her will to talk or to do anything but give in to the feelings which were spreading a warm spell over her senses.

'I sometimes think we can read each other's minds,' she said dreamily. 'It's almost frightening, is it not? I do love you so. Oh yes, Francis, keep doing that . . .'

His mouth clamped to hers, Francis stood up. Sweeping her up in his arms he bore her to the bed and they forgot about Liza and Robert as the blistering spark of their own passion flared into life.

For the next few days the twins were shown around Florence by a variety of their new acquaintances. Robert and Liza visited them often and they settled into a routine of all going out riding together.

Thomas clearly approved of their choice of friends. For a while he accompanied them on visits to the theatre and took afternoon tea with them in a variety of English establishments, but it was plain to them both that he was preoccupied.

'It's that siren with the frizzy hair,' Francis said one morning over breakfast. 'She's called Mary Wortley, I believe. It won't be long before he thinks it safe to leave us to our own devices. We must make certain that he does not suspect us of anything but good behaviour and we'll be free to go our own way. By the by, how is your friendship with Robert coming along?'

Sidonie dimpled. 'Admirably. He's so sweet. For all that he's well travelled, he's very naïve in some ways. Very shy and sensitive. It's such a delight to shock him that I'm driven to be quite shockingly bold in his company! And Liza?'

'A gem, my pet. So self-centred, pompous and certain of her own charms. I don't know how I have restrained myself from tearing off her clothes and having her just to teach her a lesson. I've an idea. As soon as we know that Thomas will be absent for a few hours we'll invite Robert and Liza for a late supper.'

Sidonie's eyes glinted wickedly.

'Do you mean what I think you do?' she said.

'I do indeed. Is it not time that we each became acquainted with the other's paramour? Intimately acquainted, as we swore to be.'

'I thought you had to be married to have a paramour,' Sidonie said teasingly.

Francis leaned over to press a fresh strawberry against her lips. Sidonie sucked the fruit into her mouth and took his finger with it. Collaring his fingertip, she sucked it and squashed the mashed fruit, allowing the juice to run down her chin.

Francis removed his finger, leaned over the table and kissed her chin, snaking out his tongue to lap up the juice before nipping her bottom lip between his even, white teeth.

'We are closer than married, my love,' he murmured against her lips. 'Joined by blood and bone and spirit. Let no man or woman put us asunder.'

Sidonie trembled. When Francis talked like that she felt like crying. No matter how many lovers she took or how many mistresses Francis had, they would never feel the same degree of loyalty to anyone but each other.

A few days later Francis was proved right about Thomas's preoccupation.

Returning home earlier than expected from a visit to Michelangelo's tomb in Santa Croce the twins were surprised to hear noises coming from the little house next to the stable. The building was normally occupied by the grooms and stable lads. At that hour the young men, devout Catholics all of them, were required to attend Mass. The house ought to be empty, but there were sounds of glasses chinking and of muffled laughter and unmistakable groans of pleasure.

Intrigued they exchanged glances. Sidonie whispered under her breath, 'I'm sure I recognise that voice.'

After dismissing their coachman, the twins went to investigate.

The house was a simple, single-storeyed building and it was easy to make their way to a downstairs window and peer inside. One room appeared to be a dormitory. It was empty. The sounds were coming from an adjoining room, visible through an open door.

Moving around to find the corresponding window, Sidonie and Francis looked into a rather austere sitting room. A wooden table, two benches and a settle against one wall were the only furniture. Thomas and Mary were lying on a rug on the floor, the remains of a picnic meal strewn all around them.

Their passion seemed to have overcome their hunger, for Mary, her dress pulled down to her waist, lay on her back amid the debris of a half-eaten loaf, crumbs of cheese and some squashed grapes. A number of wine bottles were littered around and two glasses lay on their sides, dregs of wine seeping into the rug.

'Thomas. Oh, Thomas,' Mary was groaning, her hands grasping his skinny buttocks as he thrashed away energetically between her thighs.

Grunting and puffing Thomas worked manfully, his trousers around his knees. His head, buried in her cleavage, was almost eclipsed by the huge globes of her freed breasts which flopped against his ears. Between Thomas's spread legs they could see the firm sac of his scrotum and the base of his cock as he rose and fell in time with Mary's pelvic thrusts. His cock was shiny with her dew and seemed dwarfed by the fertile swamp of Mary's sex.

Mary's sturdy calves lifted and she began to drum her feet on Thomas's back, swinging her hips up to meet him.

'Oh, that's it,' she yelled. 'I'll take you, my man. Give it to me! Oh. Oh. I'm spending!'

'That's it, girl. Tighten around me,' Thomas groaned in a voice hoarse with desperation. 'Here I come. Oh, God help me. Oh, God.'

He tensed all over and clung tight to Mary who thrashed and bounced as her pleasure overcame her.

Sidonie clapped her hands to her mouth, holding in her laughter while tears streamed down her cheeks. Thomas resembled nothing less than a ship being tossed about on high seas.

'He's in heaven, I swear he is,' Francis whispered in an awed voice. 'We should have no trouble with him for a while. Mary Wortley is enough to sap the strength of ten men!'

Chuckling, they crept away to make plans for their intimate supper.

The Honourable Elizabeth Bexham, Liza to her friends, was looking forward to having supper with Francis Ryder and his twin sister.

Her friends would be so envious. Half of them were in love with Francis and the other half were dewy-eyed over his stylish and charming twin sister. Since the arrival of the twins, the yardstick by which beauty and elegance were measured had been made anew. Everyone wanted to look like Sidonie, with her fragile, pale beauty and her great mass of strawberry-blond curls or like Francis, with his brooding good looks.

Sidonie's gowns were considered daring, even 'fast', but it seemed that she could be forgiven anything. Liza was sometimes irked by that fact. She knew full well that, should she ever try to escape the confines of what society considered 'the done thing', she would be cast aside by her peers.

Not so Sidonie and Francis. They were above the rules set for ordinary mortals. People spoke with awe about the affection between them. Francis, it appeared, was devoted to his sister. Rumour had it that he had been known to call a man out if he offended Sidonie.

It seemed most unfair that the twins could do just as they wished. They seemed touched by a kind of magic. Liza felt that it was a privilege to be walking out with Francis and she had taken great trouble to make a good impression on Sidonie. It had, of course, been a foregone thing that Sidonie would like her.

Liza was supremely confident of her own charm. It had never been known to fail.

How wonderful if Sidonie and herself were to become fast friends and share intimate, girlish confidences. She wanted to know what Francis had been like as a boy, what made him angry, and what he most liked in a woman – although she had a good idea about that already.

She recalled the feel of Francis's lips against her own. His slim fingers were cool on her skin. The last time they went out he had pulled her into the shadow of some trees and slipped his hand inside the neckline of her gown. The way he had pinched and rolled her nipple caused her knees to go weak. She burned for him. Just the memory of his caresses gave her a tingling heaviness between the thighs.

As the maid dressed her hair, she fantasised about making love with Francis. His body was beautiful, muscled and firm, but slim. She loved his tallness, the darkness of his curly hair. And his face was almost angelic, classical in its lines and hollows, but with nothing of softness about it. Just like the faces in the paintings of Raphael and Titian.

Once Francis had made love to her, he would become her willing slave. She loved the moment of conquest before her interest started to wane. Like so many other men before him, Francis was destined to become one of her love-sick followers. A pity, since he was so exquisite. The thought of the letters he would write, begging her for her sexual favours, sent a thrill of excitement right through her.

She felt a sudden pain at her nape and was rudely brought out of her reverie. The maid had caught the hairbrush in her hair. Without thinking she lashed out, catching the young woman across the cheek.

'Stupid girl. That will teach you to take care!' she said,

seeing with satisfaction that the marks of her fingers were livid against the pale cheek.

'Your pardon, ma'am,' the maid said, her eyes filling with tears. 'It won't happen again.'

'See that it does not,' Liza said, having already forgotten the incident. Maids did not have a place in her romantic thoughts. 'And make me especially beautiful. I'm having supper with the most handsome young man in the whole of Florence. He's already in love with me, but I want to sweep him right off his feet.'

When Liza arrived at the villa, she saw another coach just leaving. Ah, good. Lord Robert Godstow, a mild-mannered young man and Sidonie's current admirer, had arrived. That meant that there would be nothing to spoil her entrance.

She was shown directly into a room which appeared to be a bedroom. The rest of the villa was very quiet, almost deserted in fact. Liza felt a prickle of alarm seep into her excitement, but shook it off. How very daring to entertain one's guests in a bedroom. Why, the food and drink for supper was spread on a board placed on the bed!

The room was dark, lit only by candles placed behind red-paper shades. Sidonie and Robert sat on low chairs next to the bed.

'Ah, Liza. Welcome,' Francis said, getting up and coming to meet her.

He disposed of her cloak and she was conscious of his eyes flickering over her figure. She felt gratified by his regard, knowing that she looked her best in a low-cut gown of apricot embroidered silk. Her pale hair had been twisted into loops and secured at the back of her neck with jewelled combs, leaving her neat ears, delicate jaw-line and slender neck free – assets of which she was very proud.

Sidonie smiled invitingly. 'Good evening, Liza. You already know Robert, don't you?'

111

'How do you do?' Robert said, blushing. 'So nice to see you again.'

'Isn't this cosy?' Sidonie said. 'Just the four of us. Won't you take a seat? Supper's ready. I hope you are hungry.'

'Thank you,' Liza said, arranging her features into what she imagined was her most captivating smile. 'I have only a small appetite, but the food looks delicious.'

How striking the twins were when seen together. She felt awed by them. Sidonie was a slighter version of Francis. It was strange to see his features made soft and womanly. Usually Liza did not care over-much for female friends and much preferred the company of men. But it would be politic to court Sidonie's approval.

Suppressing the urge to eat heartily, Liza picked at some slices of meat, nibbled an orange slice, and sipped a glass of wine. Sidonie did not seem to think it necessary to show a lady-like reticence when eating and chose items from a variety of dishes. Refilling her glass at intervals, she drank a quantity of the local red wine.

The conversation was light and frivolous. Liza prided herself on her wit and her ability to entertain. Robert laughed loudly at her jokes and Francis watched her closely, his eyes lingering on her mouth – which had been remarked upon by others as being 'like a rosebud'.

The evening was going very well. She was enjoying herself immensely.

'You must try one of these, Francis,' Sidonie said after a while, passing her brother a ripe fig. The fruit was plump and had a bloom of blue-grey on its red skin.

Francis steadied his sister's hand with his own as he bit into the fruit, grinning to show the red flesh of the fig on his teeth.

'Mmmm. Luscious,' he said. 'Sweet and juicy. Almost my favourite taste.'

Liza noticed that he was looking at his twin in a strangely knowing way and Sidonie sparkled back at him and blew him a kiss. Liza felt distinctly uncomfortable, but could not have said why.

She took a gulp of wine and almost choked. Laughing, Francis thumped her on the back. With his attention solely on her again, Liza felt better. Robert seemed relaxed. He too had drunk plenty of wine. His good-natured face was flushed and there was a sheen of sweat on his top lip.

'I'll open another bottle, shall I?' he said jauntily, running a finger around the inside of his collar.

What a fool he was, she thought, but a likeable one. As the evening wore on Liza enjoyed herself even more. Sidonie was being so charming, telling amusing tales about their travels through Europe. The wine fumes in Liza's blood gave her an enormous sense of well-being.

She was vaguely conscious of laughing a little too loud and too long, but did not care a jot. What fun this was.

'And that was when Francis and I made the promise to each other,' Sidonie said into a sudden silence.

Liza had missed the first part of the sentence.

'What . . . promise . . .' she said and hiccuped. 'Oooh, dear me, sorry,' she tittered. 'What, er, promise?'

'The promise to share our lovers,' Francis said evenly. 'Or at least to examine them minutely for their suitability. We each trust the other's judgement implicitly.'

Liza held her hand to her mouth and giggled.

'Francis! You're scandalous. Did you hear that, Robert? Isn't he just too awful?'

Robert looked worried. He gave a wavery grin. 'I think he means it,' he said.

'Oh, Robert. You buffoon! Can't you take a joke?' Liza said, looking from Sidonie to Francis and back again for confirmation.

'Robert's right. We are serious,' Sidonie said.

'Really? Well, I never heard the like of it,' Liza said, the corners of her mouth trembling with mirth. For some reason she did not seem able to stop grinning. 'And what does this examination entail?'

Francis made a sudden grab for her, took hold of her around the waist and bent her backwards. She gave a

113

little scream of delight and then subsided against him as he kissed her thoroughly. When he let her go she found that the room was swimming. Her heartbeat was loud in her ears and she felt a pulse start up between her legs.

'Shall I show you, Liza?' Francis said. 'Do you want to know what I require of my lovers, you spoilt little cat? Sidonie, what do you say?'

Sidonie's voice was breathless. 'Yes. Show her. Robert can watch as well.'

'Yes, let Robert watch,' Liza said, the taste of Francis on her lips made her feel dizzy with longing for him.

'Hold on now,' Robert said, slurring his words. 'What are you all planning? I really don't think that I want to be a part of this. It's sounds very . . . ungentlemanly.'

He made as if to get up, but Sidonie pushed him down again. She reached for his hand.

'Go if you like. I won't stop you. But you'll regret it if you leave. Why not come and sit next to me? I won't bite.'

Robert grinned. 'Very well. In that case, I'll stay. I just don't want to be left out. That's always happening to me. You both seem so taken with Liza.'

'It's just a game,' Sidonie said. 'You have to admit that she's very pretty. Wouldn't you like to see more of her?'

'Well, yes, actually,' Robert agreed. 'If she doesn't mind.'

Liza giggled, basking in their joint admiration. She leaned back against Francis. The wine had made her feel wild and reckless. She wriggled as he began running his hands up the bodice of her gown and undoing some of the hooks.

'What are you doing?' she slurred. 'Oh, how wicked you are! You'll have my bubbies out in a moment. Should we not go somewhere more private?'

'Oh no. That's the idea. You're going to strip naked for me. I want Sidonie to look you over. I'd never take a mistress without her agreement.'

Liza pushed herself upright, her eyes opening wide with shock. Surely she had not heard right. She turned

114

to Sidonie and saw that she was smiling, her eyes measuring her reactions in a way that seemed almost coldly calculating.

'But I couldn't. It's too daring. I really couldn't,' Liza said without conviction, feeling her sexual tension increase.

'Of course you can,' Francis said softly. 'Nothing could be more simple. Who's to know about it? Think of it as a party game. I'll act as lady's maid for you.'

'Perhaps she does not wish to play,' Sidonie said. 'I understand. No doubt there is some bodily imperfection that she wishes to hide. You're free to leave at any time, Liza.'

At this slur on her feminine charms, Liza lifted her chin. How dare Sidonie infer that her body was less than perfect. She felt a flicker of dislike. Sidonie did not like her after all and was trying to belittle her.

Well, she'd just show *her*.

'Very well. I'll play your silly game,' Liza said and stood still as Francis began to undress her. 'Just watch this, Robert!'

All eyes were on her. Being the centre of attention was a drug stronger than alcohol. Liza felt the excitement centre in the place between her legs, where there was a pressure and a growing wetness. Her breasts felt swollen and the nipples hardened, seeming to push against her chemise.

The garments slid down her body to crumple into a heap of apricot silk and lace about her lower legs. She glanced at Sidonie and Robert, both of whom made sounds of approval as each layer came off. As her final petticoat and then her corset cover was revealed they began to clap.

Liza hung her head for a second, unwilling to reveal her flushed cheeks and shining eyes. The tension within her was almost unbearable. A pulse ticked in her lower belly and her quim felt puffy and receptive. The wetness was gathering behind the closed sex-lips, ready to spill over at any moment.

Francis took off her remaining garments, unlacing her corset and laying it aside. It occurred to her that he knew a lot about women's clothing. Finally she wore only her chemise, her knee-length stockings, and her shoes. As he took the chemise by the hem and lifted it over her head, she closed her eyes.

The close air of the room was sticky against her naked skin. Her courage failed her and she brought her two hands down to cover the triangle of hair at her groin, hunching over slightly to shield her breasts from view.

Francis stepped in front of her. He reached for her wrists and brought them up above her head. She tried to twist her body and press herself against him, but the quality of his laugh stopped her. It was harsh and faintly mocking.

'Too late now to play the innocent,' he said. 'Come over here to the light. Sidonie wants to look you over.'

Quivering with pent-up desire, Liza allowed him to lead her towards the bed. It had been cleared of the board which had held the food and was lit by two candelabra on a side table.

Liza glanced up at Robert who was watching her with an expression of scandalized lust. His hands were clamped in his lap, covering the erection which strained for release. Throwing back her head Liza laughed huskily.

'Where's your courage? Take your clothes off too.'

Robert shook his head and sank back into the shadows.

'Well, Sidonie. Do you approve?' Francis said. 'Hold your arms out, Liza. Let Sidonie have a good look at you.'

Sidonie stood up and walked around Liza. Liza held her breath. At the first touch on her skin, she jumped. She had not expected any physical contact between them. The rules of the 'game' had not been made clear, but she thought that Sidonie would pronounce her suitable and then she and Francis would retire to somewhere more private.

And then . . . Ah, then.

But Sidonie trailed her fingertips across her shoulders

116

and leaned close to place a kiss in the hollow at the side of her neck. A jolt of raw lust fizzed down to Liza's groin. It was so strange to have Francis's female-counterpart touching her – desiring her?

And oh, God. She desired Sidonie in turn. She wanted her touch, her approval. It was suddenly the most important thing in the world. The fingers trailing down her spine were all-knowing, all-seeing. She felt peeled to the bone, her every secret, dark emotion laid bare.

A little moan of distress escaped her when Sidonie's hands slid up her ribcage and took hold of her breasts. Her thumbs rubbed back and forth across the nipples and Liza trembled as they rose into hard little peaks. Sidonie smiled, squeezing and lifting the breasts, so that they jutted out provocatively.

'Very nice, Francis,' she said. 'You have chosen well. A slender waist and neat buttocks too. Rounded thighs and a good length of leg.'

Francis smiled. His eyes were hot, but the heat in them was not for Liza. Some measure of understanding struggled for life within Liza, but she pushed away the unwanted knowledge.

She was the centre of everything. Her sexual heat was a molten force, softening, swelling inside her. It was *her* body that both twins wanted to enjoy. And she craved their touch.

Sidonie slid her hands down Liza's body until they rested on her stomach. She pulled upwards, forcing Liza's pubis to pout and the outer lips of her sex to come into view. The sweat prickled all over Liza's body. Surely there could be nothing worse than this. The hidden part of her body was now to be examined.

'A neat quim, but I need to see more,' Sidonie said, as calmly as if she was talking about the weather. 'Liza, be a dear, go and lie on the bed and open your legs.'

As a deep flush rose into her face, Liza knew that the worst was yet to come. She thought of refusing. They would not force her to do anything she did not want to – but she *did* want to.

117

This was the single most erotic experience of her life. Knowing that Robert was watching, his crouched-over body making evident the fact that he was in an agony of lust, made the game even more piquant.

And she was aware that there was something different, shocking, about the twins and she wanted to be a part of it.

Slowly she walked towards the bed. Robert sat amongst the cushions in the shadows. Forgotten by the others he had opened his trousers and was stroking himself. She saw the thick column of reddened flesh sticking up in front of him and her sex fluttered, the juices welling up and overflowing.

Oh, how dreadful it was to lie down on her back, her legs hanging over the edge of the bed and the soles of her feet resting on the marble floor. Dreadful too, to know that when Sidonie looked between her legs she would see the signs of her arousal.

Francis came and stood beside her, looking down on her spread body. He began stroking her belly, circling her breasts, pinching her nipples. She gave a little cry and reached out for him, half-turning towards him. Her hips lurched and wove. The pulsing between her sex-lips was maddening. If only one of them would stroke her – there.

She yearned for their lips, their eager, questing fingers. Francis, Sidonie, she did not know who she wanted the most.

'Lie still,' Francis said softly. 'You're for Sidonie's pleasure tonight.'

A tremor passed over Liza's body as Sidonie laid cool hands on her thighs and pressed them open. With finger and thumb she peeled apart the outer lips of Liza's quim, holding her open to reveal the moist, pinkish-brown folds and the swollen pleasure bud. Liza moaned as she felt the wetness slide out of her and trickle on to the bed.

'Blonde pubic hair. How delightful. And she's wet and excited. Do you see?' Sidonie said, looking up into Francis's face.

118

Liza arched her back and let her knees fall open as Sidonie spread open her quim even wider for Francis's appraisal. Her stiff, little organ of pleasure jutted out and her vaginal entrance was revealed. She grew hot with shame as it pulsed and wept. Squeezing her buttocks together, Liza pushed her lower body into the air desperate for the easement which they cruelly withheld.

Suddenly Sidonie thrust two fingers inside her thirsting orifice at the same time as Francis pinched both nipples. Liza cried out, unable to bear the burning sweetness of her breasts, the insistent throbbing deep within her sex. Her vision fogged as the pleasure concentrated and began to build and build until she could stand it no longer.

Just as she was drawn towards the crest, she saw Francis and Sidonie lean together, their faces drawing nearer and nearer above her.

No. She screamed silently. I'm here. Kiss me. Touch me. But it seemed somehow right and natural that the twins' mouths should meet. They kissed like lovers, their mouths open, the tongues churning together. Francis nibbled Sidonie's bottom lip, murmuring words of love.

'No!' Liza breathed, not wanting the understanding that was forced upon her.

Despite her denial, she climaxed. The pleasure more intense than it had ever been. Sidonie's sopping fingers thrusting within her urged her on to another peak, which flowed out from the first and then settled gradually into lesser waves of bliss that went on and on . . .

Helplessly she writhed and moaned, threshing back and forth, forgotten and used by them both. Exhausted she rolled away from them and looked towards the place where Robert, red-faced and straining, was pumping away at himself.

She saw the jet of semen spurt on to his belly. Not bothering to cover herself, she went over to him. Taking his pocket handkerchief she wiped him clean, then snuggled up next to him.

'She did forget about me. I knew she would,' Robert said forlornly. 'I always get left out.'

'They forgot about both of us,' Liza said.

Being left out was a new experience for her and it hurt. She felt a strange sense of loss. Putting her arm around Robert, she said, 'Help me get dressed. I'll take you home in my coach. You and I have served our purpose.'

Sidonie and Franois now lay on the bed, utterly absorbed in each other. They kissed and embraced with a hunger that was alien to her. They really loved each other, she could see that. Liza felt close to tears. If only either one of the twins had kissed her or embraced her with even a fraction of that intensity, she would have been willing to do anything for them.

But they had simply used her as a spur to their own passions. The fact that she had been agreeable did not lessen the humiliation.

She was soon dressed. The twins did not look up as she and Robert walked across the room. At the door she looked over her shoulder.

'You're unnatural and heartless!' she called. 'One day you will know how it feels to be discarded. You can't just use people and throw them away. Wait and see. You'll get your desserts!'

The only sound was that of Francis's laughter and Sidonie's low murmur of pleasure.

Chapter Nine

*I*t was pleasant sitting on the terrace under the shade of a mulberry tree.

Sidonie looked towards the gardens where crumbling statues were arranged along the walks between beds planted with roses, carnations and mignonettes. Ilex and cypress cast long shadows across paths of swept gravel and the faint scent of orange blossom wafted towards her on the warm breeze.

She pushed her straw sun-hat to the back of her head and opened the top buttons of her muslin gown.

'Oh, this is all so beautiful,' she murmured. 'I'm almost reluctant to leave for Venice tomorrow.'

Francis smiled and helped himself to another glass of the wine cup in which floated slices of orange and lemon and sprigs of basil.

'It has been lovely here,' he said, sipping the ruby-coloured punch. 'Mmmm. I taste chianti in this and something else.'

He glanced at Sidonie, his mouth twitching with humour. 'It wouldn't be absinthe, would it? I know that you brought some bottles with you from Paris.'

Sidonie chuckled. 'You needn't tease me. I had only the one taste of that devilish brew. I hope you're not inferring that I need anything to give me the courage to misbehave!'

'That's plain enough, as Liza, Robert and a few others will willingly attest to! Is it not strange how certain people actually relish being humillated? You're getting quite shameless, my love,' he said, his voice deepening with admiration.

After a pause he yawned theatrically, his eyes on the open neckline of her dress where the tops of her breasts and shadowed cleavage were revealed.

'This wine and the heat are making me drowsy,' he said. 'Let's go inside. We can rest together on my bed.'

She knew what he really meant by 'rest' and was tempted. Francis looked particularly handsome in a full-sleeved white shirt, loose silk cravat, and dark trousers. His unruly dark curls spilled over his shoulders. The sun had imparted a golden light to the tops of his cheekbones and turned the light-blue of his eyes to the aquamarine tint of shallow sea-water.

It must be something about the Tuscan light that made him look so irresistible. Surely Lord Byron had looked like this when he visited the area some fifty years before them.

She shook her head.

'Not now,' she said regretfully. 'It's too risky. Someone might interrupt us. I'm not sure where Thomas is. He mentioned something about us going to the opera early this evening.'

'Oh, come on, Sidonie. Indulge me,' Francis said softly. 'The danger of being discovered adds a touch of spice. Christ, you must know that I'm dying for you. These latest flirtations into which you have encouraged me have only made me want you more. And I had an erotic dream last night. It was so strange. I was back in England. Do you remember Chatham Burney?'

She nodded, recalling the art teacher who had been her first lover. Francis too had discovered the singular delights of sharing pleasure with another man in Chatham's arms.

'He was in love with us both, you know,' Francis went on. 'It broke his heart when we left Wiltshire. I had not realised what an impression he made on me. I have never met another man who attracted me since Chatham. Indeed I do not particularly long for the embrace of any male lover, but the dream . . .'

He stopped, looking troubled. It was a moment before he spoke. 'It was so intense, so erotic, that it has quite disturbed me.'

'Tell me about it,' Sidonie said, taking off her hat and fanning herself with it. 'This is a perfect lazy afternoon for such reflections. And talking is a far safer occupation than what you had in mind.'

Francis grinned wolfishly. 'I'll tell you about my dream, but I promise you that you'll only get all excited. Next thing you'll be begging me to pleasure you.'

'Which is exactly what you wish I'd do! Try me then. I'll wager that I can hear you out and remain unmoved.'

'Oh, I think not. But we'll see. I'll take your wager. And claim my prize when I've finished telling you all about it.'

'What shall the prize be?' Sidonie was getting into the mood of their game.

'It will be of my own devising. You'll have to trust my judgement.'

Sidonie leaned back in her chair and closed her eyes. The dappled sunlight poured through the trees imprinting her face with shifting coins of light.

'Very well,' she said, sighing with contentment. 'You may begin.'

'When the dream began, Chatham and myself were in an English cornfield,' Francis said. 'It was high summer and the sky was a pure cornflower blue. You know the sort of day when the bees are droning lazily and the air is sweet with the scent of ripening wheat, corn cockles and the peculiar peppery-sweet fragrance of poppies? I always feel sort of drowsy and half-aroused on such days. Well, it was like that. Chatham said that he wanted to sketch me – naked, against the background of all that burgeoning life. Like a god of nature, was how he put it.'

Sidonie nodded. 'I can imagine him saying something like that. Go on.'

'I took off all my clothes and laid down in the corn. The warm air was like a caress on my skin. Wild flowers tickled my back and sides, and ants and small beetles ran over my limbs. I closed my eyes and felt the heat of the sun on my face. Behind my eyelids I could see the vessels in my skin. It was like watching the veins of a leaf, all aglow with orange light.

'I was very aware of Chatham's eyes on me, measuring, appraising my reactions. His request to draw me was a thinly veiled invitation to join with him in sexual union and both of us knew that. As he sketched me I could feel myself growing hard and I wanted to turn over on to my stomach to hide the fact. But I did not want to change the pose, so I did not move.

'My cock swelled and lengthened. I felt it stirring against my thigh and I could not stop it growing hard. It twitched and pulsed with a life of its own, heavy and potent. Although my eyes were closed I knew that Chatham was watching my every move. I felt his gaze flickering over me and coming to rest at my groin. I could hear how his breathing quickened and the scratch of his charcoal on the page had a wild and reckless sweep to it.'

Francis paused and took another sip of his drink. He pushed back the dark curls which tumbled forward on to his forehead, tucking one long strand behind his ear.

'Even telling you about it makes me feel hot,' he grinned. 'Anyway. It was inevitable that Chatham would put down his sketch pad and come to sit beside me. I just lay there, pretending I did not know what was going to happen. When he reached out a hand and began to stroke my chest I made no sound. He brushed his fingertips against my nipples and I groaned softly. Sliding his palm down my body he rubbed his hand across my belly and toyed with the dark curls at my groin, then he moved his hand down and placed it on my cock.

'I was so strongly erect it was almost painful; so hot and throbbing that I leapt in his hand. He began frigging me with one hand, while reaching between my legs to stroke my balls. I was shaking with desire for him and could not help bucking and twisting my hips towards him. I reached for him, but he told me to lie still. Then he drew the skin right back from my glans, exposing the swollen plum of it to the sunlight and warm breeze. Bending down, he licked the salty juices from the little cock-mouth, savouring the taste as if it were the costliest wine. He bathed the head of my cock with long, tantalising licks, now and then curling around to lick the underside where the skin joined my shaft. I thought I would spend almost at once, but he gauged me, sucking me and then stopping, keeping me thirsting for more.'

He smiled at Sidonie and when he spoke again there was a tremor in his voice.

'It was so real. I *wanted* it to be real. When I awoke I had a raging erection. My hands were clutched around my cock and I was jerking myself towards a release. I felt ... something strange. A restless hunger for a pleasure that I had almost forgotten. Can you understand that?'

She nodded and said gently, 'Was that the end of the dream?'

'No. I did not want it to be the end. I drifted back into a sort of dreamlike state and somehow managed to retrace my tracks. Chatham was still stroking me, but he was lying beside me now. He had turned me over so that I lay on my belly. His fingers were tracing the depressions and ridges that the crushed stems of corn had imprinted into the skin of my back. My cock felt like a bar of burning metal under me. I realised that Chatham was naked too now – in the way of dreams he had not disrobed, but he was also naked.

'I moved to lie on my side and he lay behind me. I felt the warmth of his stomach against my back, my buttocks fitted into his lap and his cock was pressed between our bodies. He told me to bend my knees up high in front of me and then he began to caress my taut buttocks and my balls which were jutting between my thighs, so tight and firm with my need to spend. Now and then he reached up between my thighs and stroked my shaft and my swollen, naked cock-head, but gently so that I shook and groaned with the effort of trying to come. Ah, he was deliciously cruel as he denied me the release I craved.

'In a few moments he eased my buttocks apart, sliding his fingers into the moist crack and dragging his nails ever so lightly across my anus. It felt exquisite. Yes, I thought, yes. This is the caress I crave the most. Do whatever you want to me. My cock jumped and wept with pleasure as he stroked the little aperture and then moved down to press his face between my cheeks and taste me . . . there. His tongue squirmed into me, past the tight creases and began licking the tender, bitter-sweet lining.

'After a longer while, he wetted his little finger and slipped it into me – right inside. I think I knew what would happen next. He was readying me, loosening me for the in-thrust of his hard cock. Even while I longed for this, I was afraid. I have never had a man thrusting inside me.'

Francis stopped, his voice broke and his eyes glittered with contained emotion. He leaned forward and began speaking rapidly and earnestly.

'It's something most men are scared of, Sidonie, although they will rarely speak of such things. *We* are the ones who thrust into willing bodies, conquering them, making them our own. It is what the world tells us is the correct thing to do. Perhaps that is why it is so much more difficult to give up that power. I felt all these things but still, something primeval rose up within my breast, some nameless emotion which urged me to press my buttocks back towards him, offering myself up for whatever he wished to do with me. And I felt a great surge of submissive pleasure vibrating all down my body, which seemed like a kind of freedom. Yes, take me, I thought. Possess me, as a man does with a woman. Use me for your pleasure and I will writhe and moan and weep under you.'

Sidonie could almost *see* the scene in the cornfield. She wished that it had been real and that she could have watched. How beautiful the two men would look, their strong, slender limbs entwined and the tangle of their hair – a mixture of light and dark – lying like wings against their pale skin. The sweat on their faces and shoulders would glisten in the sunlight, delineating every rise and hollow, picking out the rapid pulse at each throat-dip and temple.

Gods of nature indeed. Just like something out of a painting.

Already Francis had won his forfeit. The musk-laden heat of arousal raged through every nerve of her body.

'Continue, Francis. What happened next?' she said softly. 'Did he take you in the dream?'

Francis drew a ragged breath and said, 'Chatham reached for his cravat and wrapped it around my wrists. Oh, but I was a willing captive. The restraint simply underlined that fact, making the erotic charge between us almost unbearable. He spat into his hand and rubbed the saliva around my anus, then he lubricated his cock in the same way. He told me to kneel up and to bend over. I felt my body open to him as he parted my buttocks and nudged the head of his cock between them.

'I was trembling, my thighs shaking with the effort of keeping still. My anus was pushed out and pulsing like an eager little mouth. It hurt at first as he entered me, stretching impossibly it seemed. But he went very slowly and I was eager to accommodate him. Then he was halfway into me and murmuring breathlessly that I felt like hot-buttered silk inside.

'For some reason those words, and the fact that he was nudging against some place inside me that throbbed dully, aroused me beyond all reason. I began to move my hips, encouraging him to impale me ever more deeply. And I thought my cock would burst with the

pressure of holding back my climax. The semen threatened to boil up from my balls and splash on to my
bowed chest.

'As he pushed into the very depths of my tight
passage, I pulled against the bonds at my wrists, welcoming the way the cravat burnt and chafed my skin.
Still some dark recess of my mind fought against the
wicked pleasure, the feeling of being taken and used.
Then he was into me completely, his belly butting up
tight against my buttocks. I could no longer hold back.
A scream lodged in my throat and, as he drew back out
of me and then surged straight into my bowels in a
single deep thrust, I came. I cried and gasped, the tears
pouring unchecked down my face at the hot, wrenching
pleasure of being so soundly plundered.'

When Francis had finished there was silence. Sidonie
did not trust herself to speak. She knew that she could
not conceal her reactions from her twin – he knew her
too well. The flush of colour in her cheeks, the drowsy,
heavy appearance of her eyes, were all signatures of her
state of erotic tension.

She smiled, her bottom lip caught between her teeth.
Francis just looked at her, waiting for the acknowledge-
ment he was certain would come.

'You were right, of course. I cannot resist the magic of
such a dream. What forfeit must I pay?' she said. 'Is it to
be very wicked and depraved? Oh, say that it is!'

Francis leaned across and lifted her hand. He brought
it to his lips and dipped his tongue between each finger
in turn, then turned over her hand and kissed her palm.

Sidonie shuddered and pressed her shaking hand to
her mouth. She felt a reflection of the wet heat of his lips
and tongue in the pulpy flesh between her thighs.

'I've been thinking of the gift I bought you in Paris,'
said Francis. 'The red leather dildo. I want you . . .' He
hesitated for a moment.

She was intrigued. It was not like Francis to hold back
when he wanted something. She thought she knew what
his request would be, but she wanted to hear him say it.

'You want me to what?' she said.

'To strap on the dildo and play the man's part with me. I've never been rogered by a man, but after that dream I want to know how it feels. I have the most pressing need of your services.'

'We can't now! In the middle of the afternoon,' she said, scandalised by his daring, but already feeling her will to resist him fading. Besides the thought of doing as he asked excited her unbearably.

When she spoke again her voice lacked conviction. 'I told you before, Francis. It's too risky. Anyone might look in on us.'

'Oh, let them if they have the will to spy on us. We're leaving tomorrow. What can it matter. Now. No more excuses. Are you going to honour our wager or not?'

Sidonie stood up and shook out her muslin skirts. The blood was pounding in her ears. She held her hand out to her twin.

'Did you doubt that I would? When have I ever refused you anything?'

Hand in hand they entered the villa and made their way stealthily to Francis's room.

Thomas whistled softly to himself as he strolled along the corridor of the villa.

He was glad that they were leaving Florence early the next morning. The overblown charms of Mary Wortley had begun to pall. She was getting possessive and kept dropping the subject of marriage into the conversation.

'And I think you might drink a bit less. Your ardour is waning, my lover,' she said. 'A man with the tavern-droop is no good to himself or anyone else.'

Thoroughly alarmed Thomas sought for an answer or, better still, a way to escape. Luckily he found the perfect excuse in his bear-leadership of the twins.

'They wouldn't know what to do without me, m'dear,' he said to Mary. 'Neither of them is much good at languages or currencies. And Venice is no city to lose oneself in. They would get themselves into a fine mess if

129

I was to abandon them. Which, of course, I have no intention of doing.'

Mary sulked for a while, threatening not to see him again before he left. But she had relented at the last moment and sent her carriage for him that morning.

They had passed a pleasant few hours, strolling around some pleasure gardens and admiring the tropical plants in an orangery. Then she had ordered the coachman to take a circuitous route back to the villa and preceded to give Thomas something to remember her by.

'I'm determined not to be tearful. Even if you are going to abandon me, you rascal,' Mary said, her bottom lip trembling despite her attempt at levity. 'Oh, I'll take you anyway, my man. Once more for luck, eh?'

Thomas grinned as he recalled the way she had sucked his cock, running her thick lips sideways up and down the shaft and then drawing his bulbous tip into the wet cavern of her mouth. When he was good and stout she had lifted her skirts above her waist and straddled him, one hefty thigh placed either side of him and her knees pressed into the padded leather seat.

All he'd had to do was sit still, clenching his thighs and buttocks to keep his balance as she pressed her hands down on to his shoulders and bounced lustily up and down. As her big, fleshy quim jabbed up and down on him he sighed with pleasure, feeling engulfed by the folds and hollows of her copious femininity.

Mary emitted hoarse little cries, her breasts bouncing jauntily against his face in time with her movements. Perfumed globes cradled his face as he quested for one of her nipples. Finding the prominent, rubbery tip he worried it gently, biting harder when her breathing quickened.

Closing his eyes, he let Mary have her way with him. When he came he cried out with sheer joy. There was nothing to compare with a highly-sexed, well-covered woman – nothing in the world. The only thing that made him shrivel was the mention of marriage and, even worse, temperance.

He stopped and glanced in a mirror, which had a frame covered with gold-painted, plaster cherubs. Grimacing at himself, he combed his lank hair with his fingers and pulled down his bottom eyelid to peer at the whites of his eyes.

Oh, damnation. He did not look too good. The legacy of too many sleepless nights, Mary's zealous attempts to drain him totally and the consumption of vast quantities of the excellent Italian wines, was evident in his bloodshot eyes and the haggard lines of his already lean face.

Never mind. Tonight he planned to be abstemious. The trip to the opera was to be the jewel in the crown of their stay in Florence. Most, if not all, of the English people staying in the villas nearby would be there. The twins had been a resounding success with the 'set' and there would be many tearful goodbyes, wistful glances and promises to keep up correspondences by letter.

Pausing outside the door of Francis's room, Thomas permitted himself a moment of self-congratulation. Sir James Ryder could rest assured that he, Thomas, had introduced his children to the right kind of people. He felt certain that the twins were at last beginning to benefit from their tour and broaden their minds. He would say as much in the regular letter he sent home to Sir James and Lady Jenny.

He put his hand on the door, meaning to go straight into the room and remind Francis that it was almost time he dressed for the opera. This morning when he had mentioned the engagement he had been aware that Francis had not been paying attention. The door did not give. How odd. It was locked. He tapped softly, then a little louder, but there was no answer.

Perhaps Francis was taking a siesta. Yes, that must be it. The servants said that he and Sidonie were at home. Thomas glanced at his watch. Time was getting on. It would not do for Francis to oversleep. Arriving late for the opera was considered the height of bad manners.

There was nothing for it. He would have to go around by the gardens and try to gain entrance via the terrace. He smiled to himself, envying the capacity of the young to sleep through just about anything.

'Oh, Christ, Sidonie,' Francis moaned, reaching for her as she knelt above him on the bed.

She looked incredible, naked except for the leather harness strapped around her slim hips and the great, red phallus jutting up between her thighs. Her loose hair streamed over her shoulders, like a pale flame. And her eyes were huge and luminous in her white face.

'You look part angel, part devil, and I love it,' Francis said, claiming her mouth and opening his lips for the intrusion of her seeking tongue.

He palmed her breasts, feeling the hardening nipples swelling at his touch. She was as aroused as he was and eager to put the dildo to use, but first he wanted to watch her.

'You'd make a most enticing boy,' Francis said grinning, 'if it were not for your pretty breasts.'

'Don't you like them?' she teased. 'Ah, I can see that you do. You have the best of all worlds in me, my love. And I'm going to give you so much pleasure that you'll faint with the delight of it. Who else will ever care so much for you?'

'Dance for me, my Salome. Or are you Jezebel?' he said huskily, his mouth drying with lust and longing as he watched her.

He lay on his back, resting against the piled-up pillows on his bed. He was naked and his cock stood out strongly. He stroked himself almost absently, squeezing the moist glans within its collar of skin, keeping himself at a boiling pitch of arousal.

Sidonie, glorying in the game of being a boy, stood up and wove her hips back and forth, so that the dildo bobbed about. The weight at her groin felt strange, but exciting. There was a strap that passed between her legs and the smooth leather was slightly raised and ridged at

132

the point where it rubbed against her quim. Little shards of sensation spread outwards from the raised nub of pleasure as she worked her hips, stabbing at the air with the leather phallus.

Keeping eye contact with Francis, she closed her fingers around the dildo and feigned the movements of masturbation. Then she stood with her legs apart and sank down a little, twisting her body so that he could see her shapely buttocks, bisected by the red straps.

As she sank down further, her thighs wide, he glimpsed the light-coloured pubic hair stranding out around the straps and saw a flash of pinkish labia as the harness gaped for a moment.

'How strange it feels to have a cock,' she said giggling. 'I'd like to push it into you now. But I think it's too dry for my purposes.'

Slipping a hand under the strap which enclosed her quim, she pushed two fingers into herself then smeared her juices around the leather cock-head.

Francis watched her closely, delighting in her lewdness and erotic posturings. He thought he knew her in every mood, but he had never seen her looking so wanton, so utterly sexual. It seemed that it was the strapped-on dildo that lent her a new dimension.

'Come here,' he said thickly. 'I can't wait any longer. Let me suck your cock.'

She sashayed up the bed and stood with her feet placed one on either side of his chest. Sinking down she rested her spread buttocks on him, then put her hand behind his head and drew his face towards the phallus. Francis gave a ragged moan and parted his lips. She fed the dildo into his mouth and he sucked greedily. The cock tasted of her fragrant juices, the salty musk mixed with the flavour of new leather.

After a few moments Sidonie changed position and Francis pulled her down to lie beside him. Both of them were consciously putting off the moment when he would turn on to his belly and allow her to mount him. They were so absorbed in each other that they did not hear a knock on the door and a few minutes later were unaware of the fact that someone had pushed open the widow which led out onto the terrace.

Sidonie, raising herself into a sitting position caught the movement from the tail of her eye. She clutched at Francis and pulled him up to sit beside her.

Standing a few feet away, his face bound by an expression of shocked outrage, was Thomas. His lips worked, but no sound came out.

For a moment no one spoke. The silence was absolute. Sidonie began to shake and Francis put a protective arm around her shoulders.

'Don't,' he whispered. 'Everything will be fine. You'll see.'

'What ... what is going on?' Thomas stammered finally, his face ashen.

'I should have thought that was obvious,' Francis said dryly. 'So now you know about us. It had to happen some time. Did you want something or do you make a habit of bursting unannounced into people's private rooms?'

'Francis, don't ...' Sidonie said, her voice shaking.

He patted her hand as she tried to pull a cover over their nakedness.

'It's all right,' Francis said quietly. 'Let me handle Thomas.'

'The, er, opera,' Thomas said, trying to regain his composure. He did not seem to know where to look and settled finally on fixing his line of vision above both of their heads. 'I, um, came to tell you it was time to get ready.'

'Well, you've told us,' Francis said. 'Thank you. Is that all? Then shut the window on your way out, there's a good fellow.'

An unreadable expression flickered across Thomas's face, then he said with quiet dignity. 'I'll accompany you to the opera this evening. But I'm afraid that you'll be going on to Venice – alone.'

With that he turned on his heel and left the room.

Chapter Ten

*F*or Sidonie the opera that night was a nightmare experience.

Thomas's face, bound by a mixture of shock and disgust, haunted her thoughts. Somehow she managed to smile and exchange pleasantries with all those who came to their box bringing flowers and cards to wish them well on their imminent journey.

Beside her Francis was calm and his usual charming self, fending off all the attention with aplomb. Now and then he would lean over and say, 'Not to worry. Thomas will come around.'

Sidonie doubted that. Thomas was white-faced, the lines of strain around his mouth more deeply marked than usual. He was also sober. This more than anything was evidence of his distress.

The evening wore on and she applauded in all the right places, but she did not hear the beautiful, soaring voices or see the glittering costumes. All she could think about was that Thomas wanted no more to do with either Francis or herself.

That she was disturbed and saddened by the fact surprised her. She could not imagine continuing on their tour without Thomas. He has been so much a part of their travels; a mostly unobtrusive presence, planning excursions and visits, taking care of introductions and doing all the official, practical things which Francis and herself took for granted.

And apart from all that, she was genuinely fond of him. It was unthinkable that they should part company on bad terms.

When the interval came, she excused herself on the pretext of needing to get a breath of air and sought out Thomas. He was standing with a small group of English tourists, discussing the merits of the beautiful, dark-eyed soprano. She walked straight up to him and slipped her arm into his.

'Ah, there you are. I wonder if I might have a minute of your time?'

Before he could object she began drawing him away, smiling politely at the others in the group. Short of shaking her off, Thomas could do nothing but allow himself to be steered towards a door which led on to an outdoor balcony.

'Whatever you are planning to say to me, it won't make any difference,' he said under his breath. 'I simply cannot countenance such behaviour. I thought better of you, Sidonie. With your own brother, for God's sake!'

On the balcony they found a space where they could be alone. Thomas pulled out a chair for Sidonie.

'I won't insult you by making excuses for us, Thomas,' she said. 'Perhaps no one can understand, but we truly love each other – in every way. All our lives we've had no one but each other for company, comfort and warmth. How can anyone else know what it is like to be as close as we are? Sometimes even our thoughts collide. You have seen how often we have chosen the same gift for each other, or dressed in similar colours – all unplanned. Is this love so wrong, so unnatural? And if you deem it so, ask yourself, who are we harming?'

Thomas flushed. 'I did not want to discuss this, but since you insist. I do not wish to be indelicate, but do you not realise that you could . . . become . . .'

'With child?' she smiled sadly. 'That cannot happen.

136

We have never taken such a risk. Both of us understand that some things are forbidden to us. Oh, Thomas. Tell me that you don't hate us!'

Thomas's face softened and he reached for her hand.

'My dear child! Hate you? What folly. I could never hate you. But I cannot in all conscience go on, knowing what I now know. It would be a betrayal of Sir James's trust.'

Sidonie snatched her hand free and her chin came up.

'I've never heard anything so sanctimonious! You've betrayed his trust from the moment you took up position as bearleader. I wonder what Father would have found if he'd had the foresight to check your references. Are you quite what you seem? Oh, you've paid lip-service to chaperoning Francis and myself, but that has not stopped you drinking and whoring your way around Europe! Do you think that's what Father had in mind when he engaged your services? And do you feel qualified to make moral judgements on others?'

'I thought this conciliatory mood of yours would not last,' Thomas muttered. 'You're impossible. I find you and Francis behaving in the most outrageous, depraved manner and I'm the one who's being taken to task!'

Unexpectedly he began to chuckle.

'I suppose that my life would be duller at that, without the two of you to bait me. I thought that I was beyond being shocked, but you've proved me wrong. And it's true that I'm not one to set moral standards by. Very well, I'll come with you to Venice, although I won't say that I condone your behaviour. But you must give me your promise.'

'On what?'

'That you'll take care to be more discreet about the, er, closeness of your relationship from now on. No more of this playing fast and loose with your conquests and flaunting them for each other's amusement.' His eyes sparkled with humour. 'And take care whom you invite for intimate suppers. I had the devil's own job placating

137

a most distressed Honourable Elizabeth Bexham. And now I think I know why. So – do you promise?'

Sidonie was surprised that he had known about the supper. Dear Thomas. She imagined him comforting a distraught Liza, whose nose had been put thoroughly out of joint by being used for their pleasure and then discarded. He was far more understanding than they gave him credit for.

On impulse she reached up and kissed his cheek.

'Agreed. You do know that we *are* very fond of you, Thomas, in our own way. It's just that we're so wrapped up in each other. There's never been much affection left over for anyone else.'

'Thank you for your candour, Sidonie. I appreciate the fact that you did not insult me with platitudes. Now. The second half of the opera is about to start. Shall we go inside?'

Pink with pleasure Thomas held out his arm for Sidonie to slip her hand under his elbow. He was aware that he had been manipulated, but he did not care. It was as if something which had been troubling him had been laid to rest.

He had felt from the beginning that the twins' relationship was special. Now he knew just how close they were. Oddly enough, he sympathized with them. Each was so unique, so ethereally beautiful, that he could not imagine an ordinary mortal stealing either of their hearts. If that was ever to happen, then he feared for them. How could either of them bear to relinquish the other?

He pushed such thoughts aside. But as they strolled back towards the auditorium, he could not shake the image from his mind – that of Sidonie as naked and magnificent as some ancient Celtic goddess, wearing a leather harness slung around her shapely hips from which jutted a potent red phallus.

Early one morning, a week later, Sidonie was awakened by a loud din of voices and the sound of splashing below the balcony of her room.

Yawning, she pushed herself out of bed and padded over to the floor-length window. The oily breath of the canal reached her as soon as she stepped out into the open sir. She wrinkled her nose. The famous stench of Venice, variously described as 'more noisome than a sty' and 'a stinkpot, charged with the very virus of hell' certainly lived up to its reputation.

But the sight of the Grand Canal, so covered with rafts and barges piled with every kind of fruit and vegetable that the water could hardly be seen, distracted her from the smell. Crowds of people hurried from boat to boat, buying the grapes, melons, peaches and the other colourful fruit.

The warm breeze stirred against Sidonie's loose hair and moulded the thin nightgown to her body. Leaning over the stone balustrade she peered out over the gathering, noticing that there were many colourfully clad nobles chatting and refreshing themselves with fruit. No doubt they had been out all night revelling and were on their way home to sleep the day away.

She had been sorry to leave Florence, but Venice was beautiful in a different way. There was an aura of excitement and danger about it, especially with the people crowding into the city for the carnival.

She smiled, thinking of the invitation which had arrived late the previous night. A mysterious nobleman had asked them to visit his apartments where a gaming house had been set up. Thomas had explained that, at carnival time, everyone was welcome to these *ridotti* as long as they wore the domino and mask. If she and Francis were to accept, then they too would likely be out all night and joining the early morning crowd on the canal.

A young man, wearing the black domino cape covering his upper body, looked up and saw Sidonie on her balcony. Pushing back his tricorne hat he waved, calling out, *'Bella signorina! Bella!'* Clasping his hand to his heart, he began to sing, his powerful tenor voice rising above the clatter of voices.

Sidonie blushed with pleasure as people stopped to stare and applaud. When the young man finished singing she waved and blew him a kiss, before going back into her room and calling for her maid to help her dress.

She and Francis breakfasted with Thomas in a small waterside café. Thomas went off on an errand of his own and the twins made their way by gondola to the Piazza San Marco. There they watched rope-dancers, minstrels and magicians.

'Look there. It's the Doge,' Francis said as a carnival figure wearing purple silk trimmed with ermine walked past.

The Doge was followed by a procession of nobles wearing fur-lined ankle-length togas, coloured black, red, cream or violet. Everyone they saw was dressed in bright silks, their hair piled high and streaked with unnatural colours or concealed behind veils. The pageant paid tribute to the glory of bygone Venice.

Many people were masked or dressed in fanciful costumes resembling animals or figures from fairy-tales. One woman, tall and bedecked with a feather hat and many jewels was bare-breasted. At carnival time, it seemed as if nothing was too outrageous or too immodest.

'Look, a fortune-teller. Do let's go into the tent,' Sidonie said, dragging Francis by the hand.

He laughed indulgently and pressed a coin into the outstretched hand of the old woman sitting behind a cloth-draped table. Symbols of the zodiac were painted on the lining of the tent. A single bronze lamp cast a reddish light into the gloom.

'Ah, two who are one,' the woman said mysteriously, her voice softly accented. 'Give me your hands.'

Sidonie and Francis held out their hands and the woman studied them both, side by side. For a moment she looked down intently, then she shook her head.

'I see great distress for you, but happiness is to follow. The one must become two before you return to your homeland. That is the only way forward. Beware, young mistress, for you will lose your heart in Venice. You too, young master, and it will pain you sorely. This will surely happen. It is useless for you to resist it.'

Francis went pale. He snatched his hand away and laughed derisively. 'The devil you say! What utter nonsense is this? Come, Sidonie, the drab's a charlatan.'

The old woman grinned, showing stained front teeth. Her eyes were as bright as black beads.

'Believe what you wish, young master. The message is the same. The one must become two.'

Outside the tent, Sidonie clung to Francis's arm. She could feel how he was trembling.

'What do you think she meant by that? "The one must become two".'

'I have no idea. It was all rubbish. Don't give it a thought. Come, let's leave this place. Forget the old woman. We'll take a boat across the lagoon. Thomas has arranged to meet up with us at the glass factory on the island of Murano. I want to buy you a mirror as a momento of our visit.'

Later that evening, Sidonie stood looking into the mirror which she had hung in her room. The frame of stained-glass, covered with specks of shining gold, resembled dark brocade. It had cost a fortune, but Francis had insisted on buying it for her.

Remembering how he had looked in the fortune-teller's tent, she shivered. It was as if the mirror were intended to be a good omen, designed to deflect the pall of darkness which the old woman's words had cast over the morning. She shrugged. Francis was right. No sense in dwelling on what she did not understand.

It was time to dress for the evening. The domino cape, tricorne hat and a jewelled mask, all of which would preserve her anonymity, lay ready on the chair.

Francis alighted at the watergate and stood on the flight of steps which led to the entrance of the nobleman's house. He waited while Thomas helped Sidonie step out of the boat and then followed them into the *ridotto*.

A doorman checked to see that they were all wearing masks before admitting them. The large entrance hall of the house was tiled in gold flecked, green marble and hung with gilded chandeliers. Crowds of people stood around talking or sipping at coffees and sorbets. Through open doors on all sides, the gamblers could be seen gathered around gaming tables.

Through the slits in his mask, Francis scanned the surroundings. Apart from the many shades of pastel silk dresses and frock-coated evening suits it was difficult to distinguish the women from the men. He began to relax, realising only as his tension faded how much he had been unnerved by the fortune-teller. Although he had told Sidonie to pay the old witch no heed, her words rang in his head and he was afraid. What if Sidonie *was* to meet someone in Venice and fall in love? He did not care how many men she slept with or amused herself with. But he had never considered that she would love anyone but himself. What if she wanted to get married, to move away and live apart from him?

He did not think he could bear it. His chest hurt when he thought about losing her. Clenching his hands, he dug his nails into his palms. He would kill any man who tried to come between them.

'Francis?' Sidonie said. 'Did you not hear me? I said, shall we go into one of the gaming rooms?'

'What? Oh, yes. If you wish it.'

For a while they watched the game, gradually becoming familiar with the rules. After a time, they were invited to play. Sidonie became quite expert at throwing the dice. Luck was with her and she won a small sum, but emboldened by her success she went on to lose it all again.

There were murmurs of 'Bad luck. Try again', as she rose from her seat.

Shrugging her shoulders she laughed and replied, 'Nothing ventured . . .'

She pushed her way through the throng of people and made her way towards Francis.

'I think it is time for an iced lemonade – or something stronger,' she said.

Francis went off to fetch some drinks, noticing that people were beginning to take off their masks. It was stiflingly hot in the entrance room and he was glad to divest himself of the head-hugging cloak and hat. His dark curls were sticking to the back of his neck and his face was sweating under the mask.

As he was about to take an iced drink back to Sidonie, he became conscious of a tall figure standing beside him and a deep, throaty voice said, 'Ah, you reveal yourself. I was about to ask you to do that, but you have forestalled me.'

Francis turned around and found himself looking into the face of a tall, slender woman. Her eyes were on a level with his, something which, as a tall man, he was not used to. He found it disconcerting, but challenging.

'I have been watching you for some time,' she said boldly, her accent as thick as syrup. 'I like to study the things which interest me.'

The woman was stunning, Francis could think of no other word to describe her. She had milk-white skin, slightly tilted dark eyes, a straight nose and shapely, red lips. If anything, her nose was a trifle over-long, but that only added to her charm. Her hair, a rich chestnut colour, was coiled around her head in thick, twisted ropes and woven through with red-velvet ribbon.

Francis, taking in all these details in a single glance, was amazed at his own powers of observation.

It was as if her face were seared into his brain. He noticed too that, in direct contrast to all the pastel silks and satins, she wore a dress of sparkling black velvet. Against her white throat there lay a single gold chain, hung with drop-shaped, cabochon rubies.

'Pardon me?' he said, for once at a loss for words. 'But, have we met?'

The woman laughed, a deep brown sound that was strangely infectious and very attractive.

'You are English, no? No other race is so polite or so

reticent. How charming. Allow me to introduce myself. I am Countess Razvania Blavatsky. Will you not come into the other room with me? I would like you to meet my guardian. He too is interested in your ... companion? Is the woman your wife?'

Francis stiffened. Razvania was speaking about Sidonie. And who was the guardian she spoke of?

He had a mental image of some disreputable old nobleman, jaded and looking for fresh excitement to stir his withered passions. But it was difficult to think straight with Razvania standing at his elbow.

'My companion is my sister,' he said. 'Won't you come and meet her?'

'Certainly,' Razvania said, her small, sensual mouth parting to reveal rather pointed, white teeth. 'But will you not tell me your name first?'

Francis was annoyed to feel a flush rise into his cheeks. Damn and blast. What a fool she must think him. He had neglected to introduce himself.

'Francis. Francis Ryder at your service,' he said. 'Now, come and meet Sidonie. I'm sure she's wondering where I've got to.'

On entering the gaming room, Francis saw Sidonie craning her neck looking for him. She still wore her mask.

'There you are,' she said, a mild reproach in her voice. 'I can see now why you took so long to bring me my drink. And who is your charming companion?'

'This is Razvania,' he said. 'She wished to meet you. Why don't you take off your domino and mask? It seems that custom demands that we all reveal ourselves now.'

Sidonie took off her tricorne hat and pulled the hooded domino off, so that her hair spilled over her shoulders in a shower of red-gold. The mask still covered her eyes and nose. Slowly she reached up to remove it and was shocked to feel a hand cover hers. Strong, pale fingers closed over hers. Although they held her hands immobile, they were cool and gentle.

'Please. Wait one moment more,' a heavily accented

voice said. 'Pardon my presumption, but I have a reason for asking this. Indulge me for a moment longer, I beg you.'

Francis sensed Sidonie stiffen and took a protective step closer to her. He glared at the stranger, feeling a strong instinct to lash out at him. Sidonie read her twin's reactions and made a gesture to stop him. Oddly, she did not seem to feel threatened.

The first impression Francis gained of the man was his height, which seemed considerable, and the scent of his cologne, a mysterious blend of citrus, wood-musk and fern.

Razvania was smiling at Sidonie in an open friendly way. She laid a hand on Francis's arm.

'Do not be alarmed. This is my guardian, Count Constantin Nastase. He is a student of human nature and prides himself on his powers of observation. He also has a love of the dramatic.'

'Obviously,' Francis said coolly. 'I'm ... pleased to make your acquaintance.'

'Charmed,' Constantin said, holding Francis's eyes and choosing to ignore the slight hesitation. 'Now, my dear Razvania. Let us see if I was correct about these two young people. If my young friend here will permit me?'

Constantin untied Sidonie's mask and removed it. He made a glottal sound of satisfaction.

'Ach! Twins. I knew it. And identical in feature, but with such different colouring. How splendid. I win the wager, Razvania. Shall you pay me at once?'

Razvania smiled and held out a bulging velvet bag. She placed it in Constantin's hands.

'Of course. I was never more pleased to lose a bet,' she said. She smiled at Francis. 'My guardian has been proved correct. I thought that you might be husband and wife, or even brother and sister, your movements are so similar. And there was a conspiracy of the blood between you. But Constantin was convinced that you were twins.

145

I'm afraid I lost a quite obscene amount of money on the wager.'

While Razvania was speaking, Sidonie made a half-turn towards Constantin. Over Razvania's shoulder, Francis saw his sister's eyes widen with interest. He felt a peculiar sinking feeling in his gut as the Count lifted her hand to his lips, smiling up at her out of eyes that were darkly shining.

The man was as stunning, in his own way, as his ward.

Constantin's face seemed to be all angles, softened only by a wide, sensual mouth. There were deep hollows at his cheekbones and temples and his straight, black hair was swept back from a lofty brow. The frock-coated evening suit was made all of black velvet and his shirt and cravat was of black silk. A black diamond winked in his tie-pin.

The outfit was almost a caricature of the usual black and white evening dress-suit. It ought to have looked effeminate, but, on him, it looked merely stylish.

Count Constantin Nastase was quite simply the most striking, cultured man Francis had ever set eyes on. He exuded the supreme self-confidence of the wealthy. Francis smelt old money. This was no self-made man, as was Sir James Ryder. The Count was a man who was used to having everything and taking what he wanted from life.

And something within Francis quailed because of that.

'And now,' Constantin said, his richly accented voice low-pitched and carelessly commanding. 'If you will permit me to make amends for my incredible bad manners, I would like to invite you both to be my guests during this night's entertainment. And, when you wish to leave, I insist that you come with me to the Hôtel Leone Bianco for breakfast.'

Sidonie looked impressed. The hotel named by the Count was one of the most exclusive in all Venice. Before Francis could answer he saw Thomas making his way towards them. The introductions were made and

Thomas was included in the invitation to join them all at the gaming tables. Francis noticed that Thomas seemed very taken with the Count and his ward, accepting Constantin's offer eagerly.

Thomas took Razvania's hand and inclined his head in a courtly gesture.

'*Enchanté*,' he said. 'I would not be so churlish as to refuse the company of such a beautiful woman. You grace the room with your presence, Countess.'

Razvania smiled at the pretty gesture, her red lips parting to reveal her feral little teeth.

'How charming you are, Thomas. I do declare that there must be French blood in your veins. Or perhaps even that of my Romanian countrymen. It is settled then, we shall all spend the night together? How delightful.'

Although Francis had misgivings, he could do nothing other than accept also. He saw that Sidonie was pleased by the prospect of having the company of two such glittering beings. She seemed perfectly relaxed and was laughing at something Constantin was saying to her. It occurred to Francis that Sidonie was a lot more poised than himself.

Razvania moved away from Thomas, slid her hand into the crook of Francis's arm and leaned against him. A cloud of perfume enveloped him. It was a heavy and seductive fragrance, redolent with the notes of jasmine, rose otto and musk.

'Shall we go through to the gaming tables?' she said, her deep, throaty voice almost a purr.

Francis could imagine the effect of that voice on most men. It was playing havoc with his senses, although he was doing his best to conceal the fact. And he did not think that it was an accident that he could feel the swell of Razvania's breast against his arm and the rich curve of her hip pressing against his thigh.

His immediate reaction to her surprised him. Razvania was a little more fierce, a little wilder, than any woman he had ever met. He did not know what to think of her. To his consternation he realised that she alarmed him, even frightened him, and that added an extra piquancy to the sharpness of the desire that spiked his loins.

Razvania was like the beautiful black widow spider, irresistible to the male who goes readily to his doom.

The remainder of the night passed quickly. The Count and his ward were charming and attentive. Constantin seemed to have a never-ending supply of funds and seemed unconcerned whether he won or lost. When Thomas lost heavily in a game of dice, he took out a pocket book, peeled off a number of notes from a thick wad, and handed them over without a qualm.

'Oh, dear. I am most embarrassed – ' Thomas began.

Constantin waved away the comment.

'Think nothing of it, my dear fellow. You are my guest, remember? The invitation was unconditional. Now, are we all ready for some refreshment?' He consulted his pocket-watch, a beautifully crafted time-piece of antique design. 'It's after five in the morning. The light over Venice is magnificent at this hour.'

There was general agreement that it was time to go and eat.

They all went down to the watergate where Constantin's private gondola, high at the prow and gleaming black, swept towards them. When they were all seated the gondolier poled the vessel away from its mooring.

Francis felt for Sidonie's hand and clutched it tight, taking care to keep the gesture hidden by her wide silk skirts. For no reason that he could fathom, he had a sense of foreboding, but he said nothing as the gondola slid through the melancholy light of early morning, skimming over the fluid grey surface of the canal and passing the silhouettes of cupolas and towers which were the shade of burnished bronze against the blue-grey sky.

Chapter Eleven

Gliding smoothly past the Palazzo Pesaro, the sleek black gondola drew up before the hotel and was secured to a mooring. Everyone alighted on to the grand sweep of marble steps which led to the hotel's entrance.

Constantin led his guests towards his private apartments which were on the top floor of the Leone Bianco. He was conscious of a feeling of tightly coiled excitement within himself, but no detail of his facial expression betrayed his inner emotion.

From the tail of his eye, he saw Razvania entering the room a little after Francis, the velvet train of her gown whispering across the polished wooden floor. A look passed between him and his ward. He smiled to himself. Razvania was as delighted as he was to have discovered the two exquisite creatures at the *ridotto*.

Constantin loved to play the guessing game of imagining what was concealed behind the domino and mask of visitors to Venice. Sometimes beauty and grace was revealed, but more often it was a plain face or features made bloated and ugly by over-indulgence in food and wine. The game had revealed little enough of interest of late.

It was getting late in the season and he began to find the heat, the smell and the clouds of flies oppressive.

Even the novelty of the fabulous carnival costumes began to pall. When he had been younger the charms of the Venetian courtesans had exerted a potent pull on his senses, but they presented no challenge to him any more.

It was a rarer, more singular pleasure he sought these days – something which was not easy to have. He had been all for packing up and returning to his native Romania – the thought of the clean mountain air, the remote beauty of the forests and the Gothic edifice of his castle was like a draught of refreshing, ice-water after the cloying, overblown charms of Venice.

Razvania had had to persuade him to attend the *ridotto*. Now, of course, he was glad that he had not been so hasty as to leave. When he first caught sight of Sidonie and Francis, he knew that the tall, slender figures were special in some way – his instincts were seldom wrong. A long-buried flicker of interest stirred within him.

At first he was not sure what it was that was different about them, then he realised that it was the complicity between them – a curious mixture of intimacy coupled with a certain reticence of gesture. What was their nationality? French, he thought at first, then discounted that. And not Italian, but he was sure they were European. Ah, English – yes of course.

Disdaining to move closer in case he would overhear their conversation and, by accident, perceive some clue which would spoil the game, he watched them from across the room. And the longer he watched them, the more intrigued he became.

They did not often touch, but they communicated in some way peculiar to themselves. One might lean forward over the table to study the lay of the cards and the other, although some distance away, would mirror the first's movement.

Twice he saw them glance up simultaneously, catching each other's eye and smiling, their lips, which were the only details visible below their masks, curving at the corners. Constantin studied those mouths; the well-formed lips so alike, each mouth on parting revealing amazingly similar sets of teeth.

His eyes strayed to the slender white hands, revealed by the hem of the domino cape. The fingers, with their pale, almond-shaped nails were longer than the palms; so slender and sensitive and, again, so similar. It took him a few moments more to solve the puzzle. They were twins. He felt a surge of exultation at his discovery and made his way over to Razvania to suggest the wager.

Twins, yes. And now revealed to be a young man and young woman, as he had known they would be. But such fragile, bewitching beauty he had not been pre-pared for.

With an effort he gathered his thoughts. It would not do to forget his duties as host. Razvania was escorting Thomas around the large room, pointing out details of the Tintoretto frescos and the exquisite workmanship of the gilded wall panels.

'Please. Won't you sit here? The view along the Grand Canal to the Rialto is wonderful,' Constantin said, waving Sidonie to a window seat.

The early morning sun was pouring in through the apartment windows, picking out the jewel-like colours of the rugs and furnishings, and casting violet shadows to linger within the recesses of the intricately carved stone mouldings. The same light formed a haze around the great mass of Sidonie's red-gold hair.

She had the sort of looks much admired by painters, but who amongst them had the talent to capture her luminosity? Without the domino cape covering the upper half of her body she looked even more slender. He found himself admiring the delicacy of her shoulders and arms, the rich swell of her breasts. The pastel green of her dress was a perfect foil for her china-doll colouring.

Francis was also finely made, but his bones were heavier than his twin's. His skin had the same translu-cent quality and his pallor was even more startling than Sidonie's, due to the darkness of his hair. The shining curls lay tumbling forward on to his forehead and over his shoulders.

Constantin was as fascinated by the differences in the twins' colouring and the imprint of their gender as he was by the sameness of their features. Every last detail down to the graceful curve of their brows was identical. Extraordinary.

Feeling eyes on him, Constantin turned to find himself being studied in turn. Francis was regarding him steadily, his fine, dark eyes narrowed with concentration.

Constantin grinned disarmingly, but Francis only lifted one dark brow. 'We are used to being stared at. It will not offend us if you look your fill,' he said coolly.

Constantin smiled inwardly, but said only, 'Forgive my abominable manners. I sometimes forget that my customs are not those of other people. I mean no offence. As a connoisseur of the arts, I am always captivated by beauty.'

Francis smiled thinly, but did not reply.

Ah, the young man did not trust him. How wise. Most people were dazzled by his glamour and the aura of his wealth. It was difficult to forge true friendships. And those he could buy, he did not want. How gratifying that this young man seemed immune to his charms. The final capitulation would be all the more satisfying for them both.

'I will order breakfast for us all,' Constantin said, reaching for the bell pull. 'And while we wait perhaps you will tell me how it is that you come to be in Venice?'

Thomas and Sidonie spoke freely about their travels, both of them animated and at ease. But Francis had to be drawn out.

'And you, Francis,' Razvania said. 'Have you nothing to say about your stay in Paris? Did you not find the city beautiful?'

Constantin watched approvingly as Razvania worked her magic on the young man. Although he concealed it well, it was obvious that Francis was fascinated by his ward. Razvania's admirers fell into two categories: those who saw her as a challenge and wanted to tame her and those whose lust for her was tinged with slight wariness. The latter group, to which Francis belonged, were always the more interesting.

The food arrived and was laid out on a marble-topped table. There were great platters piled with fresh fruit, soft Italian cheeses, cold spiced meats and freshly baked bread. As well as fruit juices and a glass jug of wine cup, there was a pot of steaming coffee.

'Well then, let us replenish our strength, for I warn you, Francis and Sidonie, that I do not intend to let you have a minute to yourselves from now on,' Razvania said, pouring herself a cup of the fragrant coffee. 'You have rescued me from being spirited back to Romania where it will soon be winter, and I wish to show my gratitude. Do you know, we were on the verge of packing our bags!'

Constantin smiled at Razvania, pleased to see her looking so happy.

'I am not the monster I am painted,' he said. 'Surely I am the most indulgent of guardians, as Razvania will admit if she is pressed to comment. But it pleases her to tease me.' He reached out and took hold of Razvania's be-ringed hand. Bringing it to his lips, he murmured, 'We shall stay in Venice as long as you wish, my dear.'

Throwing back her head Razvania gave a husky laugh.

'You see? *Now* he does not mind the smell and the heat. Only yesterday he was cursing the flies and the stretches of noxious mud that border the canals at low tide. Your company has invigorated him anew. Ah, there is so much to see and do in Venice. You really *must* let me be your guide. And Constantin knows many secret places on the islands. It is magical to travel by gondola at night with only the light from lanterns reflected in the dark waters.'

'You're most kind,' Francis said evenly. 'But we have Thomas here to organise our days for us.'

'Ah, but not your nights?' Razvania murmured below

her breath, for his ears alone. 'I would show you much of the sorcery of the flesh, my English friend.'

Francis flushed, but said nothing. Sidonie looked sharply at Razvania and was treated to a winning smile. Constantin saw how Sidonie's lips twitched and her eyes glinted with a new interest.

'I would not dream of insulting your new friends by imposing my dull regime on you all,' Thomas said, beaming with goodwill and unaware of the undercurrent of tension in the room. 'You and Sidonie may do as you wish. I'm sure that the Count and Countess are perfectly capable of ensuring your safety.'

'Of course,' Constantin said. 'We would consider it an honour if you would all be our guests for the remainder of your stay.'

'I must regretfully refuse,' Thomas said. 'There are a few engagements I cannot break. But you young people must do as you think fit.'

Constantin saw the venomous look which Francis threw at the older man and bit back a grin. It really was going to be a delight to win Francis over. First Razvania would impose her will upon him and then it would be his turn.

Then there was Sidonie who looked so innocent and open-faced, but whose mouth and chin had the same firmness as her twin's. His fingers itched to stroke her pale skin. He imagined enfolding her slender body in his arms, bending her backwards and claiming that delicious mouth. Her hair would spill out around her as he covered her lips with his, pressed them open and plundered the tender interior with his thrusting tongue.

But if he were to achieve this goal, which was becoming clearer the more he weighed the possibilities, then he must play a waiting game.

His nerves felt stretched as tight as a drum and a pleasant heat and heaviness was spreading out around his groin. His cock lay in a thickening column against his thigh, pulsing with life.

He did not know which twin enchanted him the most.

But he did know that he would have them both – and by the time he was ready to take them they would be begging for his caresses.

The next few weeks passed by in a haze of enjoyment, each new day bringing something more fascinating or intriguing than the last.

Sidonie's early misgivings about the Count and his ward faded quickly. She was aware that Francis did not like Constantin and her loyalty to her twin was such that, for a while, it coloured her own judgement.

But gradually Francis was being won over. The Count and Countess were such charming hosts; nothing was too much trouble. They were intelligent, cultured and unfailingly kind. It was impossible not to be fascinated by them. Their glamour drew looks wherever they went. Both of them dressed in rich, dark colours which contrasted strongly with the fashionable pastel shades in vogue. Where the norm was for silks, chiffons, muslins, Constantin wore velvets and stiff, figured brocades, while Razvania's gowns were confections of glossy, black satin or dark, bead-encrusted gauzes; red, purple, magenta all stretched over angular frames and formed into face-framing collars.

Sidonie began gradually to imitate some elements of Razvania's style of dress. Razvania was flattered and helped her choose fabrics in deep shades of moss-green, plum and russet; colours that Sidonie would have thought unsuitable in England but which were superb against the light of Venice.

The new gowns suited her well and heads turned as she walked around the piazzas or explored the shops that lined the many bridges. Francis too approved of her new look, telling her that she had never looked more beautiful.

Their days were packed with things to do. It was true that Constantin knew Venice well. With him at their head they explored lesser known byways and narrow waterways, discovering ancient churches and crossing tiny bridges which opened out on to squares lined with tall, stone houses.

The miasma of rot and decay which hung over all the beauty of Venice added a poignant note to their explorations.

At twilight, when the boundary lights of the waterways had just been lit, they went by gondola to look at the cemetery island of San Michele. Sidonie's eyes filled with tears as she looked at its magical beauty which was tinged with sadness. A funeral gondola, draped in black gauze and topped with black feathers made its solitary way across the lagoon.

Sidonie could not help but reflect that the enjoyment of life was fleeting. She determined to enjoy it to the full while her youth and beauty were at their peak. Constantin glanced at her, his dark eyes pools of emotion, and she felt, as she often did, that he understood what she was feeling.

Indeed, she wondered if he had not brought Francis and herself to this place for the express purpose of making them face their mortality and therefore grasping eagerly for whatever pleasures were offered them.

But that would surely have been too calculating.

By day Sidonie and Francis slept, spending the afternoons entwined together on his bed, pursuing new pathways to pleasure in each other's arms as they had always done.

'Is this not just perfect?' Sidonie said against her twin's mouth. 'We have two of the most sought-after admirers in all Venice at our feet. And all we have to do is enjoy them.'

Francis laughed. 'And Thomas has given his permission for us to do as we wish. If only he knew what he was missing.'

'I expect that he has found someone to spend the time with,' she said. 'Did you know that Venice used to be called the whore-house of Europe?'

By night the twins shared intimate suppers in the

Count's apartments or went to masked balls where the drama and colour of the costumes took their breath away.

It was delightful to dress up in billowing gold tissue or yards of sequin-sewn gauze in every colour from magenta to sky-blue. The eye-masks they wore were fashioned into the likenesses of birds or mythical animals.

Early one evening, Sidonie had just finished bathing when Razvania arrived with a selection of boxes. She opened them with a flourish to reveal four Tarocco costumes.

'We wear these tonight. The ball is exclusive, only for a select few. All costumes must be based on the cards of the Tarot. You and Constantin shall be the King and Queen of Cups. Francis and myself will be King and Queen of Swords.'

The costumes must have cost a great deal and Razvania looked very pleased at having secured them.

'They were made especially,' she said. 'I ordered them weeks ago. Now you know what I was doing when you caught me measuring one of your gowns!'

Sidonie kissed Razvania's cheek, delighted by her generosity. She had never seen anything to rival her Tarot costume.

It gave her a strange feeling to put on the red-velvet domino and the tall, crowned headdress of stiffened gauze which sparkled and shimmered from the addition of hundreds of jewels. The mask of silver covered her whole face. Her full-skirted gown was embroidered with scarlet, cabalistic signs and to complete the outfit there was a pair of glittering, silver gloves which reached to her elbows.

'Don't we all look mysterious?' Razvania said, coming to collect Sidonie and escort her to the waiting gondola.

Together with Constantin and Razvania, Sidonie and Francis crossed a small bridge which led to the house of a nobleman, laughing and calling out as they passed other revellers in fantastic costumes that represented nature spirits.

157

The noise of music and enjoyment was deafening inside the vaulted room. It was impossible to distinguish any feature of the guests at the ball. At first Sidonie found this alarming, but gradually she began to find it intriguing. The anonymity of her costume made her feel quite reckless.

There were many Kings and Queens at the Tarot ball, some of the masks very similar to hers and Constantin's. She looked around trying to find Francis and thought she spotted him dancing with Razvania in the midst of the crowded room. Then Constantin took her arm and swept her on to the dance floor.

'As my Queen, you must do the King's bidding tonight,' he said, his heavily accented voice softly commanding.

Sidonie shivered as she looked into his masked face. The gold was formed to fit his features exactly, but he looked mysterious and dangerous. Although she was easier in his company now, she was made aware of the fact that he was still an enigma.

The only familiar thing about him tonight was the scent of his cologne, the usual combination of citrus, wood-musk and fern which was blended for him specially by a Paris perfumer.

'And what will you do to me if I disobey, my lord?' she said teasingly.

Constantin chuckled darkly.

'Oh, I'm sure that I'll think of a suitable punishment.'

'Some punishments are designed merely to spur the miscreant on to further sins,' she said, sparkling at him through the slanted sockets of the silver mask. 'And to give more pleasure than pain. Is yours to be that kind?'

'Perhaps the most effective punishments are those which deny you the thing you most desire,' he said.

And she had to be content with that. She turned her back and reached towards a waiter's tray for a glass of champagne.

He did not flirt with her like most of her admirers did, a fact she found puzzling. She knew that he thought her beautiful, but he had not even tried to steal an embrace. The most he ever did was to kiss her hand.

Yet he was constantly at her side, delighting in buying her gifts of jewellery and cosmetics. There were rows of exquisite glass jars in her room, boxes full of scented powders, coloured ribbons, intricately carved hat pins.

So why was it that he deflected her neatly any time that they approached the slightest intimacy? He was sophisticated enough to read the signs she gave out and could be in no doubt that she was not a shrinking virgin. She sensed that he held himself back. But why? Surely he knew that she would welcome any advance from him?

At night her dreams were erotic and complex. For the first time in her life, Francis's caresses failed to satisfy her completely. After lying naked in his arms during the hot hours of the afternoon, the shades drawn over the windows, she would leave his bed and seek her own room, ashamed that she was driven to take the leather phallus out of a drawer and place it between her thighs.

As she stroked herself until the juices flowed, holding open her labia with one hand and rubbing the head of the dildo against her bud of pleasure, she fantasised about Constantin. Would his cock be thick and strong and push into her so deliciously, as the dildo was doing now? Would he be an experienced lover and relish the delights of sucking her quim, licking her straining bud and thrusting his tongue into her willing orifice. She loved it when Francis did that.

She moved the phallus back and forth, her hips thrusting in time with the inner, sliding motion of penetration.

If only Constantin would touch her. Her breasts burned for him, her quim felt heavy, almost bruised from being in a constant state of arousal. She could smell her own intimate musk, the scent of it rising lushly from between her parted thighs.

Working the dildo faster and faster, she urged herself towards her climax, imagining that Constantin was pushing her belly-down on to the bed, raising her skirts, and thrusting his hand between her thighs. He was not gentle as he forced open her legs and pushed his fingers into her, assessing how wet and ready she was before he pressed the head of his cock against her entrance. Moaning, she imagined him sliding deeply into her in a single smooth stroke.

As she climaxed she brought her fingers to her mouth, smelling the salt-musk of her dew and savouring the taste of it on her tongue. She could almost believe that it was Constantin who pressed his mouth to her lips and that it was the souvenir taste of herself on him that she relished.

But it seemed that that was not to be. At least not for a time.

At the Tarot ball Constantin was as attentive as always, his behaviour impeccable, although she thought that she detected an unusual tension about him.

Would this be the night that she penetrated his aloofness? His reticence and perfect manners were driving her mad. No other man had resisted her for so long.

As the night wore on, the dancing and noise became more frenzied. The costume was hot and Sidonie began to long for somewhere cool to sit, somewhere where she might remove her mask for a time.

As if he realised that she needed some air, Constantin took her arm.

'Come with me,' he said. 'It is cooler out in the corridor and there is a cloistered walk with a view over the canal.'

Sidonie went willingly, her heavy silken skirts rustling on the stone floor. There were deep recesses set in the back wall of the open-fronted cloisters and she could hear the muffled sighs and rustles of the couples who occupied them. This was a meeting place for lovers. Her pulses quickened. That must be why Constantin had brought her there.

When he pulled her into an empty recess, she bit back a little cry of alarm. He seemed almost too eager, but where was the need for haste? Then she realised her mistake. He did not seek to be alone with her, but to be concealed so as to observe the couple who had stopped in front of them.

'Watch there,' he whispered.

The masked and costumed couple were leaning against one of the stone pillars in full view of any casual observer. The man's hunger for his partner shocked Sidonie. There seemed a kind of desperation about him. He pulled at her bodice of silver tissue, ripping apart the fabric and strewing the stone tiles with sequins and beads.

The woman did not care about the destruction. She gave a throaty laugh and leaned back, her torn velvet domino parting to show a length of long white throat. Careless of who watched, the man pulled down the flaps of the ruined bodice to expose the woman's shoulders and bare breasts. They were very white and high, perfect cone-shapes, each tipped by a gilded nipple.

With a groan the man closed his hands over the twin globes, massaging them between his palms and rubbing his thumbs over the golden teats. The woman sighed and sagged against the pillar as the man thrust his hand into the opening of the bodice and reached down inside her skirts, seeking to close his hand on her quim.

Sidonie's heart raced. She was acutely aware of Constantin's proximity. Surely he was as aroused as she was by the spectacle. The man was obviously passionately in love with the woman. His hips worked as he ground himself against her body as if trying to feel every rise and hollow through the many layers of silk. Breathy little sounds came from him, sighs and entreaties.

The woman must be an unfeeling monster to deny such a lover the caresses he was dying for. She seemed willing only to let him have her breasts and slapped his hand away whenever he attempted to steal a more intimate caress.

'How cruel she is,' Sidonie whispered, surprised to find that she had spoken aloud. 'Why does she torture him so?'

'Are not the best things always worth waiting for?'

161

Constantin said thickly. 'Might it not be that he gains pleasure and true knowledge of the ache of desire from anticipating that which she offers?'

He spoke knowingly and Sidonie felt a tingle go down her spine. There was the ring of truth in his words. All the nights of sexual unfulfilment, the erotic fantasies, seemed to coalesce in her breast and become one hot ache. A pulse beat strongly between her thighs. She thought of her quim as a raw and throbbing heart.

'Is that why you have never touched me in all these weeks we have spent together?' she burst out before she thought better of it. 'You want me to suffer like that man? To burn for you?'

Oh, God. It was out now. She had said it. How desperate and petulant she sounded. Now he would despise her.

But he only chuckled softly.

'It is not that simple. I want more than your suffering, more than to be the source of your sexual frustration.'

He knew about that? She felt peeled bare, exposed and vulnerable. He was far too perceptive.

'I don't understand you,' she said. 'What more is there? What else can you want?'

'I want everything. All of you. Your unconditional sublimation of self. There must be nothing in your life which is more important to you than me. Only then will I be satisfied. That day is not too far away, Sidonie. I feel how you tremble against me and how willing you are to submit. You fight this knowledge. But it is the truth.'

Sidonie was shocked. How all-encompassing that sounded. While Constantin's intensity frightened her, it also drew her strongly. Yes. He was a man for whom she could give up everything. But there was another, stronger bond, which she would not deny. She lifted her chin.

'You ask for too much,' she said, her voice quivering. 'Part of me belongs to Francis and always will. We share the same blood, the same thoughts and aspirations. Our lovers must agree to take second place to that bond. All of them have in the past. I could never bear to be parted from my twin. And he feels the same way about me.'

There was a pause before he answered, 'Are you sure of that? Look there.'

Sidonie turned back to look at the couple leaning up against the pillar. The man had torn his mask and crowned headdress free. They lay discarded on the stone floor. His head was buried between the woman's breasts and he seemed to be sobbing. Sidonie could hear him only faintly. The desperation in his voice wrung her heart.

'But I must have you. I want only you. I've never felt this way about anyone else, ever. Please. I beg you, Razvania. I'll do anything you ask.'

The man's profile was revealed as he twisted his head to one side, the outline cameo-pure against the tumbled dark curls.

With a sick jolt of her stomach, Sidonie recognised her twin. She could hardly breathe. The mask seemed to be choking her. But she could not look away. Her limbs felt like water.

Razvania laughed throatily. 'Anything? That's a rash statement. What if I wish to lie with you and Sidonie – together? Will you arrange that?'

'Yes,' Francis said, without hesitation. 'I adore you. You know that. Sidonie wants what makes me happy. She will understand.'

Sidonie could not believe it. Francis had betrayed her trust. They had sworn never to let anyone come between them. And here he was agreeing to let Razvania into their bed. Never, in all the years that they had been sleeping together, had they allowed anyone to lie with them jointly. It was an unspoken law between them, as sacrosanct as an oath.

'No. It cannot be true . . .' she breathed, unaware that she spoke aloud.

While she had been obsessed with Constantin, Francis had been growing sick with love for Razvania. And now, without Sidonie's permission, Francis was giving her over to his prospective mistress as if she were simply a toy for their joint pleasure. They had promised to love only each other. But Francis said that he wanted only Razvania, he adored her and would do anything for her.

The terrible words rang in her head. It was too much to be borne. She tried to swallow and tasted ashes.

This was all a conspiracy. Razvania and Constantin had been toying with them. We are no more than a challenge to them, she thought. They are simply two bored aristocrats who have been trying to seduce us away from each other, using as weapons their glamour, beauty and the false lure of their self-restraint.

She thought that her anger would choke her. If Constantin had not been wearing the mask she would have raked her nails down his face. She made a movement forward and, sensing that she was about to challenge Razvania, Constantin's arms tightened around her.

'This is not the moment for it,' he said. 'Believe me, all is not as it seems.'

'No?' she hissed. 'Are you trying to tell me that it is not your purpose to tear us apart? What a game this is for you. Well, I tell you now. You won't succeed. Get your hands off me and don't insult me with your damned platitudes! Take me back to the ball.'

Francis. Oh God, Francis. How could you. Her knees almost buckled and she clutched at Constantin's jewelled sleeve for support.

'Certainly. Whatever you wish,' he said coolly as if nothing had changed between them, as if her world had not just shattered and scattered around her, like the beads and sequins that glittered against the stone floor of the cloisters, like tears in the moonlight.

Chapter Twelve

Sidonie threw open the bedroom door and stormed into Francis's room.

She still wore the Tarot costume and the full, silken skirts rustled as she swept across the room. She tore free her shawl of printed gauze, paying no heed to the cloud of silver glitter that showered around her, and dropped it on to the floor.

It was silent in the room, except for the staccato sound of her wooden heels. The oil lamp was turned down low and she could just see the shadowy figure of Francis as he lay on his side on the bed. He did not move until she stood level with the bed, then he sat up and turned towards her.

Even in the dimness she could see that his expression was bleak and lacklustre.

He had a beaten look to him. For the first time in her life she despised him. Without a word she leaned over and slapped his face.

'I'm ashamed of you! Skulking here like a beaten dog!'

His head snapped back, but he said nothing.

'Aren't you going to ask me what that was for?' she spat.

He shook his head. Once he would have retaliated with angry words, even hit her back, but he only stared blankly at her. It alarmed her to see him like this. The spark seemed to have gone out of him.

She hid her consternation behind a show of anger.

'You traitor!' she said. 'I saw you in the cloisters, pawing that bitch Razvania, begging for her favours. You looked so pathetic, promising to give her anything she wished – including me! How could you? We belong to each other. You have reminded me of that fact often enough. No one must be allowed to come between us, remember? What happened to your declarations of loyalty? Are they so easily pushed aside when it suits you?'

The tears stung her throat. When he did not answer immediately she sat beside him, her own anger shrivelling in the face of his obvious distress. Feeling for his hand in the gloom, she entwined her fingers with his. His were icy cold. She rubbed his hand to warm it.

'You spied on us?' he said at length, in an oddly detached voice. 'That was unfair of you. Am I not entitled to some privacy?'

She could hardly believe he had said that. They had shared everything for so long, every emotion, every amusing anecdote about their respective lovers. No one had been sacred to them. They had gloried in the easy cruelty of mockery. Neither of them had spoken of privacy before.

Stung, she said, 'You wished to hide from me? But you did not care that you were in full view of anyone who cared to watch you. I don't call that discreet. Razvania had her bodice opened to the waist and you were kissing her breasts! I just happened to be walking there with Constantin when we saw you.'

Francis looked up and she saw his eyes flash with understanding.

'Does it not strike you as convenient that Constantin brought you to that very place? And just as Razvania allowed me to touch her breasts and kiss them – for the first time.'

The longing in his voice hurt her, but she pushed that aside.

'You mean that it was all planned, pre-arranged? They wanted me to see you together?'

Francis nodded. 'Of course. The coincidence is too marked. It all becomes clear now. We have been used. They are playing us off, one against each other.'

Sidonie wrinkled her brow.

'But why? What have they to gain? I've been trying to puzzle this all out. It can't be just a game to them. Can it? Are they so bored, so jaded, that they gain their pleasure from tormenting people?'

'I don't know. But the tragedy is that it makes no difference.' His voice broke on a sob. 'I'm sorry, Sidonie. You're right about Razvania. I've never met anyone like her. She's captivating, mysterious and cruel. Part of me wants to run away and never see her again, but a larger part of me wants to fall at her feet. She denies me everything while promising so much. I can't sleep or eat for thinking about her. I thought these feelings would pass. But they only get worse the more I see her. I think I'm in love with her.'

It felt as if a hand squeezed Sidonie's heart, but her voice was calm when she replied.

'Oh, Francis. I did not realise that you were suffering so. Why did you not confide in me? I might have been able to help. Have we not always shared the bad along with the good?'

'I wanted to tell you, truly. But you seemed so distracted lately. I thought ... I thought that you and Constantin must be lovers by now. But that you did not want to talk to me about him. And that made me feel less guilty about wanting Razvania so badly.'

He looked closely at her. 'Haven't you been keeping secrets too? Even after we had lain together you were eager to leave me. You have been pleasuring yourself whilst thinking of him, haven't you? Did you think I had not noticed?'

Sidonie felt the blood drain from her face. He was right. She had not noticed his pain because she had been so absorbed by her own longing for Constantin.

Wrapping her arms around him, she laid her head on his shoulder.

'You're right. I'm as obsessed with Constantin as you are with Razvania. And the situation is the same. He allows me to get so close and then draws away. I'm half-mad with wanting him. I dream about him, imagine how it must be to lie with him. He is charming, attentive and remote. And I could kill him for his restraint.'

They lay down together on the bed, her head pillowed on his chest. Both of them shook with emotion. Tears squeezed out of the corners of Sidonie's eyes.

'I'm sorry I hit you,' she said, in a small voice. 'I love you so much and cannot bear for it to be like this between us. No one has ever been able to shake our faith in each other before now.'

As his lips brushed against her hair, she looked up at him. 'Oh, darling. What are we going to do?' For some reason she thought of the words of the old fortune-teller at the San Marco pageant. 'The one must become two.'

And the words rang with fateful presentiment.

'And so I have accepted the Count's invitation for us all to visit his castle in Romania,' Thomas said, a few days later. 'The details are all settled.'

His announcement was meant to be a surprise. The letter from England, giving parental approval and sending extra funds for the necessary warm clothing, had arrived that morning.

'Well? What have you to say? I have gained permission for six more months of travel before we need even think of starting home.'

He had expected cries of excitement from the twins or at least a show of interest. Their white faces and shocked expressions were a little alarming. Now that he looked closely, he could see that they had lost weight. There were faint, violet shadows under Sidonie's eyes and her full mouth had a pinched look at the corners.

She had left off the dramatic, embroidered brocades she had favoured lately and was wearing one of the gowns she had brought with her from England. The silver-grey, sprigged-muslin and white collar seemed to have bleached the colour from her face and hair.

'What is it, my dear? Are you ill? You look rather liverish too, Francis. It's this heat and the smell that breeds disease. We have lingered overlong in Venice. It will be good for us all to have a change of scene. Blow away the cobwebs, eh? The Count's invitation is most generous. And Romania is a wonderful place to visit.'

He warmed to his theme. 'Few English tourists have cause to venture so far. The mountains, valleys and stretches of wild forest are spectacular. They still have wolves and bears there. How exciting it must be to ride to the hunt. There are such churches – the rich carvings and Gothic arches, the jewelled icons above the altars. Ah, you'll breathe in the culture along with the clean air.'

Sidonie and Francis exchanged doubtful looks and Thomas laughed.

'Oh, dear. I am rather going on, aren't I? Well, I'll leave you to discuss my news. We'll be leaving at the end of the week. Sidonie, I suggest you discuss your dress needs with Razvania. Winter approaches in Romania and the weather can be harsh.'

When Thomas had gone the twins looked at each other. Francis spoke first.

'So it's more than a game for the Count and Countess? At least if emotional as well as sexual conquest is their aim, the endeavour is to be somewhat protracted. A Gothic castle in Romania, eh? Sounds rather romantic, even Byronesque.'

'This is more of Constantin's manipulation,' Sidonie said sulkily. 'We ought to refuse to go.'

'Is that what you want?'

She shook her head. 'No. That's too much like cowardice. Besides we have to face this. These feelings are not just going to go away. It's best that we follow them to their conclusion. I want Constantin and you want Razvania. Very well. But I warn you. I'm not going to let

169

Razvania hurt you, I'll tear the eyes from her head first! And I don't intend to lose you entirely to her.'

Francis grinned, his eyes alight with a flash of his old humour.

'Quite a hell-cat, aren't you? Does Constantin realise what he has taken on?'

'Probably not,' she said, grinning up at him. 'And not even he will keep me from your bed.'

He moved close to her and she shivered at the softness in his face. There was sadness too in the line of his mouth, such a look of pain that it ravaged his features. He had never looked more beautiful.

'Sidonie, tell me that we can bear this. Is our love strong enough to be tested?'

She could not reply. Her throat felt too tight. As her eyes brimmed, he reached out and took her in his arms. She lifted herself up on to her toes and moaned softly as his mouth closed over hers.

Her lips opened to accept his thrusting tongue and she arched towards him as his hands pressed her close. The flame between them was as hot as ever. Sidonie felt the desire for him centre in her loins. Her womb throbbed and the juices began welling from her.

'Come with me to my room,' she said, freeing herself with reluctance from his embrace and grasping his hand. 'I want to give you something to remember when we are in Romania. If it's Razvania's cruelty that attracts you, I'll give you a taste of it now.'

The balcony outside Sidonie's room was flooded with sunlight. Far below, the Grand Canal shivered in the heat haze. Boats passed by lazily, their passengers reclining in the shade of parasols or sheltering from the heat under canvas awnings.

She rested her back against the hot stone balustrade, facing Francis who stood in the doorway. In one hand she held the red leather dildo. It swayed back and forth, suspended from the harness. Lifting her other hand she untied the ribbon and let her hair tumble over her shoulders.

Francis watched her hungrily, his eyes roving over her face and locking on to her mouth where her small teeth gripped her bottom lip in a gesture both artless and sensual. He had never seen her looking so full of purpose. It was as if she had planned this scenario in advance.

There was a new tension between them. Today they were far more like battling lovers than siblings.

'Take off your boots and trousers,' she said. 'I'm going to give you such pleasure, my darling. Remember how you enjoyed it when I told you about Gunter in Paris? I shall play Gunter for you, or shall I be Chatnam – like in your dream?'

Francis barely suppressed a gasp. He thought he knew what she intended. She was the only one who knew all his secret desires, his wish to be penetrated and used like a woman.

'You're going to lean out over this balcony while I have my way with you,' Sidonie said. 'And those below will wave and smile, little knowing what's happening below your waist. That is, unless they can read your expression. Oh, I'll make you sigh and moan.'

Trembling with eagerness and spurred on to a raging erection, Francis pulled off his leather boots. Sidonie smiled, trailing the ribbon over the thick shaft of the leather phallus. Francis could not help watching her movements and anticipating her caresses.

He was aroused beyond the ordinary level by the glint of cruelty in her eyes. As he peeled off his trousers he felt the weight of his cock bounce against his under-drawers. Unbuttoning the front he freed the throbbing stem and glanced down at himself.

Sidonie gave a low chuckle of approval. His cock was purplish-red and thickly veined, the moist glans pushing half-free of the tight cock-skin. His balls were tight and pulled in against his body as if he was dying to spend.

'Come here,' Sidonie said, kneeling down until her face was on a level with his jutting cock. 'You're fit to burst already, but I'll make you wait for your release.'

Francis clenched his hands, expecting at any moment to feel her mouth and lips pleasuring him. But Sidonie began winding the satin hair ribbon around the base of his cock, slipping a loop under his balls and then tying it close against his belly.

The pressure forced his cock to swell even more. Standing up, she urged him to approach the stone balustrade and bend over it.

'Lift your shirt. The stone will be warm against your belly. A pleasant contrast to the coolness of the leather phallus.'

Francis did as she asked and experienced a moment of shamed rebellion. He felt foolish with his bottom raised and his throbbing cock trussed-up tightly, but before he could voice his complaint, Sidonie slipped her hand between his legs and began to work his shaft.

He could think of nothing now except her encircling fingers, the way she moved the tight skin back and forth over the engorged centre. Now and then she trailed her fingers gently over his captive balls. Threads of sensations penetrated his belly and wormed their way along his stem. At the slitted cock-mouth the clear seepage gathered and began to drip down the flared tip.

Moaning he worked his hips and sank down a little, opening his thighs and lifting his bottom towards her. Sidonie cupped her palm and rested it under his glans. With her other hand she milked him, stroking patiently and gently, holding back when his thighs trembled and he threatened to climax. Eventually there was a little pool of silvery liquid in her palm.

She removed her hands and moved back. Francis did not turn around, but he knew that she was rubbing the cock-juice around the glans of the dildo. The soft folds of his anus twitched and pulsed with anticipation.

'Bend over further, Francis. And open your body to me,' Sidonie said.

His face burning, Francis did so, leaning out over the space above the canal. He did not see the crafts gliding by or the upturned faces of gondoliers and other boatmen. His whole concentration was centred on Sidonie's hands which were spreading apart his buttocks and sliding gently up and down the moist crease.

The slight scratching of her finger nail against his tender orifice made him buck and tremble. Inserting just the tip of a finger, she rotated it for a few turns, then withdrew it. When she put the head of the dildo against his anus, he tensed. Was it always to be this way? This pleasure, which he craved so, he also resisted. Perhaps it was that the forbidden held the greatest delights for him.

Sidonie reached under him and fingered the ties around his balls and the base of his cock. As she toyed with the ribbons drawing the tight sac more firmly up towards his belly, she exerted a gentle pressure on the dildo.

'Mmmmm,' Francis sighed, as the dildo pushed against the sphincter, nosing it like a blunt finger.

For a moment longer he resisted, then he felt the muscles soften. The tight creases gave way, folding inwards to admit the leather phallus. The last of his reticence faded as the leather shaft filled him, sliding into him with delicious smoothness and stretching him wide.

The sensations of Sidonie's hand masturbating him, stroking his bulging and restricted cock, and the feeling of being penetrated to the hilt seemed to run together into one white-hot spasm of bliss.

'God. Oh, God,' he murmured, his mouth sagging open and his eyes screwed shut.

He rubbed his belly against the warm stone, thrusting his hips back and forth, careless of how he looked. Sidonie whispered encouragement as she squeezed his cock-shaft, urging the jism upwards towards his throbbing glans. The dildo rolled inside him, sending wrenching, shaming waves of pleasure down his legs.

Then he climaxed, the fluid jetting out into a creamy arc over the canal.

Francis's knees buckled as he sagged over the balustrade. Sidonie removed the dildo in a single fluid movement, then swooped down to plant a kiss on each buttock. When he had caught his breath, he turned around expecting her to be waiting to untie the ribbon, a smile of satisfaction on her face.

But she had already gone into the bedroom. He followed her inside to the shaded, cool darkness.

Sidonie lay on her bed, her skirts pulled up high and her hand between her legs, rubbing away frenziedly. Her eyes were closed as if she had shut herself away into her own sexual heaven. The breath came out in little bursts from between her parted lips.

He could see the ridges of her quim, pushing out around her working fingers, the pink flesh gleaming wetly. As he watched, her cheeks flushed and her thighs jerked with tension. She cried out as she orgasmed.

Her greediness delighted him. She had not even waited for him to take her into his arms and repay her with a gift of pleasure.

Approaching the bed, he grinned and glanced downwards at himself.

'Aren't you going to free me?' he said. 'Now that you've taken your pleasure. After all, the desire you felt was at my expense.'

Sidonie was up and pulled down her skirts. There was a strange look on her faces. At first he did not recognise it as selfishness.

'Free yourself,' she said brightly. 'I have things to do now. You heard Thomas. I have to find Razvania and take her shopping with me.'

Francis watched her get up and flounce from the room, the expression of disbelief sliding from his face as the door slammed behind her.

It occurred to him gradually that a new element had crept into their relationship – an element of competition. He was not sure that he liked it. But one thing was certain. It would make their stay in Romania all the more interesting.

Chuckling ruefully to himself he began to untie the satin ribbon.

174

Chapter Thirteen

Sidonie pulled the fur collar of her cloak more firmly around her ears and thrust her hands into the fur muff. She had expected the weather to worsen as they approached the borders of Hungary and Romania, but had been unprepared for the constant, gnawing cold.

The condensation on the windows of the coach had long since frozen, the ice crystals resembling fronds of fern. She scratched at one of them now, clearing a small space with her finger-nail. Outside she could see vast stretches of forest.

Her feet were numb and she wriggled them, trying to move some life back into them. Razvania, sitting opposite, smiled at her.

'Soon we shall be stopping to change the horses. There will be time to get warm and have a hot meal.'

Sidonie peered out of the window, looking for signs of habitation. Apart from the road which wound through the frozen landscape, she could see nothing: no farms, no cultivated fields, and certainly no sign of village outskirts with a painted sign to mark the position of an inn.

It was nearing evening by the time they drew in to the cobbled yard of a coach house. Snow had begun to fall, the big soft flakes drifting down in the light of the brass coach lamps.

Sidonie put her head down and hurried towards the inn where a cheery golden light streamed out of the window and the smell of roasting meat made her mouth water. The others followed and a few minutes later they were stripping off layers of outdoor clothes beside a roaring fire.

With her hands curled around a mug of hot liquid, Sidonie felt better. She sipped at the mulled beverage, a potent mixture of red wine, spices and *pálinka*, a Hungarian plum brandy. After a dish of stew and a great chunk of home-made black bread, she felt almost human again.

'The road ahead is blocked by a fallen tree,' Constantin informed them. 'We shall spend the night here and continue in the morning.'

Sidonie was shown to a small room at the top of the inn. It was sparsely furnished. A huge bed dominated the room and a sturdy dresser stood against one wall. The only other furniture was a wooden chest, placed next to a fireplace. The one redeeming factor was the fire which burned cheerily in the grate.

Razvania followed Sidonie into the room.

'You and I are to share,' she said. 'I hope you do not mind. It is just for one night. Constantin and Francis will have to share a room too.'

The maid servant bobbed a curtsy and said something in Romanian. Razvania answered her, her tone a little sharp.

'What did she say?' Sidonie asked.

'She hopes we are comfortable,' Razvania said, waving a dismissive hand as the servant left the room.

'She seemed to take a long time to say just that,' Sidonie said dryly.

Razvania laughed, her voice low and husky.

'Very astute of you. She also asked me to give her regards to Tatjana, our housekeeper at the castle. Tatjana is a woman from this village. Now. The hour is late. I think we should sleep. I will unlace you and then perhaps you will perform the same service for me?'

Sidonie unbuttoned her woollen suit and blouse and slipped them off. Razvania's fingers were nimble as she unlaced Sidonie's corset and then laid the garment aside. Sidonie did the same for Razvania. Soon they both wore only their under-garments.

Although the fire took the chill from the room, it was still far from warm. They climbed into bed, still wearing chemises and petticoats.

Sidonie lay on her back, her arms held stiffly against her sides as she looked up at the roughly plastered ceiling. The sheets were cold against her skin and the patchwork bedcover provided little warmth. Next to her Razvania was curled into a ball. She was aware of the other woman's perfume and the smell of her freshly washed hair. It would be warmer if they bundled up together, but she preferred to lay stretched out.

She wished she did not have to share the bed with Razvania. Since watching her with Francis at the Tarot ball, Sidonie had avoided her company whenever possible. Razvania was more than a prospective friend, she was a rival for her twin's affections.

Beside her Razvania began to breathe deeply and Sidonie relaxed. Now they would not need to make conversation. Turning on to her side, she thumped the lumpy pillow into a more comfortable position and pulled the covers more snugly around herself. She was half asleep when she felt Razvania edge towards her, curl her body around her back, and slip an arm around her waist.

Sidonie stiffened, waiting to see if Razvania would speak, but she only sighed deeply and settled again. Acutely aware of firm breasts pressing into her back and the way her bottom was cradled by a softly rounded belly, Sidonie was suddenly wide awake. It was disturbing to be embraced by another woman and far from unpleasant. But she did not want that sort of contact with Razvania.

She made a small movement, testing to see whether she could escape and Razvania's arm tightened around her waist, pulling her back against her. The firm thighs pressed up more closely underneath her.

'Keep still,' Razvania murmured. 'I'm too cold to sleep. This way we keep warm. Unless you are wakeful and wish me to pleasure you?'

The words were so shocking that, for a moment, Sidonie had no answer. Then the anger she felt against Razvania surfaced. Aware of Sidonie's dislike, Razvania had lulled her into feeling secure before making any advance towards her.

'Is Francis not enough for you then?' Sidonie said, bitterly. 'You torment him with kisses and with glimpses of your body, but you refuse to lie with him. No other woman has made him suffer as you have. Now you wish to play your sexual power games with me too?'

Razvania chuckled softly and said, 'But of course, I desire you too. You are the reflection of Francis. Your resistance and the way you fight the attraction you feel for both Constantin and myself makes you most enticing. This game you speak of. Do you not realise that it is so much more? There can only be winners. All you have to do is embrace new possibilities, new freedoms.'

'Meaning what?' Sidonie said contemptuously. 'That Francis and I should allow you to become important to us? So important that the bond between us is threatened? That cannot happen. You and Constantin promise much, but you draw back from any lasting intimacy.'

Sidonie shifted against Razvania. The woman's body heat seeped into her. She felt the perspiration gathering in the creases of her body. It annoyed her that her disappointment and sexual frustration was evident in her tone. Why had she not concealed it better?

'That was in Venice,' Razvania said, her husky voice lowered by intensity. 'Constantin and myself have been betrayed by lovers in the past. Oh, it is easy to find some kinds of love – the cheap sort that does not last, the fragmentary moment of pleasure. But it is difficult to find truth within passion. We needed to know that you desired us for ourselves and not for the things our riches could give you.'

She sighed, almost regretfully. 'Oh, it would have been very easy to have become Francis's lover. I was tempted, many times, to take him to my bed. And Constantin has shown amazing restraint where you are concerned. But I promise you that in Romania things will be different. In our homeland we can be ourselves. There need be no more holding back. How can I prove that to you?'

Sidonie did not answer. Razvania's words explained so much. Instead of being jaded aristocrats, she began to see the Count and Countess as people made vulnerable by past hurts and disappointments. She felt some sympathy towards them.

'Tell me,' Razvania said suddenly. 'Have you ever had a female lover?'

Shocked, Sidonie said, 'No. I have never desired any woman in that way. Have you?'

Again Razvania laughed, but the sound was more like a throaty sigh.

'Ah, yes. Before you there was another woman, a Venetian named Adrianna. She had black hair and flashing emerald eyes. Her skin looked as if it had been dusted with gold and her lips were soft and inviting. I felt something I did not understand at first and it frightened me. Adrianna was experienced. She kept me at arm's length, playing me like a fish on a line, until I was mad for her caresses.'

Razvania paused.

'What happened?' Sidonie asked.

'One day we went by gondola to one of the small islands where no one except a few farmers live. We took wine and fruit and got a little drunk. I spilt wine on my dress and Adrianna tried to wipe it off with water. But she only made the stain worse. It began as a game ... the undressing. I recall how I sat in my shift – the red one trimmed with Burano lace. I was shy and crosed my hands over my breasts, afraid that Adrianna would see how my nipples pushed against the red silk. She smiled at me and her face looked different, somehow tender and wild at the same time. She reached out and untied the ribbon at my neckline, drew down my shift to expose my breasts. I trembled with desire and shame . . .'

Razvania shrugged. 'You can guess the rest. Adrianna seduced me. Oh, I was willing. I almost swooned when she kissed me. I had longed so for her to do that. Then she stroked and kissed my bare breasts. She pinched and rolled my nipples, rubbing them between finger and thumb until they smarted and throbbed. I could not believe how that felt. I climaxed, just from the pressure of her fingers on my nipples and the feel of her tongue in my mouth.'

She paused as if remembering, a sad smile lifting the corners of her mouth.

'After that, she taught me how to give her pleasure. I became expert at it, wanting only to hear her sighs, to feel her shudder under my hands. I had no thought for myself and would lay with my cheek resting on her inner thigh, gazing at her sex. It was beautiful, like a dewy, pink flower with a shadowed, crimson heart, all framed with silky black hair. For a while I thought that heaven dwelt between her white thighs. I came to relish the taste of her sex – so fresh and clean it was, like warm rain. We were lovers for many weeks. I showered her with gifts. Never had I been so happy. I thought she cared for me as I did for her, but she left without even saying goodbye.'

There was a break in her voice when Razvania stopped speaking. She sighed heavily.

'So you see, Sidonie, why I do not give my heart easily. I swore that no one would wound me like that again. You need not feel sorry for me. Since I met you and Francis I have not thought of Adrianna. She did me a great service. For now I know how to please a woman as well as a man. But perhaps she taught me too well how to make my lovers long for me. Have I been too cruel? Perhaps you hate me now.'

180

The tenderness and passion in the other woman's voice sent a tingle down Sidonie's spine.

'No, I do not hate you,' she said, her voice unsteady.

In truth, she was no longer sure what she did feel. Her emotions seemed to have been turned upside down. No wonder Francis was besotted by Razvania. Her mixture of beauty, boldness and vulnerability was heady indeed.

Razvania moved a hand down to caress the curve of Sidonie's hip.

'I'm so glad we're friends again,' she purred. 'Because I desire you strongly. And I mean to give you proof of that. Did you know that there is a singular pleasure in exploring a body that is very like one's own? And you are so beautiful. Shall I show you what I learned in Adrianna's arms? It would please me greatly to do so.'

Sidonie lay still as the long fingers slid down over her thigh. She dared not speak or the fragile spell between them might shatter. Somehow they had become cocooned inside a web of intimacy. Razvania's story about Adrianna had stirred her senses. The heated body pressing so closely against her own was redolent with the promise of fleshly delights.

Between her thighs, she felt the heavy pulse of arousal start to beat. Razvania's hand slid upwards now, passing the indentation of her waist, and caressing the bottom curve of her breast.

'Turn over and lie on your back,' she whispered.

Slowly, Sidonie did so. There was still time to stop this, but she felt reluctant to do so. The soporific warmth of the bed, Razvania's perfume and the hand which was gently stroking her breast were sending a potent thrill all the way down to her toes.

'But what about Francis?' she murmured. 'Should you not lie with him first? He is sick with love for you.'

Razvania bent over to kiss the corner of her mouth. Her lips were hot and tender.

'How delightfully unselfish you are. Francis will be enchanted when you tell him about this,' she said. 'Or perhaps I shall tell him, when he lies in my arms. When I kiss his mouth like this . . .'

The thought of her twin making love to Razvania was a powerful and arousing image. Sidonie made a sound deep in her throat as Razvania lay across her and began to kiss her thoroughly. Sidonie wound her arms around the other woman's back as she returned the kiss, enjoying the novelty of the soft breasts pressing against her own.

Silky chestnut tresses spilled around her as Razvania's tongue probed her mouth, tasting and exploring. The kiss went on and on, deepening until Sidonie's senses swam. Razvania's hand described little circles on her breast, working towards the nipple which was pressing against her palm.

Sidonie arched her back, eager now for whatever was to happen. She moaned softly when Razvania's fingers closed on her nipple, pinching and teasing it into an aching peak. The many layers of lace-trimmed cotton formed a barrier between their bodies and suddenly she wanted to be naked, to feel the caresses on her bare skin.

'Wait. Please. Let me undress . . .' she whimpered against Razvania's mouth, but the other woman shook her head.

'It is better like this. Do you not relish the thought of hidden caresses, stolen pleasure? Your sex is like a jewel hidden within so many garments. A jewel I must seek.'

Sidonie drew in her breath as Razvania moved away a little and looked down on her. The slanting dark eyes were drowsy with desire and her pale skin was tinted gold in the dying light of the fire.

How beautiful Razvania was with her straight nose, strong chin and small, sensual mouth. That mouth looked so red, so moist – it put Sidonie in mind of other, more intimate lips and she flushed deeply.

How would Raszvania feel and taste – *there*? Francis had told her that all women tasted different. When he spoke of it, she had fantasised about touching a woman's quim, even tasting it. Did they taste as she did herself –

sweetly musky, a fragrance that lingered on the fingers so enticingly? When Razvania spoke of tasting Adrianna, Sidonie had felt a stab of lust deep within her belly.

Razvania lay down alongside her and began kissing her neck and nibbling her earlobe. All the time her hand kept stroking Sidonie's breasts, stimulating each of them in turn until they were swollen and her nipples stood out as hard as beads. The sensations of pleasure spread down Sidonie's body and centred in the soft furrow between her thighs.

Razvania's hand moved downwards, stroking her belly and cupping her mound. Her grasp was firm, possessive. Sidonie surged against the hand which was rubbing her mons in circles, feeling her contours, discovering the purse-shape of her quim. The soft flesh gave under the probing fingers and her quim opened, the hardening pleasure bud rubbing against the layers of cloth. The pressure was subtle and hypnotic, a hint of what was to come later.

The whole area between her thighs felt warm and sticky. As she moved under Razvania's expert fingers, she grew hotter. Her armpits prickled and a trickle of sweat ran down the division of her breasts. She pushed against the bed covers, wanting to throw them off, but Razvania stopped her.

'Relax, my darling. All you have to so is enjoy this,' Razvania whispered. 'Is it not a delight to be so warm?'

Sidonie tried to lay still, while the stroking and exploring went on. Little shards of sensation were transmitted to the liquid heart of her quim. Her juices trickled out to mingle with the sweat on her thighs and the hot, swollen labia seemed to flutter with eagerness.

The caresses continued, while she grew hotter. Tendrils of hair stuck to her forehead. Her skin felt feverish.

'Perhaps I will uncover you now,' Razvania said, taking pity on her.

Dipping her head, she mouthed the hollow at Sidonie's throat while beginning to ease the petticoats up her calves.

'Mmmm. Salt-sweet,' Razvania murmured. 'Your skin is so smooth and the heat is delicious on my tongue.'

Sidonie squirmed at the ticklish sensation as the tongue lapped at her skin. In a moment Razvania slid her mouth downwards, trailing a burning path over the damp skin of her chest.

Sidonie lifted herself, eager to feel the lips and tongue on her breasts. She was so hot, she seemed to be burning up. But she gloried in the heat, loving the wet stickiness of her skin, the fecund, spicy smell of her creases.

Pushing aside the loose neck of the chemise, Razvania closed her mouth over a nipple. Collaring the thrusting point, she tongued it back and forth.

As the folds of her petticoats slipped up to lie on her belly, Sidonie opened her legs. The tension had pooled inside her and she felt as if she was bearing down, pushing out her quim receptively. Her sex pulsed and trembled as Razvania's questing fingers parted the slick folds. Sidonie felt ashamed at the evidence of her lust and tried to close her thighs on Razvania's hand.

'Open to me, darling,' Razvania murmured. 'I love to feel how your honey seeps from you.'

Her thighs shuddering with agonised lust, Sidonie did as she was asked, bending up her knees. She felt her labia opened wide as gentle fingers parted them, pressing them up and backwards so that the tiny cone-shape of her bud stood proud of the surrounding folds.

'I shall tease out the delight from your body,' Razvania said. 'And I shall relate every detail of this night to Constantin.'

'No, oh, don't do that,' Sidonie implored. 'I could not bear him to know.'

'But I must. Have I not just stolen what he most desires? It would be too cruel to keep this pleasure all to myself. Besides, you want him too, don't you? You do not answer. Tell me the truth or I'll stop doing this . . .'

Sidonie moaned and threshed, her dew wetting the fingers that stroked and manipulated her so soundly. Razvania held her sex wide with one hand and used two fingers to rub delicately up either side of the stiffly swollen pleasure bud.

Flexing her knees, Sidonie lifted her pelvis and rotated the slippery sex-flesh against the knowing fingers. The sensation was exquisite. It was unbearable to think of such pleasure being withheld.

'Tell Constantin then,' she whimpered. 'It's true that I want him as much as Francis wants you. Please don't stop doing that. Oh, God. It's wonderful. Do anything you like to me, but don't stop that . . .'

Pressing on the jutting nub of flesh, Razvania smoothed back the tiny hood and tapped gently on the exposed protuberance. At the same time she moved back up to claim Sidonie's mouth. Her lips were no longer gentle and the tongue that plundered the inner recesses was firm, claiming and demanding her utter submission to pleasure.

Sidonie's hips bucked and she rubbed herself shamelessly against the hand that was buried between her thighs. Her tongue meshed with Razvania's in an erotic dance. Razvania tasted of warmth and sex and plum brandy. The threads of a climax began to interlace and she gave herself up to the gathering sense of total surrender.

Her quim was soaking now, but she no longer felt any shame as her juices trickled into the crease of her bottom. Razvania's slim fingers slid up and down the folds, now and then pinching the engorged little stem until it burned and throbbed for its release. Pressing her bottom against the bed, Sidonie lifted herself ever higher, yearning for the feelings to go on and on as Razvania pulled the pleasure bud gently back and forth between two fingers.

Just as Sidonie's neck fell back and she began tossing her head from side to side, Razvania thrust two fingers deep inside her. As her climax washed over her, Sidonie cried out, sinking down to impale herself on the fingers which pressed downwards towards her rectum, the knuckles rubbing at her vaginal entrance.

The unexpected pressure, the uniqueness of the action, tipped her over. Her orgasm rose to a crest, began to spiral and then was pushed on to a higher level by the thumb which pushed against her anus.

'No. Please . .' she begged, afraid of being penetrated there.

An image of Francis, impaled rectally by the leather phallus, swam into her mind. And a surge of fresh lust throbbed in her groin. She tried to fight the onrush of sensation, but it broke over her, swamping her, wiping her mind clear of everything else. The shock of it stole her breath.

She opened her legs to lie flat against the bed, her belly taut and her hips rotating as the thumb went into the creased tightness, hurting her with a peculiar, hot smarting pain as it pushed past the virgin orifice.

'Yes, oh, yes . . .' Sidonie breathed, wanting to be plundered, to be claimed by this woman who was such a mixture of strength and vulnerability.

The thumb and fingers moved inside her as she came again, wave after wave of pleasure sweeping over her lower body. She hardly noticed when Razvania withdrew and lay beside her. No wonder the French called a climax, *la petite mort*. She had all but passed out.

It was a few moments before she recovered. Razvania held her tight, stroking her face soothingly and kissing her from time to time.

'You come so beautifully,' she said, her eyes glinting with triumph. 'I love how you fight the pleasure until you cannot help but give in to it. Now you see that I am not truly cruel. For I have suffered also. Many nights I lay in my lonely bed, giving myself pleasure. Do you know how much I have longed to lie with you? Ever since I first saw you and Francis I have hungered to possess you both.'

She stroked back the tangle of damp, red-gold hair.

'And when I tell Constantin what has happened between us he will burn to possess you also.'

Sidonie pushed herself up on to one elbow.

'The night is not yet over. Let us make sure that you have plenty to tell him. Take off your clothes. It is my turn to pleasure you now.'

Chapter Fourteen

Constantin was eager to get to the castle now. The mountains and streams of his homeland seemed to call out to him.

As the coach toiled up the valley of the Cris Repede towards the great horseshoe of the Carpathians his heart soared. How sweetly the slopes fell away to one side of the road. He had almost forgotten how his eyes longed for the sight of mountains.

Here and there he glimpsed a single-storey farmhouse, the walls painted in pastel shades of lavender or pink. There would be beechwoods and alpine meadows to explore come the spring, but for now the iron grip of winter held sway. He did not mind. He loved his country in all her guises.

'Look there, my friend,' he said to Thomas who was looking broodingly out of the window. 'Our destination is just over that range.'

'It seems an awfully long way,' Thomas said. 'Especially in this weather. It has not stopped snowing since we left the village.'

Constantin laughed with the ease of a man mountain born and used to long journeys and harsh terrain.

'Nonsense. It is only another day's journey. And I have sent on ahead to order my sleighs to be readied.

You can enjoy the countryside from a new vantage point.'

He beamed at the others who all looked refreshed from their night's sleep. Razvania and Sidonie, bundled up in fur coats both held hand-warmers between their gloved palms. The warmers were small tins which held stubs of candles.

Constantin smiled at Razvania, pleased to see the rosy tint to her cheeks and her softly glowing eyes. She too looked pleased to be returning home. There was a look of conspiracy about his ward and Sidonie. He was sure that they had made love. The signs were unmistakable. No doubt Razvania would furnish him with all the details later.

He wondered whether Razvania could see the same look of complicity about himself and Francis. His cock stirred into life as he thought of the pleasure they had enjoyed. How fortuitous that they had been forced to share the small upstairs room. The bed was hardly big enough for two people and Thomas had had to be provided with a collapsible pallet which he slept on in the narrow corridor.

Francis had seemed reluctant at first to get into bed.

'It's very small,' he had said, taking off his outside garments.

'Then we'll keep each other cosy,' Constantin replied. 'If you get in first you can warm my side for me.'

With the cold of the room Francis had needed little persuading. Leaving his clothes in a heap but keeping on his shirt, he slid under the covers. With the dark curls tumbling over his shoulders and the shirt collar opened to reveal his smooth, hairless chest, he looked very enticing.

Constantin stripped naked, not bothering to hide himself and conscious of the way Francis's glance flickered over the planes of his body.

Laying on his back, his hands linked behind his head, Francis watched closely as Constantin stood before a tin bowl of water and began splashing it over his face, neck and chest.

189

'Good grief, man, that water's stone cold. You must be freezing,' he said. 'How can you stand it?'

Constantin grinned, throwing back his loose black hair and letting the droplets run down his flat belly. His nipples tightened and the cold air raised gooseflesh on his skin.

'We mountain folk are hardy souls. But I must admit that I only remember why when I return to my country,' he said ruefully, rubbing himself dry with a rough cloth. 'There are not the luxuries of Venice here. But perhaps there are compensations.'

The firelight flickered on his pale skin and sparkled on the water drops which bedewed his pubic hair. Francis's eyes still lingered on his body and Constantin felt a stirring at his groin. He did not turn away, but allowed the other man to see the way his penis thickened and grew heavy.

He knew that he had a good body. His shoulders were broad and his limbs were slim but well muscled. There was not an ounce of fat at his waist. Sliding his hands over his belly, he scratched the hair at the base of his cock, the movement making his penis bob against his hand.

'Get in, why don't you? The bed's warm,' Francis said, with forced lightness.

It was evident from the rise in the covers that he was trying to hide an erection. As Constantin lifted the bedcover and slid his body between the sheets Francis turned over, drawing up his knees and pressing his hands to his groin.

The bed was too small for them to lie without touching and Constantin made no effort to put space between them. He lay on his side, one arm cradling his head, facing Francis. Francis could not help but be aware of the cock that pressed up against his buttocks.

For a while they lay still, the tension between them almost tangible. Neither of them said anything, but body spoke to body. Finally, with a muffled groan, Francis turned around into Constantin's embrace.

Constantin's arms went out to surround the firm,

young body. His lust was tempered by tenderness as Francis rested his cheek against his upper chest.

'I was wondering how long it would take you to do that,' he said. 'Is it so difficult to admit that you desire me?'

Francis shook his head. 'Difficult? No. Just strange. Love between men is such a taboo. I desire you strongly, but my emotions are all mixed up. It is Razvania who has been tormenting my senses these past weeks. And you who have been pursuing Sidonie.'

'Do you not realise that next door Razvania is likely pleasuring your twin?' Constantin said hoarsely, rubbing his chin affectionately against the top of Francis's head.

'I thought as much, but strangely I do not mind. I am jealous in a way. But then . . .' He paused as if not sure how to explain himself, then rushed on. 'I would be jealous as hell if Sidonie was lying with you tonight. There, I have said it. But you know this, don't you? That is why the two of you have been holding back. You and Razvania were not sure which one of us you desired the most.'

Constantin gave an exclamation of delight.

'That is true. I am so glad you understand this. It makes things so much . . . I was going to say easier, but that's not true. It certainly makes things more interesting.'

He tipped up Francis's chin, smiling down into the troubled blue eyes.

'Let's not worry about that now. Do you want to waste the whole night talking?'

Under Constantin's hands Francis awoke to passion. The muscles corded under his skin, standing out like ropes as Constantin ran gentle, exploratory fingers over his body.

Where was the arrogance, the pride? Constantin mused in delight. Francis quickly became a willing supplicant to the needs of his body.

'Take off that shirt,' Constantin ordered and threw

back the bedclothes so that he could gaze upon the perfect young body.

Francis lay shivering but quiescent while Constantin manipulated his limbs into different positions, all of them designed to teach him that he was simply a creature to be pleasured and to give pleasure.

'Whatever you wish,' Francis breathed, trembling with wonder as Constantin made him lie curled up on his side, his cock jutting downwards between his closed thighs.

Then, with a slow, almost insulting rhythm he stroked the cock, smoothing the skin over the covered glans and feeling how it grew slippery with the juice of pre-emission. Francis arched his back and thrust towards the hand that had the power to grant him release.

'Ah, not yet,' Constantin said. 'I want more from you. I demand everything from my lovers. Roll over, Francis.'

He laid him spreadeagled on his back, his arms above his head so that his ribcage stood out and his belly formed a shallow slope. The reddened shaft jutted out proudly from the cluster of curls at his groin. As the cock throbbed and jerked, Francis moaned softly, twisting against the sure grip of the strong, white hands.

His eyes pleaded with Constantin. Take me, use me, they seemed to say.

But Constantin just looked him over, his mouth curving with satisfaction. Bending suddenly he bit at the tight male nipples and moved to lay across Francis so that his leg partially covered the slim hips. With his weight pinning the slender form, he could feel how the trapped sex pulsed, like a heartbeat or a ticking clock. It felt hot and bursting with life.

Still holding his wrists captive, Constantin kissed Francis for the first time. The kiss was not gentle. He used his mouth as a weapon, claiming, punishing the young man for being so irresistible. The lips opened under his own, allowing the assault of his tongue.

Drawing away, he looked down into the wide, blue

eyes, loving the way Francis's cheeks grew red with shame and need.

Removing the leg that had pressed Francis closely against the bed, he said, 'Bring up your knees and hold them apart. I am almost ready to take you.'

And Francis did as he was told, as if captivated by the novelty of responding to a direct order. His eyelids swept down to veil his troubled eyes. As Constantin bit his nipples again and pushed his fingers between the tight buttocks, seeking out the tight puckered folds of his anus, Francis arched his body into a bow and his still-covered glans dripped a clear fluid.

'No, oh, no . . .' he gasped as Constantin pushed a finger inside him, curving it to press on the sensitive spot high up in his bowels.

When the passage grew soft and the anal ring relaxed, Constantin inserted two more fingers, feeling the way the folds of skin stretched tightly around them. He pushed them in slowly, letting Francis get used to being opened. At the pressure Francis's glans squeezed out of the cock-skin as if pushed from the inside.

Little grunts escaped Francis's wide-stretched lips and his face was screwed into a rictus of pleasure. His orgasm was not far off. The heavy sac of his balls had drawn in tight to his body and his cock was a rigid, tortured column. Judging the moment correctly, just as Francis began jerking and bucking, rotating himself on the buried fingers, Constantin withdrew them in a single, swift movement.

'Oh . . .' Francis whimpered. 'Please. Let me come . . . I can't stand this . . .'

Constantin only laughed and told him to wait.

He moved up until he was sitting astride Francis's chest, his balls resting on the muscular heated skin. Then he pushed the big, purplish tip towards those sculpted lips.

'Suck me,' he ordered. 'Give me your mouth.'

When Francis's mouth opened eagerly to receive him, Constantin closed his eyes. Francis licked the thick stem and used loose lips to collar the glans. Gently he pushed back the cock-skin, before sucking the shaft firmly and drawing it into his throat. Constantin rose on to his knees, sinking so deeply into the willing cavern that his dark pubic curls brushed against Francis's mouth and chin.

The sweet ache boiled upwards in Constantin's balls, but he withdrew from the hot mouth and slid back down Francis's body. Lifting the bent knees higher, he pressed the head of his cock against the loosened anus and pushed. As he leaned inwards, burying his spittle-wet shaft in the silky warmth, Francis's cock leapt frantically with frustration.

Moaning incoherently Francis worked his hips, lifting his bottom up to match Constantin thrust for thrust. The movement was lascivious, practiced. This was not a unique experience for the young man. Constantin felt a thrill go right down to his root at the thought of someone else's cock having been pushed into Francis's body.

'Who had you before?' he demanded, gritting his teeth and pressing the captive wrists more forcefully into the pillow. He withdrew completely and jabbed at the tight creased hole, wincing at the tightly squeezing pleasure on his cock-tip.

'Tell me, who taught you to enjoy being taken like this?'

Francis shook his head in helpless arousal, begging for Constantin to penetrate him again. Leaning forward, Constantin ground his stomach against Francis's cock, which throbbed with a dull and heavy note, stimulated almost to giving up its seed by the threshing of their joined bellies.

'Tell me, damn you!' he said. 'Or I'll take my pleasure and leave you wanting!'

Francis's face grew shiny with heat and tears as he sobbed with pleasure. He threshed against the hands which held him captive, the nipples like tight beads against the painfully stretched chest.

'All right. But make me come or I'll die of frustration.'

Constantin pushed the moist, flaring tip past the

closure of the flesh ring. Then he inched into the silky channel. Between sighs and gasps, Francis twisted his head to one side and blurted out a string of words.

'It was – Oh, God. Yes. Deeper. Go deeper. Chatham. His name was Chatham. My art teacher. He was my first male lover. He taught me to relish the taste of . . . his come. God. Oh, God. I'm spending . . .'

As Francis came, the creamy sperm splashing between their bodies, Constantin again drew almost all the way out of him. His own climax built as the anus spasmed, sucking and scraping deliciously over his glans. Even as his semen left him and he cried out with the wrenching pleasure of it, he slammed back into the depths of the hot, narrow channel.

Afterwards, slumped across Francis's body he propped himself on an elbow and lay looking down on the finely wrought chest and slim waist. How gratifying it was to be in control, to be the custodian who meted out pleasure. He loved to see the look of helpless passion on a lover's face.

And Francis was a potent mixture of arrogance and vulnerability. It was such a delight to see the strong made weak by the tyranny of desire. With the twins the pleasure was more than doubled.

Between them they promised so much . . .

In the carriage the following day, Constantin dragged his thoughts back to the present.

He could hardly wait until they reached the castle and Sidonie gave herself to him – or rather he took her. She had been ready to fall into his bed for weeks now. It was simply a matter of fate that Francis had capitulated first. Razvania and himself had exerted almost super-human restraint over the past weeks. It was no surprise that both of them had finally weakened last night.

No matter. There were so many possibilities, so many erotic scenarios to dwell on. His mind filled with images of joined bodies, seeking mouths, eagerly offered sexes.

At that moment Francis caught his eye. It seemed that he glimpsed what Constantin was thinking. Sidonie flashed her brother a knowing glance then and a delicious flush spread over each of the delicate faces, both light and dark eyes taking on the hazy look of desire.

The inside of the carriage was fraught with sexual tension. Razvania reached for Sidonie's hand and gave it a knowing squeeze. Only Thomas seemed unaware of what was going on.

Constantin's erection swelled and his balls tightened. He had to shift position to accommodate the pressure. Francis smirked at the movement, his eyes flicking down to rest fleetingly on the pronounced bulge in Constantin's trousers.

Christ. He felt like tearing off the handsome bastard's clothes and driving into him in full view of his twin. Now that was a thought.

He had an insane desire to stop the carriage and drag Francis into the woods. In front of all of them he would bend him over a branch and tear down his trousers. Perhaps he would spank him before having him. The thought of pushing his cock between the sore, reddened buttocks was very appealing.

And what would the watching Sidonie do?

He imagined her begging him to be gentle, or offering herself in place of her twin. Or perhaps she would just watch avidly, the liquid excitement gathering between her thighs and soaking into her chemise.

The throbbing heat at his groin was uncomfortable and the blood pounded in his head. He needed to relieve the pressure or his balls would start to ache. It was the remembered pleasure of last night that had him in this state of pained arousal. After all the self-control of the previous weeks it was as if a dam had burst inside him.

He needed to come. And he did not think he could wait until they reached the castle.

He began fantasising about masturbating. Even better if someone else would pleasure him. And then that was all he could think of. Somehow he would think of a way of being alone with one of the twins.

Then he had an idea. A secret smile hovered around his lips.

Sidonie was delighted when she saw the horse-drawn sleigh.

She walked around them, stroking the velvet noses of the horses that stood waiting in harness. The sleighs were open to the elements. The driver sat on a high platform in front, while the body of the vehicle and the couch-like seat in the back was piled high with fur rugs.

The others were all inside the coaching inn, finishing off the remnants of a meal. Then the door opened and Constantin came outside to stand next to her.

She almost caught her breath. He had changed out of his beautifully tailored suit and wore loose, leather trousers, tucked into knee-length boots. A padded waist-coat covered his black-silk, collarless tunic. Around his broad shoulders he had slung a floor-length cloak, lined and collared with thick, shaggy black fur. A hat of the same fur topped his head and his loose hair streamed down his back.

'You look different,' she said, thinking that the words sounded inadequate. Which they were. He looked magnificent.

He grinned, the sculpted lips parting to reveal very white teeth.

'Different clothes for a different life,' he said, handing her a steaming mug of coffee laced with brandy. 'I brought you this. It's to warm you on the inside. We have to cross the frozen lake before we reach my home. Will you ride with me? We can leave at once. Razvania will go with the others.'

She looked sharply at him but he was drinking his coffee. Had there been the hint of an invitation in his tone? She hoped so. Razvania had told her that the waiting game was over. The night spent in her arms had attested to the truth of that, but Constantin had yet to prove that anything was different between him and herself.

It was hard to believe that he would unbend and welcome her to his bed. But perhaps at the castle he would be more relaxed. Certainly he seemed to be in a strange mood. Looking sideways she studied him. His features had become familiar to her over the past weeks, but she seemed to see him anew. In the peculiar, blue-white light of a Romanian winter he looked even more stark and dramatic than usual.

The sharp angles of his face, his hollowed cheekbones and deep-set dark eyes were softened only by the wide, sensual mouth. The smooth, pinkish-brown of his lips was the single spot of colour on his monochrome persona.

She drained her coffee, feeling the brandy spreading its way through her veins. Handing the empty cup to him, she smiled. 'Yes. I'll be happy to ride with you.'

Snow began to fall again as they set off. Everything was blanketed in white. Even the forested hills showed no glimmer of green. Constantin directed her attention to a hill-top in the distance.

'That's our destination,' he said with more than a hint of pride. 'My ancestral home.'

The Gothic spires and towers of the castle were clearly visible, the stone the bluish-grey colour of gun-metal against the bleached surroundings.

Sidonie could hardly believe they were almost there. The journey had been far longer than she had anticipated – in every sense, England seemed a world away. Surely the house in Wiltshire, their dreary childhood and the enforced closeness between Francis and herself belonged to another life.

For an instant it seemed that she had a glimpse into another existence where the world did not revolve around her twin. It was too terrifying a prospect, like gazing into an abyss. She drew back, not wanting to face such a possibility.

'Your castle. It is beautiful,' she said to Constantin, who was waiting for an answer. 'And this country is so wild, almost savage. It seems a hard land to live in and must demand much of its people. But I can understand how you long to return here after all your travels.'

'Can you? Can you feel the pull of it too? I'm so glad,' he said, his voice rough with sudden emotion.

Icy winds stung her cheeks as the sleigh sped over the lake's frozen surface and snow flakes melted on contact with her skin. She was glad of the big, circular fur hat which covered her hair and a good part of her face. The speed they were going was exciting. Sleigh bells rang and the harnesses jingled in time to the pounding hooves.

How delightful this journey was. She turned to smile at Constantin and almost caught her breath at the intensity of his gaze. He looked as if he wanted to devour her. His eyes were dark pools in his white face. The shaggy black fur of his hat gave him a dangerous look. Long strands of his hair were whipping across his face, blown by the hectic wind.

'What is it?' she faltered. 'You look so strange. You're frightening me.'

His hand searched amongst the furs. Pulling off her fur mitten he closed his hand possessively over her fingers. He said earnestly, 'Do not be frightened. This is who I really am. The courtier, the tourist, the rich, sexually jaded fool, those are façades to dupe people who wish not to look too deeply. But you are not one of those. You are different. Look into the face of reality, Sidonie. My reality. There's no holding back here. Life's for the taking. This can be yours too, if you wish it.'

'I . . . I do not understand.'

'Oh, I think you do. We spoke of it earlier. I told you that I wanted you. In every way. Are you ready for that yet? There's one way I can show you what I mean.'

She felt his other hand pushing aside the furs, gathering her skirts into folds and raising them. He surely could not mean to make love to her now? But she saw by his face that he did.

'Here?' she said, alarmed and excited in equal measure. 'But you can't! What about the driver? He'll see us.'

He gave a throaty chuckle. 'He'll not notice. He has

orders to keep his eyes on the way ahead. Besides he'll see nothing under these furs. Although he might hear us. That's up to you.'

His hand was becoming more insistent, delving beneath her skirts. He let go of her fingers and encircled her waist, pulling her down to lie under him. She felt his other hand on her knees and then her bare thighs. His fingers were cold and thrilling against her skin.

She could not believe this was really happening. All his reticence, his carefully guarded remoteness, had gone. He truly had become as wild and unpredictable as the landscape. His new persona aroused her. There was a heat and recklessness about him, an almost desperate urgency, something she had not seen before.

Something inside her unfolded and rose to meet the challenge he threw out. Then he thrust her legs apart and closed his hand on her quim. A dart of pure lust centred low down in her stomach. Without preamble he pushed two fingers in, exclaiming in delight at her wet tightness.

'You're ready to take it now,' he murmured, his pronounced accent evidence that he was almost beside himself with desire. 'I'm going to give it to you hot and hard. That's the way you want it, isn't it? Answer me. Tell me what you want from me.'

She ought to have been shocked by his crudity, but she relished it. Her inner walls pulsed and sucked at his fingers, welcoming the invasion. She felt herself softening, growing wet.

'Yes. Oh yes,' she said, snared by his dark eyes, the heat flaring unbidden into her cheeks. 'I want you now. As much as you want me. And I beg you – do not be gentle.'

His fingers penetrated her still, curving inwards and moving back and forth so that her juices gathered and ran down his knuckles. He rotated the fingers as if exploring her, then moved them apart, opening up her vagina.

The feeling of being stretched, assessed for her readiness, was delicious. The swollen bump of her pleasure bud ached for his touch, but he ignored it. Intent on his own pleasure he fumbled with his clothes and his cock sprang free.

Sidonie squirmed under him, eager for the moment when his mouth would close on hers. His breath hissed against her ears turning into mist in the freezing air. She caught the clean scent of his fur collar and clutched at it, dragging his face close to hers.

'Do it. Fuck me,' she whispered.

His dark eyes glittered and she loved what she saw there. She did not need any subtlety or finesse. She was ready for him. Ready to be impaled, torn into. It was what she had been longing for.

He pushed aside the layers of skirts and petticoats and she felt the kiss of his bare skin against hers. His hips and belly were hot and smooth, his pubic hair brushing against her inner thigh. For a moment longer his cock rubbed against her quim, then she felt the blunt glans slipping between her parted labia.

As he found his target, she lifted her hips to aid him. He pushed into her in a single, smooth stroke, letting out his breath on a sigh of pleasure. Then they were kissing, frantically mashing their mouths together, thrusting their tongues against each other.

His hard flesh surged within her. Leaning into her, he pressed her legs more widely apart and drove downwards, the big glans butting against the neck of her womb. She worked her hips joyfully, feeling her juices sliding down her open slit, accepting the almost animal coupling.

It seemed so right to do it this way, surrounded as they were by the snow and the freezing wind.

Constantin seemed a creature of the elements, his cock within her was strong and primeval. The raw, unrefined pleasure spread over her lower body as they toiled frantically towards a joint climax.

With the sleigh bells in her ears and the snow flakes falling on to her eyelashes, Sidonie squeezed Constantin's lean hips between her thighs and rode him hard. He pumped away at her, the strokes fast and deep, pulling against her labia and sending a referred pressure to her stiffly erect bud.

When she came, she buried her face in his shoulder, muffling her cries against the fur collar. And the feeling of exultation and tenderness that swept her was almost chilling in its intensity.

Chapter Fifteen

Seen close to, the castle was almost overpowering in its magnificence. It brooded on its secluded perch like a great crouched eagle, the Gothic spires and ramparts soaring high overhead.

Their imminent arrival had been noted and the huge brass-studded front door swung open as the sleigh drew up in front of it.

A tall, statuesque woman, wearing a high-necked dress of crimson silk, descended the steps, her lips curved in greeting.

'Welcome home, Count Nastase,' she said. 'I received word that we were to have guests. The rooms are ready.'

'Efficient as ever, Tatjana, even in my absence, eh?' Constantin said, smiling. 'This is Sidonie. Her brother Francis and Thomas, another Englishman, will be here soon with Razvania. You are to treat all of my friends with the same courtesy you normally reserve for me. Is that clear?'

'Perfectly,' Tatjana said, giving Sidonie a measuring look. 'It shall be as you wish. I hope you will enjoy your stay here, madame.'

As they went inside, Sidonie glanced sideways at Tatjana, taking in her strong features, ruddy cheeks and coronet of glossy brown plaits.

The name seemed familiar. She remembered where she had heard it before. It had been at the village, where they stayed the night. Razvania had mentioned that the castle housekeeper had been a village woman. So this was she. Sidonie hid a smile. What a formidable creature. She was very handsome in a severe sort of way. Although her manner was diffident, Sidonie was sure that it would not be wise to cross her. She could not wait to see Thomas's reaction to her. The housekeeper was just the type of woman he found attractive. An army of servants waited in line to welcome the Count home and he nodded at each of them as he passed by.

'Perhaps you'd like to go straight up to your room?' he said to Sidonie. 'I'll have Tatjana send up some hot water for a bath. Then you might like to join me downstairs and I'll show you around. It will take you a few days to get used to the size of the castle. It's quite a maze. My great-Grandfather built the place and he had a love of grandeur.'

Sidonie followed the housekeeper who led her towards a stone staircase which was guarded by two carved, seated lions. More lions, this time on their hind legs, marched up the wooden banisters, each of their heads topped by an ornate iron lamp.

They passed down a corridor, lined with richly carved and decorated panels. Tapestries were hung at intervals and there were many paintings and collections of weapons. Tatjana stopped before a set of inlaid double doors and threw them wide.

'Your room, madame. I hope you will find it comfortable. The fire has been lit and the room is warm.'

'This is beautiful,' Sidonie exclaimed, stepping into a large room which was decorated all in red and gold. 'Thank you, Tatjana. And you've even put some flowers in a vase. How thoughtful. But where did you find them at this time of year?'

'There is a garden room at the back of the castle. We have flowers all year. I'll show you later if you wish. I'm glad that you like the room. The Count asked for you to have this one,' Tatjana said, a glint of pleased pride in her eyes. 'The view over the mountains is the best in the castle. This adjoining door leads to the room I have had prepared for your brother.'

She went off to arrange for hot water and towels to be sent up. As Tatjana closed the doors behind her Sidonie looked around the room. It had a kind of barbarous splendour. The furnishings were all of some kind of heavy, dark wood, much of it decorated with gilding and precious stones. Curtains of blood-red velvet, encrusted with gold embroidery, hung at the windows. The upholstery of two large settles, placed either side of an enormous walk-in fireplace, was in figured silk in the same colour.

But it was the bed that captured her attention. Taking up the whole of the wall opposite the fireplace, it was encased from floor to ceiling in a massive, flamboyantly carved wooden box which was decorated with scrolled carvings, gilded lions' heads and shields. More of the red silk was looped up around the bed to form a headrest and curtains. A matching counterpane and cushions completed the picture.

When she turned back the covers she saw that the sheets were also of red silk. The bed did not seem to be a place for sleeping – rather it seemed to invite one to luxuriate in its sumptuous depths, preferably with a lover. It was the most garish piece of furniture she had ever seen. She loved it, even though, she thought with a grin, a whole family could live in it.

By the time the hot water arrived she had almost finished undressing and was ready to put on the dressing gown of stiff brocade, thoughtfully provided by Tatjana.

As she stripped off her under-garments she was aware of the wetness between her thighs and the warm animal scent emanating from her vagina, evidence of the hasty coupling in the sleigh. Her pulses quickened as she recalled the rough pleasure of Constantin's caresses.

There would be many more opportunities for them to make love, but nothing would replace the memory of that first coming together while the sleigh slid over the frozen lake, snow fell around them and the winter winds tore at their faces.

A maid arrived with hot towels and stood by to help Sidonie bathe. It was a luxury to have her limbs rubbed with herb-scented soap and her hair washed and then dried. Accepting the maid's offer to rub her limbs with perfumed oil, Sidonie lay on a spread towel in front of the fire.

The woman's hands on her body were firm and efficient. The oil smelt of something heavy and exotic. It made her feel drowsy. Pillowing her head on her bent arms, she closed her eyes and fell into a slight doze as the maid massaged her limbs.

The slippery pressure continued on over her shoulders, breasts and belly and downwards to her toes. In a while, at the maid's gentle urging, she turned over and the same attention was given to her back and buttocks. The massage took a long time, the long strokes lulling her into a state bordering on a trance.

She was conscious only vaguely that the hands on her seemed to be lingering, dipping into the parting of her thighs and applying oil there. Now and then, on the upward stroke, the fingers brushed gently against her pubis. Enjoying the sensual feelings she opened her thighs a little wider and stretched voluptuously, lifting her bottom so that the woman could rub more of the oil into the tender skin on the inner surfaces of her thighs and buttocks.

As the oily stroking continued, she rested her cheek against the back of her hand and settled down again to doze. For a while she enjoyed the way her buttocks were pummelled, the flesh lifted and rolled between strong fingers. Then the whole length of her legs and feet were given a similar treatment.

She felt so relaxed that she could hardly move. The warmth from the fire on her naked skin and the penetrating fragrance of the oil made her feel toned and pampered.

Then she became aware that the massage had changed rhythm. Slowly, almost stealthily, the fingers worked towards the crease of her bottom. In a feather-light caress they trailed down the opening and began to move over her quim, pushing against the closed sex lips.

Now and then the exploratory fingers paused as if testing to see if she was awake. When she made no sound, the stroking continued.

Sidonie was not sure whether she was imagining it, but it seemed that the maid wanted to examine her body more intimately. Just to make sure, she made a movement and let out a little sigh. The hands were swiftly, almost guiltily withdrawn. She knew then that she had not been mistaken. The woman's fingers had been deliberately stroking her quim, apparently for her own gratification.

She realised that she had a clear choice. Either she could challenge the woman and demand to know just what she thought she was doing or she could feign sleep and enjoy the experience. She chose to do the latter.

Soon the maid resumed her ministrations. Sidonie bit her lips as the fingers stroked her quim, taking each of the lips and pulling them open. Soon her labia stood out thickly, pouting around the fingertips which still penetrated her crevice only shallowly.

It took a supreme effort for her to lie still and not push her bottom towards the maid's hand. The traces of oil on the woman's fingertips made her flesh swell and burn a little as the fingers rubbed at her folds, but that only added to the sense of illicit pleasure. Then she felt a finger push into the open slit of her sex, edging along the moist groove and searching for the hardened tip of her bud.

Sidonie bit into the back of her hand, caging her sighs behind her teeth. The whole of her quim was quivering with pent-up pleasure. The movements against her erect nub were maddening, the pressure not quite enough to bring her to a climax. They were without rhythm, diffident, as if the maid was not really sure what to do.

Sidonie yearned to give her instructions but did not want to spoil the mood. The pretence of being asleep while the young woman examined and stimulated her was almost overpoweringly erotic. As if moving in her sleep, she opened her thighs wider and lifted her bottom a little higher. As before, the hand was removed for a few seconds, until it appeared that Sidonie had settled again.

Holding her breath, she waited for the maid to put her hand back between her thighs. When the explorations continued, she let out a mock-sleepy sigh, unable to hide the evidence of her enjoyment. Her juices seeped out to mingle with the oil. Spurred on by this, the maid pushed two fingers between the wet, open labia and rubbed gently back and forth.

On the forward stroke, the fingertips butted against the swollen bump of flesh, smoothing it down towards her belly and then pulling it with the backwards stroke. The movement was subtle and indirect, but it was exquisite. Imagining how lewd she must look with her sex all pushed out and reddened, the inner lips hanging down a little and the whole vulva protruding below her buttocks like a purse, Sidonie felt herself moving towards a climax.

The pleasure peaked and tipped over. Somehow she kept still, her buttocks and thighs relaxed as the sweetly tearing sensation flowed down over her. The subterfuge of being innocent of what had happened added to the pleasure. Her breath came fast and she was sure that a flush had spread over her skin.

It was obvious that she had come, but she and the maid kept up the pretence.

The maid removed her fingers and began almost casually to stroke the skin of Sidonie's lower back. Sidonie managed to catch her breath and pretended to wake up. She stretched and yawned, turning on to her side away from the fire. Her whole body felt relaxed and glowing.

'Madame?' the maid politely and with a measure of

distance. 'Ah, you are awake now. I have finished the massage. I will leave you now. Unless there is anything else I can do for you. May I say that madame is very beautiful. Your skin is so fine and white. It would be a pleasure to serve you again, at any time, in any way that you wish.'

Sidonie sat up and yawned again. For the first time she really looked at the young woman.

She had a pretty, small-featured face somewhat marred by her mouth, which was thin-lipped, and a small chin which sloped sharply backwards. There were a few stray brownish curls visible at her forehead, but the rest of her head was covered by a white scarf. Her high-coloured gown was black and her apron snowy white.

'What is your name?' Sidonie asked.

'Izána,' the maid said, smiling at the unexpected question and looking shyly at Sidonie.

Then she blushed as she saw Sidonie's expression, her eyelids sweeping down to veil her mild black eyes.

'Well, Izána. You are adept at massage. But do you know how to do a manicure?'

'Yes, madame,' she said, looking pleased.

Sidonie pulled the towel up to cover herself from breast to hip, and held out her hands. 'My nails need shaping. Will you attend to them, Izána?'

'Certainly,' the maid said. 'Is that *all* madame wishes for? I have many skills.'

'I'm sure you have. But after that wonderful, relaxing massage, I need little else,' Sidonie said, feeling somewhat amused by the maid's eager manner.

She seemed almost frantic to please. It was as if Izána had been ordered to make certain that Sidonie was physically satisfied – in every way possible. She had a thought.

'Tatjana sent you to me, did she not?'

Izána nodded, a look of fear creeping over her face.

'Yes, madame. But why do you ask? If I have offended you, forgive me. Please do not tell Tatjana.'

'I have no intention of doing so. Tell me what were your orders? Your specific orders.'

Izána's eyes slid sideways. Sidonie had to insist that she answered, but then she explained readily enough.

'I'm new at the castle. If I fail in my duties, I shall be sent back to my village. I must stay here. My family relies on the money I send them. I . . . I was told to serve you in whichever way you might wish. Even to offer to give your body pleasure.'

'I see,' Sidonie said. 'And then to report back to Tatjana, no doubt? Well, there will not be anything for you to tell her. Will there?'

The maid shook her head. Sidonie was satisfied that Izána took her meaning.

'Good. Just concentrate on doing my nails and then you can go. And do not worry. I shall tell Tatjana that you did just as she told you to.'

As Izána filed and then buffed her nails, she thought about the housekeeper. It seemed to her that Tatjana had sent Izána to her as a test. Perhaps she felt her power threatened by the arrival of herself and Francis and wanted to get their measure.

She was willing to bet that Francis would be subjected to a similar test. Her first instincts regarding the woman had been proved correct. Tatjana was a powerful influence within the castle and would certainly bear careful watching.

By the time the connecting door between the two rooms opened and Francis stepped inside, Sidonie was sitting in front of a dressing table, drawing a silver-backed brush through her loose hair.

Francis walked straight up to her, gripped her shoulders and bent down to kiss the side of her neck.

'This is quite a place, is it not? I never dreamed that Constantin would own somewhere half so grand. Just look at this room and that bed! But you, my darling, look as if you belong here.' He gave a dry chuckle. 'Isn't it decent of Constantin to put us next to each other? I'd

210

hate to have to go creeping down dark corridors by candle-light, trying to find out where your bedroom is.'

Sidonie leaned back against him, raising her arms and running her fingers through his dark curls as he slid his hands down to her waist. He unbuttoned the front of the dressing-gown and slipped a hand inside. Palming her nipple, he murmured against her ear, 'Would I be right in thinking that there was a reason why you and Constantin set out for the castle before us?'

Despite herself, Sidonie blushed. How ridiculous it was to feel as if she had been caught out at some schoolgirl misdemeanour. But the heat in her cheeks was there for a second reason. Francis's lips on her neck and the pressure of his hand against her breast had caused an immediate reaction.

'If you mean, has Constantin made love to me,' she said dreamily, her eyes on his in the mirror, 'Yes, he has. And it was wonderful.'

Francis's face darkened and he pinched her nipple cruelly until she winced with the pain of it.

'Worth waiting for, was it?' he said, twisting and pulling her nipple out into an elongated tube. 'Tell me. Was he better than me?'

It was a question neither of them had ever asked the other. In the past it had not been necessary. None of their lovers, however adept, could compete for either of their affections.

The fact that Francis had felt the need to ask her about Constantin underlined the subtle difference in their relationship. When she did not answer straight away he slid his other hand inside her dressing-gown and pinched the other nipple – hard.

As he kept up the pressure, her eyes watered. 'You're hurting me, Francis,' she said quietly.

'Good. I'm repaying you for the cruelty of keeping secrets from me. But the discomfort isn't unbearable, is it?' He twisted the twin nubs of flesh, pulling them out even more until the tips of her breasts stood out in little, flattened cone-shapes. 'Look within the pain and go past

211

it. Take a deep breath and ride it. And tell me, my treacherous lover, whose kisses thrill you the most? Mine or his?'

She had never seen him this way before. He was still playful, still her adoring twin, but there was an underlying sharpness to his words. His eyes on her in the mirror were dark and intense.

'Do you feel it yet?' he asked.

Her nipples burned and stung. She drew her breath in deeply as he ordered her to, letting it out slowly and gradually. For a moment longer she could concentrate on nothing but the pain. Then the strangest thing happened. There was a sense of soaring out of herself and she saw colours. The pain centre shifted, dissolved.

A hot, thrilling spasm fizzed down to her groin.

God. The feeling was like an orgasm. Between her legs she felt the soft little pad of her pleasure centre throb and throb. How sweetly it pulled and it had not even grown swollen with desire, let alone received any direct stimulation.

She let her head fall back, her lips parting as a soft cry broke from her. Francis dipped his head and, pushing aside the heavy fall of her red-gold hair, pressed his lips to the little bump at the top of her spine.

'Him or me?' he insisted, his lips trailing down the ridge of her backbone.

'Oh, Francis. How can you ask? Can't you see how I react to your touch? I've loved you for so long. Do you think I'd let anyone change how I feel?'

He gave a groan and let go of her tortured nipples. Coming around to face her, he knelt down and buried his head in her lap. She stroked his bent head, twirling one of the dark, twisting curls around her finger.

'I'm afraid,' he said. 'Forgive me, but I can't bear anything to change.'

He looked up and his eyes were brimming with tears.

'You see, I have lain with Constantin too. It was too wonderful to explain. I loved it when he took me. It was so much more intense than with Chatham. And I was glad to submit to him. But he's too greedy. He demands everything, and the power game is not confined to when he is in bed with a lover. He told me that he wants all my emotion, total submission on all levels. And I . . . I . . .'

'You're afraid that you'll give in? Is that it?'

He nodded miserably. 'He's so strong-minded. The pleasure he gave me . . . It was devastating – like a drug. All I can think of is lying with him again. Well, apart from lying with Razvania, that is. But she is just like him. The pair of them are ravenous for control. That would not matter if it were just for enjoyment – just sex. But it's different this time. Don't you feel it, Sidonie? Constantin and Razvania are not just casual lovers. Why do they mean so much to me – to you too?'

She chuckled softly. So that was what this scenario was all about. How like Francis to punish her for something he felt guilty about.

But she was painfully aware that she had lied to him when he had asked her how she felt about Constantin. She too was almost blinded by the power of his persona. It would be so easy to let Razvania and Constantin rule the two of them.

Francis had so eloquently put her own doubts into words. He was more honest than she.

'Perhaps Constantin is wiser than we think him,' she said. 'Remember that night in Venice at the *ridotto* when we were masked and he bet Razvania that we were twins? He is very astute. Human nature is something of a hobby of his. I don't think he does demand our complete surrender. This is a game to him. I think he is forcing us to take a very close look at ourselves, although I'm not sure what his motives are. I'm certain that he knows we are lovers, but I also think that he approves.'

Francis looked taken aback.

'He can't know, surely! I'd never tell him. What makes you think that he knows?'

'By his thoughtfulness. He could have put us in rooms some distance from each other. This place is a maze.

213

There must be fifty or more rooms and all separated by miles of corridors. But we have adjoining rooms. That is no accident. So I think that he does not wish to tear us apart.'

He brightened and dashed a hand across his eyes. 'Then what do you think he wants?'

Sidonie bent down to kiss his trembling lips. She could not bear to see him looking so troubled. For so long he had appeared to be the stronger of them, but now she realised that he needed her far more than he thought he did.

And for herself, she intended to make sure that they were always together. Whatever Constantin planned, it *had* to include the two of them.

Smiling fondly, she said, 'I can't help thinking of that old fortune-teller's words. Remember? She told us that, "The one must become two". I think I'm beginning to understand what she meant.'

Francis looked puzzled.

'Well, I don't. It still sounds like gibberish to me.' She laughed. 'Never mind. Forget about it for now. Come here. I want to hold you.' Her eyes sparkled. 'Something happened just before you came in that rather excited me. I could tell you all about it, but perhaps I should wait until you've had a visit from Izána.'

'Who?'

'Oh, she's a maid. Tatjana sent her to attend me or rather to spy on me. She's rather sweet and has some unusual skills! Which you'll soon discover for yourself. Now, why don't we try out my bed? Isn't it just too splendid? I'm certain that Tatjana will be examining the sheets for signs of sexual activity and then running to tell tales to Constantin. Let's leave something for her to find! And I want to ask you something, you wretch!'

'What's that?' he said, scooping her up in his arms and kissing her soundly. 'You smell divine. What is it?'

'Some sort of spicy oil,' she said airily. 'But never mind about that. Just who taught you how to do that trick with a person's nipples?'

214

Chapter Sixteen

*T*homas left his room and slipped quietly into the corridor.

His hands shook slightly and there was a taste like mud in his mouth, but apart from that he had little to show for an almost alcohol-free evening spent around the roaring fire in the main hall. The Count kept a good table. The food was wonderful. Roast birds, glazed vegetables, and a dessert of dried plums, toasted nuts and whipped cream which tasted heavenly.

After the meal the housekeeper had brought in a silver tray bearing a pot of strong coffee and tiny glasses for the plum brandy which everyone drank in Romania.

The moment Thomas laid eyes on Tatjana, he felt something give way inside him. It was as if a tight string that connected his heart and his loins had snapped. He was riveted, spellbound. She had barely glanced at him as she laid down the tray, but her sharp black eyes had glinted and her severe face softened a fraction. As she left the room, she looked back at him and Thomas was lost.

He had been able to think of nothing but Tatjana all evening and had drunk only three glasses of brandy, just enough to impart a warm glow, but not impair his faculties. Any more than that and he would not have a clear head in the morning.

Now it was not long after daybreak and he was on his way into the bowels of the castle. He had a vague notion of going outside for a walk and then returning via the kitchen, his excuse being that he had lost his way.

Tatjana would be there overseeing the breakfast preparations. He smiled as he imagined her inviting him into the warm kitchen, her severe, handsome face softening with pleasure as she offered him a mug of spiced eggnog.

As he opened the door which led on to a courtyard a blast of icy air swept in. The view was magical. Weak sunlight slanted through the morning mist and made the ice-bound trees and statues shimmer as if covered in silver glitter.

Thomas shivered, chilled to the bone within seconds. This was no weather to go strolling in. He decided to forgo the walk and go straight to the kitchens.

The noise of pots and pans rattling reached him before he was halfway down the corridor. He followed the din, marching purposefully towards the huge iron-bound door which stood open a few yards away.

There were a number of stone archways leading off the corridor and he glanced in them as he passed. The spaces under the arches were lined with rough brickwork and seemed to be storerooms, most of them piled high with sacks of flour or beans, some of them hung with strings of onions and stacked with boxes of root vegetables, jars of honey, sides of cured ham and red, sausage-shaped salami.

He caught a movement in one of the store rooms and slowed his steps. Surely that had been Tatjana. He was sure that he had glimpsed a flash of crimson silk.

Moving forward curiously he walked into the vaulted space. At the very back, behind a stack of boxes, he saw the flash of colour again. Ah, he had not been mistaken. But as he moved forward and saw behind the boxes, his throat dried.

Tatjana was indeed there, her red-silk sleeves rolled up to her elbows to reveal brawny forearms. But she was so engrossed in the matter at hand that she did not notice Thomas. He made a sound of surprise and she looked up.

Her eyes were bright and her cheeks ruddy from her exertions. In her hand was a small bunch of birch twigs, the sort of thing used to whip up egg whites in the kitchen.

The young man who stood against the wall, his wrists secured to heavy rings set in the brick, hid his face against his shoulder. Thomas's horrified glance was drawn to the man's groin where a huge erection jutted upwards. It was obvious what had been taking place. He could not ignore the scratched and reddened areas on the inside of the man's thighs, the blushing skin of his cock and balls.

'Ah, come in, Thomas,' Tatjana said cordially, completely unruffled by his unexpected appearance. 'György here will not mind if his punishment is witnessed. Will you, György? And I would welcome your company.'

She reached out to stroke the young man's hard belly, then moved her hand down to his cock. He moaned slightly as she closed her fingers around the sore shaft and smoothed the skin back from the tip. The cock-skin was tight and slid reluctantly from the glans to reveal the moist purplish bulb.

'Not yet, György. Hold back,' she said. 'Now you can put on a good show for our guest.'

Thomas was ashamed at the rush of lust he felt from just looking at Tatjana's bare arms. She had large, capable hands and strong work-worn fingers. They moved in a sure and efficient manner over the man's straining penis. He imagined how it would feel to have those hands on him, punishing, chastising, using him as if he were a thing for her amusement alone.

He realised with a shock that he envied György.

'Take a seat, Thomas,' Tatjana said, slipping her hand between the spread legs and palming the taut scrotal sac.

Pinching the loose skin together at the top of the balls,

she exerted a pressure until the egg-shaped testicles jutted against the fine skin. Stroking them gently, she smiled and looked into György's eyes as if enjoying the trace of fear she saw there.

'Well, if you're sure,' Thomas mumbled inadequately, and took a seat on one of the wooden benches set into the wall opposite where György was fastened.

'This is the place of punishment and reward,' Tatjana explained equably, letting go of the scrotal sac. 'I designed it myself. Those who have pleased me with their hard work and dedication are allowed to watch offenders being punished. It serves to remind them that I am a strict task mistress.'

'What has György done to deserve this?' Thomas asked, hoping to find out, for future reference, how one incurred Tatjana's wrath.

'Tell him,' Tatjana said, moving back a pace and beginning to flick the underside of the tortured penis with the bundle of sticks.

'I . . . I stole food,' György said, wincing and tightening the muscles of his belly.

'A whole salami, to be precise,' Tatjana said. 'I will not tolerate theft. Everyone has enough to eat here. György knows he has done wrong and he has accepted his punishment. Is that not so?'

'Yes . . .'

'Yes what?' Tatjana rapped, flailing the cock back and forth with the birch until it jerked and pulsed.

'Yes, mistress!' Gyorgy almost yelled.

He arched his back and pumped his hips, the abused cock swinging back and forth like a club. It looked heavy and potent, the reddened shaft almost bursting with pressure and the foreskin lodged back behind the flaring tip.

Horrified and aroused in equal measure, Thomas could not look away. He had a rampant erection himself and jammed his hands between his legs, trying to push it down.

'Open your legs, György,' Tatjana ordered. 'Wider. Make yourself available to me. And sink down a little.'

György did so, the bonds at his wrists stretching tight. His heavily muscled thighs bulged with the strain and the cock and balls appeared to be thrust into even greater prominence.

Tatjana threshed the birch back and forth between each thigh in turn, until the skin flamed with hectic colour. Now and then she paused and brought the tips of the birch up between his spread legs, pressing on the centre of his scrotum so that his testicles bulged out, one on either side of the switch.

Thomas squirmed on his seat, fascinated by the expression of mixed pain and pleasure on György's face. He would have expected the man to cringe away from the bite of the birch, but instead he seemed to relish the punishment, weaving his hips and pushing his cock forward as if lusting for each sharp caress.

Tatjana's broad face was sheened with sweat. Thomas caught her scent. Female exertion; it was an earthy smell like new-baked bread and there was an underlying sharpness of perspiration; something like lemons and spice with a touch of salt. He wanted nothing more than to bury his face between her large breasts and breathe in her exciting smell.

His mouth watered as he imagined her taste. He just knew that her quim would be plump and generous, the hair covering her mons would be bushy and coarse. His belly was speared by a dart of wanting. By God, this was a woman who would engulf a man; drown him in the luxury of her rich flesh.

'And now, György. It is time,' Tatjana said.

Time for what? Thomas wondered. Then he realised what Tatjana meant. She was giving her permission for György to spend. He felt a thrill of absolute delight as he watched her urge the young man on to a climax.

The birch moved up and down the rigid, crimson shaft but gently now, drawing out the pleasure from the suffering flesh. The fine twigs scraped across the tender glans, nudging at the little mouth, persuading it to give up its bounty.

György gasped, runnels of sweat snaking down his chest and pooling in his navel. A pearly drop gathered at the tip of his cock and hung there, trembling as his balls tightened and drew up close to his body. His nipples were as rigid as tiny beads, pink and new-looking against the golden skin of his chest.

Thomas had never desired another man in his life and despised those who did, but he found the sight before him uniquely erotic. And he felt ashamed to admit to himself that it was because he identified with György.

He wanted to be secured like that, to have Tatjana's attention focused solely on chastising him.

The bound man groaned and the tendons on his neck stood out like cords. Another syrupy drop of juice dripped from the slitted cock-mouth and hung down in a long shining thread. Tatjana gathered it up on to the birch and wiped it on to György's stomach. Massaging the moisture into his skin with one hand, she used the birch in a light, back and forth motion, almost tickling his tight sac.

György's mouth hung open and his breath came in hoarse gasps. The cock throbbed and jerked, tapping against Tatjana's circling hand.

'Now. Do it now,' Tatjana ordered.

And to Thomas's astonishment, György cried out, tightened every muscle in his body and obliged. The semen shot from him in a long, milky arc that spattered the wooden floor of the storeroom.

Tatjana smiled with satisfaction and closed her hand over the spurting penis, milking him efficiently and completely. While he slumped forward and trembled from head to toe, she slipped the birch into a compartment that hung from the belt at her waist. Then she reached up to free György's wrists, all the while looking over her shoulder at Thomas.

'You see?' she said. 'It is possible to train servants to

obey your every command. Even the demands of the body are subject to a greater will.'

As at the moment of their first meeting, Thomas felt a hot movement inside him. It was as if something unfurled and spread tingling through his veins, reaching right down to each fingertip.

He knew with absolute surety that Tatjana was the woman he had been waiting to meet for the whole of his life. Standing up, he inclined his head in a gesture that was both stiffly polite and full of admiration.

'Might I invite you to take a walk with me in the grounds?' he asked. 'Or perhaps you would like to ride with me in a sleigh?'

Tatjana's hard mouth curved in a brief, dismissive smile.

'I'm afraid that I do not have much time for relaxation at present. My duties are many.'

Thomas knew that his face showed his disappointment. He felt as if someone had thrown a bucket of cold water over him and that only made his desire for her all the more intense.

'I understand,' he said, trying to sound as if he really did not care very much. 'You must be very busy. Forgive my presumption. I spoke out of turn. I apologise.'

Tatjana seemed to consider for a moment. Then her sharp black eyes sparked with understanding. For an instant her face relaxed into a pleased smile. She ushered György out of the room, telling him to get back to his work and then turned back to Thomas.

He saw that her handsome face wore its habitual expression of sternness, but there was a flush high up on her broad cheekbones.

'It is so early for a guest to be up and about,' she said briskly. 'You will not have eaten yet. I will bring food and drink up to your room. Perhaps I can spare a few moments.'

Thomas felt as if he had just been granted a reprieve from nameless suffering. His heart hammered against the cage of his ribs. He could not stop the delighted grin from spreading across his face.

'Yes. That would be ... be splendid,' he stammered. 'I'll go back up to my room now, shall I? Will you be very long?'

She shook her head. 'There will just be time for you to prepare yourself.'

Thomas looked at her in puzzlement, his mind still churning with the enormity of what was happening. She had accepted his invitation. They both knew that this was something special. And he also knew that she understood the nature of her attraction for him.

'Prepare myself?' he said, trembling with eagerness and hanging on her every word.

'Make sure that you are naked and stretched out on the bed. I want to see your erection standing proud and ready to do me service. Make no mistake, Thomas. You will have to work hard before I reward you. And remember that I carry the birch with me everywhere. One word out of turn, one action which displeases me and I shall use it.'

'Yes, Tatjana,' Thomas whispered, his mouth dry with awe and lust.

'Very well. You may go,' she said. 'Oh, one other thing. I do not want to taste wine on your breath. You are not to touch another drop until I order it. Those are my terms. What do you say?'

'As you wish,' he mumbled.

And Thomas hurried from the storeroom, hardly able to walk for his raging erection and the sexual heat that suffused his entire body.

Francis stretched luxuriously, feeling his skin tingle with good health and vitality.

He would get out of bed in a moment and throw wide the heavy curtains, let in the winter sunlight which was pushing dusty fingers through a chink in the figured velvet. But just for a moment he wanted to savour the feeling of lying there on the rumpled silk sheet with the promise of a full day before him.

He was going riding with Razvania in an hour or two. There was time to wash and have breakfast first, but he decided that he would rather spend the time in Sidonie's bed. Padding across the room in his bare feet, he pushed open the connecting door.

Her bed was empty. That meant one of two things. She had spent the night with Constantin or she had risen early. Once, Francis would have been deeply wounded by her failure to keep him informed about her every movement, but now he simply shrugged and went back to his own room.

Throwing open the curtains he peered out of the window. The magnificent view never failed to move him. The ice-bound forest was wreathed in mist and the frozen lake glistened like a sheet of silver. He could just see the tiny island which housed the ruined chapel. And then, emerging from some trees, he saw the horse-drawn sleigh and knew that the two figures snuggled down amongst the fur rugs were Sidonie and Constantin.

A cold hand touched his heart. It was still too early for him to feel happiness for her without it being coloured by jealousy. She had been his for so long. Would he ever be able to let her go free? He doubted it and he did not think that she wanted that.

Annoyed with himself for his gloomy thoughts and feeling his good mood begin to evaporate, he crossed the room to the dresser and splashed his body with cold water. Then he rubbed himself dry with a coarse towel, buffing his skin to rosiness. Despite his intention to let nothing distract him from the pleasures of contemplating Razvania's company, he could not help thinking about Sidonie.

Were Constantin's hands on her even now, his lips pressed to some sweet fold of flesh, some perfumed crevice? Or was Sidonie mouthing his white skin, running her fingers over the planes of his muscles, pinching his tight nipples? Instantly Francis experienced a physical reaction, his cock lengthening and growing heavy. He remembered the taste and feel of them both so well.

What pleasures he had experienced lying in Constantin's arms. But it was no use to think of that now. Constantin wanted Sidonie. And Sidonie could love whomever she wished. She had always taken other lovers and he had never cared. But Constantin was different, unique. And worthy of finding a place in both their hearts.

But damn it to hell, why did admitting to that have to hurt so much?

Deep in thought, he did not notice the door to his room opening.

'What a charming sight,' Razvania said, sitting down in a chair next to the hearth. 'I see that you were expecting me.'

Francis smiled at her, seeing how her eyes lingered at his groin where he was more than half-erect, his cock lolling a little to one side.

'Ah,' she said. 'Not for me? Then who were you thinking of? Sidonie perhaps – or Constantin? Is it not a tragedy when one has so many lovers?'

She gave a peel of throaty laughter, the sound rippling around the room. Francis laughed too. It did sound ridiculous when put like that.

'Come here,' Razvania said huskily. 'I want to taste you.'

Obediently he crossed the room and stood before her. His hips were on a level with her shoulders. She looked up at him, her dark eyes wide and compelling. His breath caught in his throat as she leaned forward, her cheek brushing against his cock.

Then she put her hands around his hips and clasped his buttocks. For a moment she did not take him into her mouth, but continued to let her soft cheek rest against his shaft. He shifted and thrust towards her as she kneaded his buttocks and she smiled at his eagerness. When she opened her lips and placed them gently around his covered glans he went weak at the knees.

She drew him right in, letting her throat relax so that it formed a deep, warm well. As he pushed gently through the soft cushion where tongue and palate met he felt his bones dissolve with raw pleasure. Razvania sucked him avidly, her fingers straying into his moist cleft to play over his anus and scratch gently at the firm pad behind his balls.

Francis screwed his eyes shut and let the sensations wash over him. Behind his closed eyelids he could see the image of Sidonie entwined with Constantin. Sidonie was lying on her back, her hips tipped up and her thighs held open, while Constantin lay between her legs, his muscular buttocks clenching and unclenching as he pushed his cock into her.

Francis could have wept with envy, but the feelings that were radiating outwards from his groin were all-encompassing, driving away all emotion. And the woman who was driving him to ecstasy was Razvania. The beautiful cold-hearted witch, who had lately become transformed into his partner in pleasure.

He gave a sigh as Razvania flicked her tongue lightly around the flaring rim of his glans. Strands of her loose chestnut hair brushed softly against his belly and thighs, teasing his sensitised nerve endings.

Then she dug her fingers into his buttocks, pulling them open and exploring his damp crease ever more intimately. At the same time she urged him to plunge into her mouth, her lips nudging his pubic hair as she swallowed almost his whole length. God, her mouth was so warm, so tight around him. Francis went rigid from head to toe, the climax boiling up in him.

When he came it was in great tearing spurts. Razvania swallowed, then licked him clean. When she pulled away he saw that there was a smear of creamy sperm at the corner of her mouth. He fell to his knees and gathered her in his arms, kissing her mouth and licking his taste from her lips.

She returned his kiss, her tongue pushing into his mouth, claiming and conquering the dark space. Francis shivered, feeling anew the glorious sensation of her power over him. No other woman had been able to order his actions like Razvania. He was a puppet, dancing gleefully on the end of the strings she pulled.

In a few moments Razvania stood up and put him gently from her, making it clear that nothing more was required of him at present.

'If we're to go riding, you had best get dressed,' she said, smiling. 'Where would you like to go?'

He had no hesitation in replying. 'To the ruined chapel. Across the frozen lake.'

She gave him a searching look and said, 'Where Constantin and Sidonie have gone? Why not.'

Chapter Seventeen

The stone rim of the fountain pressed into Sidonie's back.

Constantin loomed over her, his beauty stark in the clear light. He looked a little dangerous but that was part of his attraction. She trembled with contained emotion. Sunlight gleamed off the powdery snow that frosted Constantin's dark hair. His hands, already pushing aside her fur cloak, were hot and thrilling on her skin.

Under the cloak, she was naked. The warm fur caressed her shoulders and back as she pressed herself close against him. He wore a tunic and trousers of leather. She drew her breath in sharply when the cold fabric touched her breasts and belly.

Constantin laughed and held her tight, unwilling to let her pull away. Her nipples were chafed into hard points by the chilled leather. She made a sound of protest against his mouth and twisted in his grip, but he put his hands on her waist and lifted her easily, settling her on the stone rim.

'Tenderness is for later,' he murmured.

The determination in his face unnerved her. She knew that he wanted her at once and was not minded to be sidetracked with soft caresses and kisses, but that only excited her all the more.

She parted her thighs to admit him as he pressed into her, his fingers at his belt. The leather was cold on her inner thighs, but beginning to warm with their combined body heat. Glancing down, she saw that Constantin had merely opened the front of his trousers.

His cock sprang free and reared up powerfully against the darkness of the leather. It was flushed and dark, the glans tinted a deep purplish-red. How potent, how beautiful it looked. She wanted to suck him, stroke him. But he was impatient to possess her.

Then his lips were at her throat, his tongue lingering at the hollow before trailing a path along her collar bones. Buried within her desire for him was a spark of fear. She sensed that this was to be a turning point in their relationship. There was something of purpose in the way his hands moved over her skin, demanding, claiming that she give herself up to him completely.

Perhaps it was time that she stopped resisting the inevitable. Francis was ready to give in to the power of the Count and his ward. But some stubbornness in her still fought against them both.

Constantin moved against her, his hands slipping under her buttocks and lifting her up to meet his hard flesh. She put her arms around his neck, her cheek against his jaw where there was the slight roughness of new beard growth under the skin. When he went into her, she whimpered softly.

He drove downwards, into her upturned channel. As he tipped her hips towards him and leaned into her, taking her with deep, penetrating thrusts, she linked her legs around his hips. Violently they pleasured each other. Sidonie digging her ankles into his taut buttocks, urging him on to pound into her. Constantin's mouth hung open, his breath coming in short bursts, fogging around them in the icy air.

His cock felt hot and hard. She welcomed the surging strength of it and imagined it filling her, her eager, swollen membranes parting to allow him access. The big glans butted up tightly against her womb on each inward stroke, the almost painful pressure drawing out the sensations of spiked pleasure.

Sidonie threw back her head, feeling the fur hood slip off and her hair tumble down her back. Sunlight fractured in splintering prisms on the icicles hanging from the fountain. She drew in a deep breath of the cold air and it slipped down her throat like smoke-tasting water.

'Ah, yes. Oh, yes, my love,' she murmured, as Constantin surged into her in a deep, satisfying volley.

'Yes. Yes. I am your love. Give yourself to me,' he murmured, kissing the corner of her mouth.

His lips were cool before she warmed them with her own. His tongue moved strongly in her mouth, meshing, threading with hers, the movement echoing the rhythm of his enclosed man-flesh.

Sidonie could think of nothing but the demands of her body. There was no subtlety in their joining. The whole of their energies were centred in their loins. Neither, at that moment, yearned for tenderness. There was only one word for what they were doing. Fucking.

And fucking like this was rich and raw, primeval. Her thighs flexed as she urged him into her, rising up to match him stroke for stroke. Their joined sexes merged juicily, the lewd sounds adding an extra note to their passion.

'God. Sidonie,' Constantin moaned as his body grew taut and his thrusts became rapid and shallow.

She hung on him, lifted clear of the stone rim, suddenly still and clasped so close that their pubic hair was meshed together. When he came, she felt the hot splashing of his semen inside her. She needed only to push herself against his belly, grind her erect bud against the base of his cock and her own climax spilled forth.

Constantin was still hard and he rode her furiously, urging her on to another paroxysm of pleasure. She dissolved against him a second time, her hands brushing over his cheeks, fingers playing over his lips in a tender, grateful gesture which she did not entirely understand.

It was as if her body had capitulated to him, even

229

while her mind still fought against giving way to her emotions.

What was it about this man that moved her so? It was something more than his beauty, his nobility, his complex and subtle character. No wonder that Francis desired him as strongly as she did. She was surprised to find tears in her eyes.

Constantin held her firmly against him as if unwilling to relinquish her flesh. His softening cock slipped from her and he moved away and put his clothes to rights. A warm trickle of semen snaked down her thigh. She smelt the sharp animal scent of it, mixed with her own musk, and wished that she could hold the trace of him inside her for a little longer.

Whatever was wrong with her? She had never been given to strange fancies, but she did not seem able to think straight and the tears were spilling down her face.

Enfolding her in his embrace, Constantin captured a tear on one finger and smiled down at her.

'For whom do you weep, my love? Not for me, surely. Or for yourself? No – for you are happy, are you not? I suspect it is for something less tangible, for your loss of innocence, perhaps?'

'My innocence?' she said, her voice trembling with wry humour. 'I lost that a long time ago.' She laid her cheek against his broad leather-covered chest, gaining comfort from the feel of his heart which beat so strongly against her skin.

'I think not,' Constantin said. 'You lost the innocence of the flesh perhaps, but I speak of a certain naïvety of mind. Did you really think that it would be possible for you and Francis to love each other so completely for the whole of your lives? To keep yourselves pure and to be untouched by anyone or anything else?'

She nodded miserably, unwilling to talk of such precious things but unable to keep silent.

'It was what we wanted,' she said. 'Can you imagine how it feels to be so close to someone that they seem like an actual part of you? Our thoughts, our desires and needs, overlapped so much that it was often difficult to separate them. And neither of us wanted to. We were a little selfish and cruel at times, using people for our pleasure, taunting them in front of each other, while swearing to stay true only to each other. It worked too. We never let any of our lovers get too close. Until now, that is.'

'Ah,' Constantin said, his voice deep and husky. It was a sound of deep satisfaction and for some reason it angered her.

How dare he be so certain of himself?

'You know that you have some power over me, Constantin. I will admit that no other man has affected me like you have. Perhaps I love you in a way. But Francis is part of me and that can never change. You are expecting me to stay here with you, aren't you? I might do that. But only if Francis agrees to stay on too. No one will ever tear us apart!'

He smiled tenderly. 'Yes. You must stay. But I have no wish to separate you and your twin. My God, that would be too cruel.'

'You don't? But I thought –'

'You thought that I wanted you all to myself? To possess you utterly?'

'Well, yes. You said as much.'

He slid one hand up to cup her fragile skull, his fingers moving against her hair.

'Do you think I am some kind of unfeeling monster? You misunderstood me. I wanted only for you to love me as much as you love Francis. And that is a great deal, no? I do not think that I can ask any more of you than that. It is certainly more than you have ever given anyone else. Perhaps it is the most you can give me.'

He was right. Sidonie knew that. She had never thought herself capable of feeling this way about anyone other than Francis. All her fear, her anxieties, had been because she felt herself weakening, slipping into the sort of intimacy which seemed in itself to be a betrayal of her love for her twin.

She had been terrified that he would demand that she give up her twin-lover. But now Constantin was telling her that he did not wish to separate her from Francis. She could love them both and there need be no betrayal, no lies.

They might even be able to express their love in public, for no one would dare show disapproval. Constantin was too rich and powerful to be affected by the petty morals of lesser beings.

Oh, she could not wait to tell her twin!

'You mean that? You and Razvania will allow Francis and me to continue as we have always done? We can share a bed whenever we wish?'

He nodded.

'Of course. I honour the expression of true love in whichever guise it is found. And it is enough for me that you will stay. We shall all be very happy together, no?'

She gazed up at him, her face rapt with grateful thanks.

'Oh, Constantin. I never dreamed that you were so wise and generous. Just wait until Francis hears this. He'll be so thrilled.'

'Hears what? Why don't you tell me now?' Francis said, stepping out from behind a crumbling archway.

His face was white and strained. She saw that Razvania was with him. They must have left their sleigh on the far side of the ruins and picked their way through the spaces littered with ancient stones.

How much had he heard? From his face it seemed that he had only drawn near at the end of the conversation.

'Let's have no more secrets,' Francis said tightly. 'What is it that you are about to tell me? No. Let me guess. You are sick with love for Constantin and have decided to stay here with him when I return to England.'

He paused and searched her face for expression, his pale eyes bright and somewhat unfocused by pain. 'That's it, is it not? Oh God, I can see it in your face. You're in love with him. Look at you, still flushed from his lovemaking! Have you nothing to say to me? Where's

232

your courage? We swore that we would be honest with each other. You were supposed to tell me if you were going to leave me – ' His voice broke on a sob.

She could not bear to see Francis looking so stricken. His lips were a thin, pale line and his jaw was clenched and set-looking. When Razvania moved close and held out her arms to him, he shook his head and stumbled blindly towards one of the still-standing archways.

'Get away!' he said, leaning a shoulder against the cold stone, his head bent so that his dark curls tumbled forward to mask his face. 'Both of you! You and the Count set out to destroy us. Well, you've done your worst. I hope you feel pleased with yourselves.'

'No! You've got it all wrong,' Sidonie said, struggling to free herself from Constantin's embrace. 'Let me explain. Listen to me, Francis – '

'Why bother. It's self-evident,' Francis cut in bleakly. 'Stay with your damned lover then. I'll have nothing more to do with you! You faithless bitch!'

Sidonie shrank from the bleakness in Francis's expression. He could not mean that. The venomous words spewed from him, but she could see only the hurt. Constantin's arms tightened around her.

'It might be best if I speak to him. Wait here, Sidonie.'

Her eyes blurred by tears, she nodded, sinking down to sit on the rim of the fountain. Francis shot her a look of hatred and she almost cringed from the heat of it. He began backing away.

'How touching. You defer to your lover instead of me. Well, there's nothing more to be said. I'll leave for England at once – '

'Oh, be silent, man,' Constantin said, grasping Francis's shoulders and dragging him into his embrace. 'Don't be a fool. Come here.'

Lowering his head he claimed his mouth. For a moment longer Francis struggled, but Constantin was by far the stronger of the two. He held Francis close, kissing him roughly and expertly, until Francis gave a sort of shudder and lay still against his chest.

'Is that the kiss of someone who wants to send you away?' Constantin murmured against Francis's mouth. 'Now kiss me back and show some sense.'

Francis moaned softly as Constantin slid a hand down to the small of his back and pressed him even closer. His head was tipped up to Constantin, his mouth opened wide for the onslaught of the invasive tongue.

Watching them both, Sidonie felt a mixture of emotions. The two people she loved best in all the world must be able to reach some agreement. She did not think she could bear it if Francis was to leave now. But he had to accept that he must share her. As, indeed, she must learn to share him.

Razvania walked over to Sidonie and sat beside her. Sidonie had her hand pressed to her mouth, the knuckles showing white through the skin. Razvania reached for her hand and squeezed it affectionately.

'Constantin can be extremely persuasive when it pleases him,' she said dryly. 'But I have my own ways of making a point.'

Tipping Sidonie's chin up, she placed her lips softly on to her mouth. The tender, questing tongue slipped between Sidonie's lips and she felt a shudder of desire travel down her body. The kiss was deep and became more insistent, less gentle, until Sidonie felt quite faint.

In her own fashion, Razvania was as demanding and captivating as Constantin. When Razvania drew back, Sidonie looked at her in astonishment. It was as if scales had fallen from her eyes.

Razvania laughed her deep husky laugh. The sound of it was like something syrupy and golden. It was an engaging, warm sound and Sidonie felt an echo of it in the heat spreading outwards from her groin.

'You see everything clearly now?' Razvania said. 'Constantin and myself – we wanted you both from the very beginning. We both of us desired each of you. And is that not true of you and Francis? But your bond was so close, so all-encompassing, that no one could get near to you. It seemed that you had built an opal darkness for yourselves to dwell in. Oh, it glittered and shimmered like a precious jewel, drawing others to it, but admitting no one. Constantin and myself did not care to become casualties, as so many of your lovers had. The only way to penetrate that was to make each of you fall in love with us.'

A slow smile spread over Sidonie's face. How well Razvania put it. An opal darkness. A dark jewel that surrounded Francis and herself. It was true. She saw that now.

In time, perhaps, Francis and herself would have worn out their love. How sad, how tragic, it would have been for them to grow old, both of them living alone in their togetherness, childless by choice and cut off from any number of prospective friends.

This way they could have it all. She might even have a child one day.

Francis and Constantin walked towards them, still embracing. Francis's pale eyes were shining. The desire for them both bloomed in Sidonie's belly. She reached for her twin and Francis moved forward and took her in his arms.

There was no more need to hide how they felt. It would be liberating to be able to express their love in public. For the first time in the company of their lovers they kissed unashamedly and with passion, while Constantin and Razvania looked on approvingly.

'So it is settled,' Constantin said, looking from Sidonie to Francis. 'You both stay. A joint wedding, I think, to make everything official. A sumptuous Romanian event which will be remembered in the district for years to come. Then, in the spring, we shall travel to England to visit your parents.'

'Yes. Oh, yes. Anything you like,' Sidonie said, not knowing whether to laugh or cry. 'What do you say, Francis?'

'Marriage? Why not? The title of Countess will suit you,' Francis said, clinging to her arm, his fingers digging almost painfully into her skin.

He was still bemused and a little intoxicated by Constantin's kiss, she realised. She put her hand over his. It was all going to be so perfect. She must write to her father at once to explain. At the thought of her father's surprised face and Lady Jenny's look of pleased pride, she smiled fondly.

Then she had a thought.

'What about Thomas? I wonder what he'll say to all this. It will be quite a shock.'

Constantin grinned. 'Oh, I think you'll find that Thomas too will be agreeable to staying. And I doubt whether he will want to return to England.'

'Oh, why is that?' Sidonie said.

Constantin and Razvania looked knowingly at each other and spoke one word with perfect accord.

'Tatjana,' they said and burst out laughing.

Thomas lay flat on his back, looking up adoringly at the woman who straddled him.

Tatjana's meaty thighs were pressed one to either side of his lean hips, her bottom hovering over his groin. Thomas's mouth dried as she loosened the laces of her bodice. The red silk seemed packed tight. He could not wait to see what the fabric contained.

Tatjana sank down a little, the generous lips of her quim parting to admit his glans. Her labia were firm and muscular, settling around his shaft as closely as fingers. Thomas bit his lip, not daring to move. He did not want to displease this goddess, this woman whom he had adored on sight.

He felt humbled by her presence. She was as proud and fierce as an Amazon. Whatever she demanded of him, he would give it.

He moaned softly as she eased herself down on to his cock, loving the way her silken heat enclosed him. She moved gently at first, her fingers still unthreading the laces of her dress, moving unhurriedly, prolonging the moment of revelation.

Thomas held himself back in an agony of anticipation

as the red silk bulged, moved liquidly around its contents, and finally opened.

As Tatjana pressed down on to him, her buttocks grazing his belly, she leaned forward so that the lush, pendulous globes of her breasts spilled free.

'Oh, Lord God bless me,' he sighed, reaching up to palm the twin wonders.

The soft white flesh spilled over his hands and he moved his fingers over the big nipples, feeling them grow firm at his touch. The nipples were like small saucers and as brown and textured as bark.

Wonderful. He could not wait to taste them, to run the tip of his tongue around the jutting tips.

Tatjana began bouncing up and down on his cock, her huge breasts jiggling in time with her movements. Her cleavage was deep and mysterious and exuded a spicy perfume. The slippery sheath of her quim squeezed and massaged his aching sex. Her inner muscles gripped him firmly, beginning to milk him and draw him forwards to new places of pleasure.

'Now then, Englishman. Show me what you can do,' she said, her snapping black eyes fastening boldly on to his face.

Thomas groaned and worked his hips, breathing in her exciting smell. He raised his back off the bed and thrust manfully as she jammed herself down on to his cock.

Oh, God. She was liquid heat. It was as if there were some kind of slippery creature inside her quim.

Tatjana reached for the belt at her waist and took hold of the little bunch of birch twigs. As she rode him hard, she brushed the birch back and forth across his erect nipples.

'That's it, Englishman,' she said, the perspiration beading on her top lip. 'I like a lover who works hard.'

Thomas squeezed Tatjana's big, rubbery teats, loving the way her soft breast-flesh oozed between his fingers. She circled his nipples with the birch. He cried out at the gentle, scratching pleasure, imagining other more painful delights to come.

Her spread buttocks ground against his belly and her moisture smeared his root and balls. He vowed not to wash for a week, wanting to retain her smell and the memory of this, their first coupling.

He was in heaven. Tatjana was the woman of his dreams.

As he felt his balls tightening and the skin of his sac shrinking in towards his belly, the tendrils of pleasure moving through his veins, he thought that he had met his nemesis.

He wanted to stay with Tatjana always and repeat this experience night after night.

Tatjana gave a shriek and sat upright, her quim tightening around him as she came. A flush spread over her exposed chest. As she raised her hands to link them behind her head, her breasts lifted and hovered above him like twin moons.

Awed and humbled, he began flooding into her, the pleasure seemingly torn from him, overflowing into something beyond ecstasy. When Tatjana fell forward, almost burying him under mounds of fragrant flesh, Thomas wrapped his arms around her and drew her close. To his delight she did not resist, but lay quietly on him, her hot, muscular body covering his.

Soon she slept, her soft snores echoing in his ears. Thomas felt protective then, although he knew that the roles would be reversed when she awoke.

What a woman. He needed a lifetime to explore all of her facets.

Was there any way, he wondered, that he could persuade the twins to stay on at the castle for a while?

LOOK OUT FOR THE ALL-NEW BLACK LACE BOOKS – AVAILABLE NOW!

All books priced £6.99 in the UK. Please note publication dates apply to the UK only. For other territories, please contact your retailer.

THE HEAT OF THE MOMENT
Tesni Morgan
ISBN O 352 33742 7

Amber, Sue and Diane – three women from an English market town – are successful in their businesses, but all want more from their private lives. When they become involved in The Silver Banner – an English Civil War re-enactment society – there's plenty of opportunity for them to fraternise with handsome muscular men in historical uniforms. Thing is, the fun-loving Cavaliers are much sexier than the Puritan Roundheads, and tensions and rivalries are played out on the village green and the bedroom. **Great characterisation and oodles of sexy fun in this story of three English friends who love dressing up.**

WICKED WORDS 7
Various
ISBN 0352 33743 5

Hugely popular and immensely entertaining, the *Wicked Words* collections are the freshest and most cutting-edge volumes of women's erotic stories to be found anywhere in the world. The diversity of themes and styles reflects the multi-faceted nature of the female sexual imagination. Combining humour, warmth and attitude with fun, filthy, imaginative writing, these stories sizzle with horny action. Only the most arousing fiction makes it into a *Wicked Words* volume. This is the best in fun, sassy erotica from the UK and USA. **Another sizzling collection of wild fantasies from wicked women!**

Coming in January

STICKY FINGERS
Alison Tyler
ISBN 0 352 33756 7

Jodie Silver doesn't have to steal. As the main buyer for a reputable
import and export business in the heart of San Francisco, she has plenty
of money and prestige. But she gets a rush from pocketing things that
don't belong to her. It's a potent feeling, almost as gratifying as the
excitement she receives from engaging in kinky, exhibitionist sex – but
not quite. Skilled at concealing her double life, Jodie thinks she's
unstoppable, but with detective Nick Hudson on her tail, it's only a
matter of time before the pussycat burglar meets her comeuppance. **A
thrilling piece of West Coast noir erotica from Ms Tyler.**

STORMY HAVEN
Savannah Smythe
ISBN 0 352 33757 5

Daisy Lovell has had enough of her over-protective Texan millionaire
father, Felix, and is determined to get away from his interfering ways.
The last straw is when Felix forbids her to date a Puerto Rican boy.
Determined to see some of the world, Daisy goes storm chasing across
the American Midwest for some sexual adventure. She certainly finds it
among truckers and bikers and a state trooper. What Daisy doesn't know
is that Felix has sent personal bodyguard Max Decker to join the storm
tour and watch over her. However, no one can foresee that hard man
Decker will fall for Daisy in a big way. **Fantastic characterisation and lots
of really hot sex scenes across the American desert.**

SILKEN CHAINS
Jodi Nicol
ISBN O 352 33143 7

Fleeing from her scheming guardians at the prospect of an arranged marriage, the beautiful young Abbie is thrown from her horse. On regaining consciousness she finds herself in a lavish house modelled on the palaces of Indian princes – and the virtual prisoner of the extremely wealthy and attractive Leon Villiers, the Master. Eastern philosophy and eroticism form the basis of the Master's opulent lifestyle and he introduces Abbie to sensual pleasures beyond the bounds of her imagination. **By popular demand, another of the list's bestselling historical novels is reprinted.**

Coming in February

LIBERTY HALL
Kate Steward
ISBN O 352 33776 1

Vicar's daughter and wannabe journalist Tess Morgan is willing to do anything to pay off her student overdraft. Luckily for Tess, her flatmate Imogen is the daughter of infamous madam, Liberty Hall, who owns a pleasure palace of the same name that operates under a guise of respectability as a hotel. When Tess lands herself a summer job catering for 'special clients' at Liberty Hall, she sees an opportunity to clear that overdraft with a bit of undercover journalism. But when she tries to tell all to a Sunday newspaper, Tess is in for a shocking surprise. **Fruity antics aplenty in this tale of naughty behaviour and double crossing.**

THE WICKED STEPDAUGHTER
Wendy Harris
ISBN O 352 33777 X

Selina is in lust with Matt, who unfortunately is the boyfriend of the
really irritating Miranda, who was Selina's stepmother for several years
until her poor old dad keeled over years before his time. When Miranda
has to go to the US for three weeks, Selina hatches a plan to seduce the
floppy-haired Matt – and get her revenge on the money-grabbing
Miranda, who Selina blames for her dad's early demise. With several
suitors in tow, the highly sexed Selina causes mayhem, both at work – at
the strippergram service she co-runs – and in her personal life. **Another
hilarious black comedy of sexual manners from Ms Harris.**

DRAWN TOGETHER
Robyn Russell
ISBN O 352 33269 7

When Tanya, a graphic artist, creates Katrina Cortez – a sexy, comic-strip
detective – she begins to wish her own life were more like that of
Katrina's. Stephen Sinclair, who works with Tanya, is her kind of man.
Unfortunately Tanya's just moved in with her bank manager boyfriend,
who expects her to play the part of the executive girlfriend. In Tanya's
quest to gain the affection of Mr Sinclair, she must become more like
Katrina Cortez – a voluptuous wild woman! **Unusual and engaging story
of seduction and delight.**

Black Lace Booklist

Information is correct at time of printing. To avoid disappointment check availability before ordering. Go to www.blacklace-books.co.uk. All books are priced £6.99 unless another price is given.

BLACK LACE BOOKS WITH A CONTEMPORARY SETTING

☐ THE TOP OF HER GAME Emma Holly	ISBN 0 352 33337 5	£5.99
☐ IN THE FLESH Emma Holly	ISBN 0 352 34498 3	£5.99
☐ A PRIVATE VIEW Crystalle Valentino	ISBN 0 352 33308 1	£5.99
☐ SHAMELESS Stella Black	ISBN 0 352 34485 1	£5.99
☐ INTENSE BLUE Lyn Wood	ISBN 0 352 34496 7	£5.99
☐ THE NAKED TRUTH Natasha Rostova	ISBN 0 352 34497 5	£5.99
☐ ANIMAL PASSIONS Martine Marquand	ISBN 0 352 34499 1	£5.99
☐ A SPORTING CHANCE Susie Raymond	ISBN 0 352 33501 7	£5.99
☐ TAKING LIBERTIES Susie Raymond	ISBN 0 352 33357 X	£5.99
☐ A SCANDALOUS AFFAIR Holly Graham	ISBN 0 352 33523 8	£5.99
☐ THE NAKED FLAME Crystalle Valentino	ISBN 0 352 33528 9	£5.99
☐ ON THE EDGE Laura Hamilton	ISBN 0 352 33534 3	£5.99
☐ LURED BY LUST Tania Picarda	ISBN 0 352 33533 5	£5.99
☐ THE HOTTEST PLACE Tabitha Flyte	ISBN 0 352 33536 X	£5.99
☐ THE NINETY DAYS OF GENEVIEVE Lucinda Carrington	ISBN 0 352 33070 8	£5.99
☐ EARTHY DELIGHTS Tesni Morgan	ISBN 0 352 33548 3	£5.99
☐ MAN HUNT Cathleen Ross	ISBN 0 352 33583 1	
☐ MÉNAGE Emma Holly	ISBN 0 352 33231 X	
☐ DREAMING SPIRES Juliet Hastings	ISBN 0 352 33584 X	
☐ THE TRANSFORMATION Natasha Rostova	ISBN 0 352 33311 1	
☐ STELLA DOES HOLLYWOOD Stella Black	ISBN 0 352 33588 2	
☐ SIN.NET Helena Ravenscroft	ISBN 0 352 33598 X	
☐ HOTBED Portia Da Costa	ISBN 0 352 33614 5	
☐ TWO WEEKS IN TANGIER Annabel Lee	ISBN 0 352 33599 8	
☐ HIGHLAND FLING Jane Justine	ISBN 0 352 33616 1	
☐ PLAYING HARD Tina Troy	ISBN 0 352 33617 X	
☐ SYMPHONY X Jasmine Stone	ISBN 0 352 33629 3	

To find out the latest information about Black Lace titles, check out the website: www.blacklace-books.co.uk or send for a booklist with complete synopses by writing to:

Black Lace Booklist, Virgin Books Ltd
Thames Wharf Studios
Rainville Road
London W6 9HA

Please include an SAE of decent size. Please note only British stamps are valid.

Our privacy policy
We will not disclose information you supply us to any other parties. We will not disclose any information which identifies you personally to any person without your express consent.

From time to time we may send out information about Black Lace books and special offers. Please tick here if you do <u>not</u> wish to receive Black Lace information. ❏

Please send me the books I have ticked above.

Name ....

Address ....

....

....

....

Post Code ....

Send to: Cash Sales, Black Lace Books, Thames Wharf Studios, Rainville Road, London W6 9HA.

US customers: for prices and details of how to order books for delivery by mail, call 1-800-343-4499.

Please enclose a cheque or postal order, made payable to Virgin Books Ltd, to the value of the books you have ordered plus postage and packing costs as follows:

UK and BFPO – £1.00 for the first book, 50p for each subsequent book.

Overseas (including Republic of Ireland) – £2.00 for the first book, £1.00 for each subsequent book.

If you would prefer to pay by VISA, ACCESS/MASTERCARD, DINERS CLUB, AMEX or SWITCH, please write your card number and expiry date here:

....

Signature ....

Please allow up to 28 days for delivery.